BY THE NUMBERS

Other Titles by
New York Times Bestselling Author
JEN LANCASTER

Bitter Is the New Black

Bright Lights, Big Ass

Such a Pretty Fat

Pretty in Plaid

My Fair Lazy

If You Were Here

Jeneration X

Here I Go Again

The Tao of Martha

Twisted Sisters

The Best of Enemies

I Regret Nothing

JEN LANCASTER

By *the* Numbers

 New American Library

NEW AMERICAN LIBRARY
Published by New American Library,
an imprint of Penguin Random House LLC
375 Hudson Street, New York, New York 10014

This book is an original publication of New American Library.

First Printing, June 2016

For more information about Penguin Random House, visit penguin.com.

LIBRARY OF CONGRESS CATALOGING-IN-PUBLICATION DATA:

Names: Lancaster, Jen, 1967– author.
Title: By the numbers/Jen Lancaster.
Description: New York, New York: New American Library, [2016]
Identifiers: LCCN 2015041935 (print) | LCCN 2015045292 (ebook) |
ISBN 9780451471116 (hardcover) | ISBN 9780698167001 (ebook)
Subjects: LCSH: Sandwich generation—Fiction. | Divorced women—Fiction. |
Domestic fiction. | BISAC: FICTION/Humorous. | FICTION/Contemporary
Women. | FICTION/Family Life. | GSAFD: Humorous fiction.
Classification: LCC PS3612.A54748 B9 2016 (print) | LCC PS3612.A54748 (ebook)
| DDC 813/.6—dc23
LC record available at http://lccn.loc.gov/2015041935

Printed in the United States of America
10 9 8 7 6 5 4 3 2 1

Penguin
Random
House

For the crews at LFHF and IBJI
because you had the technology and you had the capability

BY THE NUMBERS

CHAPTER ONE

To: christophersinclairjr@calmail.berkeley.edu, jessica@sinclairsartorial.com

From: the_bride@kelseylovesmilo.com

Date: May 30

Subject: Greetings from Bridal Central!

Hi, you guys!!

I'm soooo excited to see you both! I can't believe I'm getting married in a week—WOOOOOO!! It's, like, *everything* that the fam is going to be together one last time in the house, except for Barnaby, which, OMG, don't get me started or I will be sobbing all over again.

Listen, I need you two to have my back on something—Mom says Daddy can't stay over Friday night, which is ridic because there's oodles of space. Like, he's supposed to drive all the way back down to his place with Stassi in the city after the rehearsal dinner, then turn around and come back to the burbs first thing in the morning? What if he's so tired he crashes on the Edens or something? I mean, WEDDING DAY RUINED, right? I kept pleading and pleading and she was finally all, "He can get a hotel room, an Uber, or a time machine and a code of ethics. His choice." She's THE WORST. When you guys get here, please, please help me change her mind. Like, we can make up a spreadsheet or something—those are always her jam.

Bee-tee-dubs, she's been *such* a bitchacrite about everything. She's all, "Are you sure you want to decorate the tent with rusty birdcages? Happy to buy you new ones if you'd like. Would you prefer champagne glasses? Might they be easier to drink out of than Mason jars?" Why is she so controlling? She *so* doesn't get my curated aesthetic, which is gonna be great, right?

I think that's it as I'm currently tied up sourcing an iron bathtub to hold craft beers at the reception—and it will be EPIC.

Big love,

Kels

P.S. Milo is bringing his food truck as a surprise for the after-party following the reception!

P.P.S. I just got a flock of sparrows in flight tattooed across my collarbone. Bridesmaids don't HAVE to get a coordinating sparrow inked, but it's my gift to them, so they're strongly encouraged to opt in. Don't tell Mama Killjoy.

To: christophersinclairjr@calmail.berkeley.edu

From: jessica@sinclairsartorial.com

Date: May 30

Subject: Flight info

Toph,

What day are you coming home? My flight arrives from JFK on Wednesday at noon. That's as late as I can possibly get in without (a) making Kelsey absolutely banana-sandwich-crazy by not being there sooner and (b) still being able to hit the party at Mimsy and Gumpy's club. You know I love me some cocktails with the grandparents.

Other than dinner with the oldsters, I'm not looking forward to any of this. For real. From the nosy cousins grilling me, all, "Since when is fashion blogging a career?" to the three-ring-hipster-shitshow of a wedding party to the tremendous passy-aggro question mark that is what'll happen when our mother comes face-to-face with Dad and Stassi (who's actually really chill), this will NOT be fun.

I feel like the only lucky one is Barnaby. At least he had the good sense to die before Kelsey could proceed to drape his noble self in daisies and trot him down the aisle with the rings. Did we break some sort of record for world's oldest beagle? Wait, I'm sure our mother knows the exact longevity statistic and will tell us *all about it.*

TTFN,

Your favorite sister

P.S. I am not getting Kelsey's basic bird tattoo; I want to be crystal clear about that.

P.P.S. If Kelsey doesn't shave her pits for the big day, I will hold the bitch down and shear her like a sheep.

To: jessica@sinclairsartorial.com

From: christophersinclairjr@calmail.berkeley.edu

Date: May 30

Subject: Re: Flight info

Jess,

I don't start my new job with Goldman until June 15th, so I'm coming home on Monday and flying back to San Francisco a week later. Really looking forward to being in Chicago—it's been way too long. Think I can sneak away to catch the Cubbies on Thursday?

Hey, saw your latest Instagram—not to sound like a cousin, but how *do* you afford the sweet Chelsea loft and boots with a comma on the price tag? Maybe you should have been the one to go into finance, because clearly you know something we don't about cash flow.

Anyway, see you soon.

Topher

P.S. Kelsey's higher than usual if she thinks I'm wearing the straw boater AND the bow tie AND the arm garter. I'm a groomsman, not a member of a goddamned barbershop quartet.

P.P.S. R.I.P. Barnaby. You were a real good boy.

P.P.P.S. No more Mom bashing, though, okay? Don't forget, I'm on her team.

say, "I'm Penelope Bancroft Sinclair—Penny—and I can tell you when you're going to die." Then I raise my wineglass.

Kelsey gasps and claps her hands over her eyes. Jessica makes a moue of disgust, grimacing with a delicately curled lip. That's when I realize I've said the wrong thing and embarrassed my daughters.

Again.

In my defense, that line kills at corporate dinners. When all of us executives go around the table to introduce ourselves, this is my go-to greeting, and it brings down the house every time. Granted, I'm an actuary, and there's not a ton that's funny about the business of predicting life expectancy for insurance industry clients. I mean, one of the biggest jokes regarding my profession is, "How can you tell when you meet an actuary who's an extrovert? He looks at YOUR shoes when he talks to you!" so we're not exactly famous for being toastmasters.

A silence best described as "awkward" overtakes everyone in the private dining room. Of course, me falling flat had to happen here at the Centennial Hills Club, the hub of my parents' social network and the epicenter of almost every one of my childhood humiliations.

My mother was determined that I connect with the right kind of children, so I was subjected to an endless stream of activities at which I was destined to fail. Through forced participation on these grounds, I discovered early those undertakings at which I did not excel. I guess the silver lining is I learned what activities to avoid as an adult, such as tennis *(e.g., black eye—1974, second black eye and fractured orbital bone—1975, broken wrist—1975, sprained ankle—1976, broken nose—1977)* due to poor hand-eye coordination.

I know I lack the intestinal fortitude to guide one thousand pounds of tempestuous Arabian over a gate jump *(fractured tibia—1977, sprained coccyx—1978, broken collarbone—1979)*, so horses did not turn into a lifetime love as they did with my equestrian friends who still spend their weekends mucking out stalls. And that's fine, because those thigh-strangling jodhpurs do no one any favors. Every time I see a woman in riding pants at Starbucks on Saturday morning when I'm grabbing a skim latte, I glance down at my flattering legwear and think, *Dodged a bullet there.*

My ex should count himself very lucky that I never took a long-term shine to clay pigeon shooting *(replace clubhouse window—1979, send flowers and Get Well Soon muffin basket to Range Master Rick at Highland Park Hospital—1980)* because I imagine my aim would have improved had I not been banned from the sport entirely. (Unlike me and jodhpurs, Rick did not dodge my bullet. I still feel terrible about that even though I know his shoulder healed nicely.)

Someone coughs into a napkin and the only other sounds are the clink of ice cubes melting in glasses and the creak of the swinging door opening and closing on the far side of the room as headwaiter Miguel gathers his team of servers in the back with the salad course. A minute ago, I was so looking forward to Centennial's signature spring mix blend with caramelized walnuts and goat cheese tossed in a warm balsamic dressing, but now my stomach is suddenly twisted in knots.

I can feel the pink tinge of shame starting to flower across my chest and up my neck. My cheeks begin to burn.

Most of the people here know that I just gave my big actuarial meeting opening line, yet they're all looking at me as though I'd confessed my deep and abiding love for practicing white witch-craft while frolicking naked in the moonlight to the music of John Denver, who's actually probably so retro he's cool again, especially on vinyl.

(By the way, Kelsey and Milo's apartment is full of vinyl records—full of them! They have knotty-pine paneled walls with spider-leaved plants suspended in macramé and lots of bright plastic chairs and owl-based knickknacks. Their tufted couch is made from crushed, burnt-orange velvet with paintings of big-eyed poodles staring down from the walls. They even have a horseshoe-shaped bar. Essentially, they've re-created the den in my parents' house, circa 1974.)

Why couldn't I have just introduced myself to Milo's extended family as Kelsey's mother and left it at that? Why did I have to try to be clever or cute? I'm neither of those things and that's perfectly acceptable; I have lots of fine qualities outside of comedy or country club endeavors. I make a mean heart-healthy frittata with garden-fresh herbs. I've never once been ticketed for speeding. My tax return is impeccable. (Not kidding; I should audit the IRS.) I have permanent premier status on two major airlines because of all the miles I've flown. Clever and cute aren't even blips on my radar, so why did I try to haul them out this evening . . . here . . . now?

I'm not one to feel sorry for myself or to make excuses; that's simply not my style. I feel there's little to be gained by dwelling in the past, by rehashing old hurts, by pulling off the scab again and again to see if the skin has healed.

For the most part.

But if I were to allow a moment of self-indulgence, I'd applaud myself for having held it together as well as I have in the past year and a half since my fiftieth birthday. For example, Karin, my best girlfriend since grade school, got a trip to Santorini, Greece, for her big 5-0.

Me? My husband got a girlfriend and I got a divorce.

Honestly, I thought we had it together, Chris and me. Our lives weren't perfect and we were quite young when we got married. Technically, we were the same age as Kelsey and Milo are right now, although we certainly felt older. That's likely because we didn't request vintage comic books on our wedding registry. (Not a judgment, just a statement of fact, and, oh boy, did my mother have something to say about *that* social faux pas.)

Chris and I had our share of ups and downs over the years, but I felt like we were on a definite upswing; we were finally empty nesters, with Topher at UC Berkeley, Jess in New York, and Kelsey in an apartment downtown with some of her friends. How lucky were we to have everyone out of the house in this economy, with a minimum of parental help? We were beating the odds, as thirty-six percent of all children between eighteen and thirty-six still live at home with their parents.

Look at poor Karin—her kids tell her they have no intention of leaving her house until they're at least thirty because they'll never be able to afford to live so well on their own. They say it's *her* fault for getting them accustomed to such luxury. I can't say I disagree with their logic. Who'd want to live in a hovel when they can stay rent-free in a sprawling home with a full-time cook, maid, laundress, and BFF all sewn into the perky package that is Karin?

Karin says all she wants is the freedom to walk down to the kitchen in her underwear. I kept telling her she should and maybe that would be the impetus to chase everyone out of there. Well, she finally took my advice . . . and now all her twenty-three-year-old son's friends have seen her in a thong. On the bright side, she says the Pilates has paid off and her boy's buddies called her a "smokeshow."

Again, not a selling point.

Anyway, I thought with the kids gone, Chris and I could finally have our own moments alone, whatever that might entail. We had so little time to be a couple on our own before Jessica was born—less than a year. Having lucked into the house so soon (although we weren't as fortuitous as we thought, we were soon to find out), Chris spent all his off time that whole year priming, painting, stripping, or sanding, and when I wasn't at work, I was cramming for my first set of accreditation exams. We were never wild and free newlyweds, so into each other and unencumbered by other responsibilities that we didn't even bother to turn on the television. We were both so exhausted every night, TV was pretty much all we could do. Heck, I'm still nostalgic for those days anytime I see a rerun of *The Golden Girls* as I flip through the guide.

While having a house and kids in such rapid succession wasn't our original plan, we made adjustments. We adapted. We thought, *We'll just roll with this. If we have our kids young, then we'll still be vital and vibrant when they're on their own. We'll pay off our mortgage and we'll travel the world with our original kneecaps and hips. Win-win.* So I thought we'd finally rediscover our whole lives together, and maybe give Dorothy, Rose, Blanche, and Sophia a rest, wink wink, but . . . turns out it was not me with whom Chris decided to wink wink.

Is it wrong to hate how damn comfortable Chris looks tonight with his new girlfriend? While Stassi isn't That Hussy Who Wrecked Our Lives, she is practically Jessica's age, which is almost worse.

Oh, hi, young lady for whom gravity is yet to be a factor! Love that you didn't want or need to wear a bra to this intimate pre-wedding family gathering!

I'm generally not so catty, but (a) thin fabric and (b) cold room. Do the math.

Patrick, my cousin and best friend since our mothers would stick us in a playpen together while they smoked and drank Gibson martinis, insisted I "glam it up" tonight, ditching my usual tailored suits for something more on trend. He said I should wear a cocktail dress cut a little lower, maybe with some sparkle at the neckline. But I'm here in my usual Elie Tahari two-piece with a tasteful silk shell. I figured if I tried to mix it up, everyone would see right through me, especially my daughters, and I'd never, ever hear the end of it.

I'm just going to say it—my daughters are the Mean Girls at the lunch table that is my life.

Here's what no one tells you in the parenting books—regardless of how many times you take an earlier flight home from your trip, giving up your business-class ticket to fly standby, squeezing into the middle seat between two gum-snapping, deodorant-eschewing, close-talking amateur sumo wrestlers just to capture on videotape your kid picking her tree costume out of her bunghole in the school play, and irrespective of all the years you pilot to work the Cheerio-encrusted, juice-box-filled, humiliation-mobile better known as a minivan solely for the children's safety and comfort (while rocking out to Radio Disney, which is so ubiquitous, you accidentally listen even when they're not in the car), and notwithstanding the dance moms and soccer dads and myriad other obnoxious booster parents with whom you have to make nice over the course of your children's quickly discarded and surprisingly pricey interests, it's entirely possible that sixty-six percent of your offspring will grow up to be Regina George, despite your best efforts to love them, feed them, house them, and buy them the exact kind of light-up sneakers that will ensure their positive self-esteem.

(P.S. God help you if those sneakers aren't Skechers.)

Everyone in the room looks at me expectantly. Again, I normally don't have to explain myself with this intro. "I . . . I . . ." I stammer. "What I mean is—"

My mother, the septuagenarian vixen better known as Marjorie Bancroft, snorts audibly. She's imperious as a queen in her seat, handmaiden and mini-me Jessica at her side, both of them with coordinating upswept platinum chignons and both sporting Marjorie's signature red Passion by Chanel lipstick, impeccably applied and contained entirely within their natural lip lines. (How do they manage that? Every time I wear bright lip color, I consider just rubbing it on my teeth from the start, simply to get the inevitable over with.) They're consuming matching Gibsons, too. I've yet to understand the allure of a cocktail featuring an onion. What's wrong with wine?

While my mother isn't without charm (mostly when she wants something), she can turn into the demon spawn of Judge Judy and Lucille Bluth once that first cocktail hits her system. I swear I feel a chill go down my spine every day at 4:00 p.m., Central Standard Time, earlier on weekends and special occasions.

Marjorie drawls, "Penelope, darling, do sit down."

Oh, and two drinks in, she forgets she's not British. I suspect this recent occurrence is due to the one-two punch of an influx of British snowbirds in her retirement community and her newfound fascination with *Downton Abbey*. Someone *wishes* she were the Dowager Countess is all I'm saying.

My knees buckle and I fall back into my seat without having explained my opening line. I glance at my cousin Patrick, who's at a table across the room with Auntie Marilyn, his mother; Uncle Leo, his dad; and Michael, his longtime partner. Patrick raises his glass in a mock salute and mouths, *Swing and a miss*, at me. I'd rage at him for not being supportive had he not specifically cautioned me about veering off-script earlier today.

"On a scale from one to ten, how sexy is tonight's outfit, with ten being the full Sofía Vergara? I'm talking sequins, sparkles, color, and no, taupe is not color. Nor is gray. I want to see Vegas, baby. I'm even lifting my moratorium on feathers. This is the first time you're meeting That Hussy, so you should glam it up."

"Different hussy," I reminded him. "Not the Original Hussy, remember?"

"Doesn't matter," he replied. "They're all hussies." Patrick has always been on my team, so the "tough love" he dispenses is a minimum of ninety percent for my benefit and ten percent for his own amusement, at best.

I asked, "Who do you consider a one on this scale, to make sure I have an accurate basis for comparison?"

Seriously, I wanted to set realistic expectations. I mean, I'm never going to be any kind of Kardashian for a variety of reasons, starting with age and ending with dignity. But I'd have been very happy to place the ten marker on the sexy scale at "Sandra Bullock" or "Helen Hunt" or "Diane Keaton a decade ago."

I feel I should be awarded a bonus for my ability to do long division in my head, like when a figure skater automatically is scored on a higher scale for including a quadruple jump in her program. The math part of me has to be a selling point. Patrick says it isn't, but women don't appeal to Patrick so he shouldn't be the arbiter of what counts. Plus, who never has a problem divvying up the bill equitably when the waiter forgets separate checks? Even when there are nine people at lunch and some ate the appetizer and some didn't, some had wine and some had water, and that one vegan only consumed a veggie kebab with tabbouleh and wouldn't shut up about not paying more than eleven dollars, no matter what? Who can always run the numbers, to the penny? *This* Penny.

He said, "Already I'm concerned you're placing the bar too low."

"I specialize in data analysis! I must be familiar with all the parameters to make an accurate calculation!"

He sighed. "Fine. Um . . . ahh . . . I should have known you'd ask. How about Queen Elizabeth?"

"Her? A *one*? She's such a badass. Remember reading how she insisted on driving King Abdullah around her Scottish estate herself in a Range Rover? Such an elegant screw-you gesture, considering the Saudi Arabian ban on women driving. So British, and I mean *real* British. Not Madonna British. Not Marjorie Happy Hour British."

I heard Patrick exhale on the other end of the phone. "No one's arguing that the queen's not a badass. On the scale of badassery, Liz goes to eleven. Only she could diminish the magnificence that is Kate Middleton, you know? Those post–Baby George volleyball shots where she still has a perfectly toned midriff? I die."

"I love her so much," I squealed, and I am generally not a squealer.

Patrick and I are obsessed with Kate Middleton, which makes some sense, considering how insane we were for Princess Diana back in the early 1980s. However, *one* of us wore Shy Di's feathery haircut better than the other, *ahem*, Patrick. During Royal Baby

Watch II, Patrick was calling me every hour to check in before Charlotte finally arrived. Mind you, he wasn't that invested with *my* children and he's Topher's godfather.

"Please. I love her more. If I could make a suit of her skin and wear it around, like Buffalo Bill, you know I would. But back to the queen—on the sexy scale of fussy hats, low heels, and dowdy dresses that don't show off the royal ta-tas, she's a one. Which tells me *you're* wearing a pantsuit tonight, aren't you? Don't lie, you lying liar."

The downside of having a cousin who's more like an evil twin is never being able to slide anything past him. It's impossible to hide anything from him because he has a sixth sense. He was at my house the morning after I had sex with Chris for the first time, with two bottles of Tab and a box of melba toast, ready for the dish. I didn't even tell him; he just knew.

"I'm already going to be uncomfortable enough with Chris and the New Hussy, so let me just wear the one thing that makes me feel confident, okay?" I begged. "Please? I swear on my love for the duchess that it's my nicest pantsuit—it's designer and has pin-stripes!"

"Fancy. Not." But I could feel him capitulating. "Then it's Let's Make a Deal time. You are going to give me final approval for your mother-of-the-bride dress; that is nonnegotiable. I will need to see shoulder, thigh, or cleavage. Not all three; I'm sure the New Hussy will have that (not) covered. But at least one. You have to do this. Not for me. For you."

"I promise I'll let you choose. I have two highly appropriate dresses—one's a rose red Carmen Marc Valvo sleeveless sheath with a peplum at the side, and the other is an Escada off-the-shoulder cocktail dress in navy with laser-cut lace covering a nude overlay."

"Neither sounds horrible," he grudgingly admitted.

"My God, it's as though Anna Wintour herself has given me her blessing. I'll let the saleswoman at Neiman's know neither 'sounds horrible.' I'm sure she's been standing by the phone, waiting."

"Ooh, sarcasm. Hit a nerve. Anyway, moving on." His voice took on more of a cheerleading tone, like he was revving me up for battle, which he sort of was. "I want you to think of the next four days of wedding events like this—they're a marathon, not a sprint. Pace yourself, kiddo. Don't run balls-out for the first eight miles and then call it quits. You'll be tempted, but ultimately that won't be satisfying. Also, don't let the bitches get you down. Yeah, most of the bitches are related to you, but you're not going to let them get you down. You're going to repeat the words of the famous philosopher Jinkx Monsoon with me—'Water off a duck's back.'"

"Water off a duck—wait, who?"

"Jinkx Monsoon. She won the fifth season of *RuPaul's Drag Race.*"

"Unfamiliar."

"Then put it in your Hulu queue; it's must-see. One more thing. As your best friend, as your family, as your *consigliere*, I beg of you: no actuary jokes. Not kidding. They only work when you're with your nerdzilla consultant buddies. Trust me. When you get scared or nervous, you start spouting off numbers and statistics and it's off-putting to everyone who isn't a human calculator. Please just be you, except for the actuary part, because that is *what you do*, not *who you are.* Leave work at the office."

So I can't say I wasn't warned. However, leaving work at the office isn't so easy for me. That's largely because Patrick is wrong; work *is* who I am at this point.

I mean, a few years ago, I had other roles—I was a wife. I was a mother. Now? I feel like what I do professionally is pretty much the sum total of who I am. And I *love* who I am at work—I'm the one who's in charge, not just because of my title, but because of the respect I've earned along the way. I'm the one other consultants come to when they have a problem they simply can't solve on their own. I'm the person who ensures the project is completed on time and under budget. I'm the one tasked with keeping the clients happy.

When I'm in my office, I'm competent, I'm in control, and I'm in demand. And when I finally have a chance to work with the data, which isn't as frequent as I'd prefer because of my other responsibilities, I feel such a sense of calm because of the utter predictability of the numbers. And then, at the end of the day, I come home and I'm . . . nothing anymore. What other purpose do I serve?

While I take responsibility for misreading the room tonight, I'm not sure I should be faulted for trying to introduce the one part of my life that's going exceptionally well to a situation that's so patently uncomfortable.

Topher, my only considerate offspring, pats me on the back and hands me a fresh glass of Riesling as I slink down into my seat. He smiles at me, and I see my own hazel eyes and same sprinkling of freckles mirrored on his kind face. I clutch the glass and glance over at Jessica. She has her arms crossed tightly over her chest, her cheeks sucked in, her lips pressed into a line, and she's scrutinizing the whole room, visually assassinating anyone who dares make eye contact. Patrick informed me this expression is called her Resting Bitch Face. I dare not meet her gaze, lest she turn me into a pillar of salt, all Lot-in-the-Old-Testament-style. (A quick deviation, if I may? Why salt? I'm a good Episcopalian, and I never figured out why his punishment was being turned into a pillar of salt. To me, that seems random.)

I quickly turn away to admire Topher's profile, noting how the corners of his lips are permanently tilted up, like he has a delicious secret, and is always on the verge of a full-on grin. That he inherited from his father. He has the sort of face that makes people comfortable approaching him for directions. I'm sure they'd request he watch their bags at the airport, were that allowed anymore. Before I realize what I'm doing, I run my hand over his wiry light brown hair, and he presses his head into my palm, exactly like Barnaby used to do once we finally realized that all we had was each other.

I'm thankful for a thirty-three percent success rate with offspring who have a fondness for me. He's such a good kid, through and through. Levelheaded and fair and honest. (My genes, obviously.) I have to wonder if he's cut out for the world of high finance—I certainly wasn't. How long did I last? A minute? I'm surely the only person who looks back on Black Monday as one of the best days of her life.

As for today? Not such a good day. I wonder how many times I'm going to replay this mortifying scene over again in my mind. A lot, I predict. Perhaps this gaffe will replace my stress-dreams where I've forgotten to study for my accreditation exams or show up for them naked.

"Penny can tell you when you're going to die because she beats the odds for a living."

I snap out of my reverie. Chris, who'd been seated at the polar opposite end of the room from me—at my request—is now standing. (Actually, my request was that he not be here at all. Ignored—thanks, Marjorie. All the decades she considered him beneath me, now she has to come around?) For a second I don't even realize it's him; he just seems like some handsome stranger attempting to dissipate the awkwardness and not like the person I'd most want to kick in the thorax.

Honestly, he doesn't look terribly different from when we met so many years ago. There's a fair amount of salt and a dash of pepper mixed in with his short blond curls, and there's considerably more wear and tear than when I spotted him for the first time in my tenth-grade speech class, but overall, he's not so changed. If he were a car, he'd be considered classic and not a junker. He'd have one of those fancy vintage license plates the State of Illinois issues.

Chris is still tall and ruddy with eyes the color of faded jeans and a quick smile. He's a bit weathered from spending so much time outside at job sites, and I can tell that Stassi isn't on him about diligent sunscreen application or cutting down on nitrates, which is a shame.

However, his health is no longer my problem or my responsibility. Although melanoma is the fifth most likely occurring cancer for males and his probability for contracting it is increased dramatically since he's over fifty. And he stands a sixty-seven percent higher chance of contracting pancreatic cancer than those who consume the fewest processed meats.

But again, not my business.

He continues. "See, she's not a bookie or a psychic—she's an actuary. She uses mathematical theory to assess risk. She was making a joke. Y'all need to laugh or you're going to make her feel bad, and then she's going to lower *your* life expectancy."

There's something about his still-boyish charm that warms the room and breaks the mood. People chuckle and raise their glasses to me. My mother nods toward Miguel, the headwaiter who's been working here for as long as we've been members. He's been my buddy ever since I was a little girl, always serving me extra cookies or the biggest cinnamon roll at the annual Christmas brunch or the end cut of triple-chocolate cake with the extra side of frosting. Foster, my older brother, used to get so jealous of the blatant favoritism Miguel showed me at meals. However, I'm convinced he felt sorry for me because I was perpetually in some kind of cast or brace or cervical collar. I suspect he worried my mother was abusing me . . . at least until he witnessed me playing a game of mixed doubles and realized I actually *was* that uncoordinated.

Miguel's the one who finally convinced me to start swimming in the club's pool. "Maybe you don't hurt yourself so much in water," he'd suggested. Turns out I was a strong swimmer, which is how I eventually came to work here as a lifeguard once I was old enough.

A tuxedo-clad staff begins deploying Centennial's signature salads with great efficiency, serving all thirty guests in a flash. Kelsey and Milo are sitting with his family, and they're both as excited about their salads as they are about each other. They're mooning over each other between bites, so I guess she must have forgotten her abject mortification at my introduction. Kelsey's even reaching for a second sunflower-seed roll, buttering it with gusto. Funny, but I lost my appetite right before my wedding, to the point that the seamstress had to add a couple of darts to compensate for my weight loss at my final fitting.

Milo's family seems somewhat uncomfortable in the country club setting. I'm not sure they're used to dining in a place with a strict dress code. Milo's dad's suit is ill fitting and his older brother's shirt still has creases in it from the store. His little brother was forced to wear one of the club's jackets, as he didn't have his own sports coat.

Kelsey doesn't tell me much, but from what I've pieced together, his family owns some kind of restaurant in conjunction with their small farm in Ohio, which is why Milo started a food truck instead of going to college. I suspect his people are more on the blue-collar side, not that there's anything dishonorable about working with your hands for a living. Rather, this is exactly why I told Marjorie the idea of an extended-family dinner at the club might be too much. I suggested we do something more casual to bring the families together initially, perhaps a barbecue or a picnic, but she wouldn't hear of it.

Still, Kelsey and Milo seem so happy together, and they do make a gorgeous couple, in an old-school, hippie-Coke-commercial kind of way, both of them with their flowing dirty blond locks and layers of ironic hemp-based clothing. Milo has a cherubic face, even with the scruffy beard. He looks like he'd be as comfortable playing a flute in a 1970s yacht rock band with Michael McDonald as he would be palling around with Jesus back in the day. As for Kelsey, she takes my breath away with her mineral-blue eyes and that fringe of black lashes . . . that are far too often narrowed at me for some unspeakable offense. She'll be a beautiful bride, though, resembling a wood nymph in her flower crown instead of a traditional veil, as it is her plan to look as natural and earthy as possible.

But not *too* earthy; I paid the price for that.

I promised myself I wouldn't interfere. The last thing I want is to turn into Marjorie, given how she railroaded my entire wedding day. I wanted a quick ceremony with a justice of the peace; I got three hundred people on the lawn here at Centennial Hills with a formal reception to follow in the grand ballroom. There was and is no middle ground or compromise with Marjorie.

Still, I'd be damned if Kelsey were to walk down that aisle in a strapless dress with tufts of fur under her arms. Not for me, because honestly I don't care. She's an adult and it's not my day. I just didn't want her to regret the decision later and then blame me for not having been more vocal.

Fine.

That's not the entire truth.

Maybe I made the deal a little bit for me, if you factor in having to listen to Marjorie for the rest of *her* life, all, "Why didn't you *force* her to shave?"

Oh, *Marjorie.*

As though *forcing* my daughters to do anything has been an option for at least a decade. Chris used to say that I spoiled the girls, but I didn't spoil them so much as I bent to their will because to do otherwise would have been like crossing the path of a speeding train.

The difference is subtle, but crucial.

The negotiation cost me honeymoon tickets to Portofino, the foolishness scheduled for tomorrow, and a portion of my sanity, but I got the job done, like I always do, and that's what's important.

Seems like grooming would have been one area where I could have enlisted Jessica's help, but she's so distant and oppositional. If I'd even mentioned the idea, she'd have taken the counterpoint, despite having written a whole treatise on waxing on her Sinclair-Sartorial blog. Per Jessica, everything below the eyelashes must go. Everything, even the tiny blond hairs on the pinkie toes. (Without my reading glasses—thanks, middle age—I can't see well enough to be sure I even have hair on my pinkie toes, but I shave them diligently anyway.)

I observe Jessica and Marjorie working their salads in unison, removing every morsel that contains calories or carbs or pleasure, forming a pile of croutons, dried cranberries, bacon, cheese, and nuts on the side plate between them, nothing but desiccated leaves remaining. When he thinks no one is watching, my father, the esteemed Maxwell Sullivan Bancroft, Centennial Hills Club gold-standard member and CEO emeritus of Bancroft Custom Cabinetry, snatches and then quietly mixes all their salad castoffs into his own.

I want to tell Milo's family to please relax and feel at home here, and that for all the pomp and circumstance of this stuffy place, ol' Sully and Margie Bancroft weren't exactly to the manor born. Had he not been a hardscrabble carpenter with an entrepreneurial spirit and she not been a looker, none of us would be eating signature salads right now. (And P.S. if Miguel is on his game tonight, he'll diplomatically remove breadbaskets and extra butter bells before the whole lot of them mysteriously find their way into the backseat of my father's car. Again.)

The thing is, we're all going to be family now, so I guess Milo's people and ours have the rest of our lives to learn each other's secrets.

After I finish my salad, Miguel clears my plate. "Hi, Miss Penny. You look so pretty tonight. I like your nice pantsuit. You are like a young Hillary Clinton."

"Hey, Miguel, thank you. You're looking quite distinguished yourself." He preens, smoothing back his pomaded silver hair and straightening his bow tie. "How are you? What's new? Haven't seen you in ages."

I know, *I know*, it's horrible and classist and exclusionary that this gracious older gentleman who has been my friend for decades has to call me "Miss" and I'm to call him by his first name. There's a reason I never wanted any part of the whole country club non-sense, and it's not just because I was bad at all terrestrial sports.

"Everything is so, so good! I will retire this year, and I'm gonna live winters back home in Puerto Rico and summers I will live here."

I have no idea what Miguel's job might be like, or the challenges he faces having to kowtow to the upper middle class on a daily basis, yet I've never seen him without a smile. His eyes are perpetually set to twinkle, which delights me, especially given that longevity is absolutely linked not just to quality of life but also to quantity.

"That sounds amazing. But why not stay there full-time? Who'd want to be in the boring old Chicago suburbs when you could be on the beach?"

"My granddaughter Alicia, she goes to University of Illinois at Chicago. Hey, you know, she studies to be an actuary, too. I bet she is going to like your joke. I will tell her tonight."

Before the next course is served, I've already set Alicia up with HR to join our summer internship program. Yes, I pulled some strings, which is something I never do. In fact, I wouldn't even help my own daughters secure summer jobs with my firm. However, if Alicia is anything like her grandfather, then my consulting firm will be lucky to have her on board. (And let's be honest, far better off than they would have been with Jessica or Kelsey.)

As I glance around the room, I inadvertently catch Chris's eye. He gives me that half grin that's become as familiar to me over the years as the sunrise, and as constant and as expected.

I feel the knot in my stomach return.

Chris raises his eyebrows and nods at me, the look we'd used once upon a time to telegraph to each other whether or not it was all clear to tiptoe out of the room of a sleeping child. Eventually, as the kids grew and no longer needed us to slay dragons in the night, this gesture just became shorthand and second nature for "Hey, are we cool?"

I don't return the nod.

Because he and I are not cool.

Not by a long shot.

CHAPTER TWO

mmediate family is huddled in the front pews at the church, with a few of our dearest friends gathered close behind us, everyone clad in appropriately somber colors, Bishop Gartner presiding over us.

There's no casket at this service; instead, just an elegant copper urn on a marble pedestal, surrounded by two grand wreaths woven out of ivy, white lilacs, pale pink peonies, and brilliant Nikko blue hydrangeas. The smell of sandalwood mixes with the flowers' perfume and permeates our senses with an almost overpowering sweetness. In the corner, in front of the apse and the altar, his portrait sits propped on an easel in a heavy gilded frame, as though watching us from the shadows. I do miss him so, much more than I'd ever imagined.

I have no doubt he's looking down on us right now, but I'd be hard-pressed to gauge his thoughts on the proceedings.

The clouds outside part and crepuscular rays of light shine in from the stained-glass window, casting a heavenly glow on the proceedings, almost like he's bestowing a blessing on us from the Other Side.

The bishop bids us to bow our heads in a final prayer for this memorial service. He says, "Amen," and before we even raise our eyes, we hear the haunting lyrics of "Ave Maria" being belted out by a trained baritone, emanating from the robing room off the north part of the transept.

I watch as the man attached to the beatific voice exits the robing room and stands in the center of the transept. He fills the room with his voice and his presence. A woman who's singing soprano follows him, and she's trailed by an entire gospel choir in full gowns with sashes that perfectly match the floral arrangements.

I fear this color coordination may not be an accident. I'm taken out of the spirituality of the moment and the bittersweet remembrance of a true gentleman as I mentally add this cost to the rapidly growing tally already accrued. In my head, the calculator hums along, adding in line items such as the out-of-season Nikko hydrangeas, the urn, the portrait, and the pedestal.

I no longer hear the dulcet lyrics of "Ave Maria" reverberating throughout the church—I can hear only the *ching! ching! ching!* of an imaginary cash register.

When the choir finishes the song, which was absolutely glorious, Kelsey turns to the rest of us and says, "He would have wanted us to end on a high note. Okay, guys, hit it."

The choir jumps into a particularly upbeat rendition of Kanye's "Jesus Walks."

Oh, this week keeps getting better and better. And it's still just Thursday.

Topher whispers, "The song samples the hymn 'Walk with Me,' which is I guess why Kelsey found this to be the appropriate finale."

"Sure, of course," I reply, because what else can I say here? As we observe the performance, I wonder if I have to pay for the ASCAP rights as well. My guess is yes. I imagine Kanye will need to get paid because Kim Kardashian does not strike me as one to use a Groupon.

Ching! Ching, ching!

"Listen, Mom," Topher says. "The pause right there? 'Where restless—pause—might snatch your necklace?' The choir's editing out the profanity and the use of the n-word, I guess with this being a church and all."

Patrick leans in on my other side and says, "Blasphemy's certainly top of mind when one's conducting a *dog funeral*."

Oh, did I not mention we're having a funeral for the dog?

Ever mindful, Barnaby passed peacefully in his sleep last weekend after never having been sick or showing any signs of discomfort. In terms of timing, he went at the best possible moment as to not disrupt any of the wedding plans. I suspect he took one look at the floral harness, the bow tie, and the straw hat Kelsey intended to strap on to him and death was his way of politely declining the invitation.

But poor Barnaby was not to be let off the hook so easily.

Kelsey insisted we do something to include him in the big day, and having a memorial service seemed to be the least offensive way to accomplish that. And since it's a Thursday morning, most people are at their day jobs and can't be here . . . or at least that's what I told Kelsey, because I made as few of those calls as possible.

I had today circled in my calendar, hoping I might be able to have some normalcy between wedding events, some adherence to my usual routine. The country club event was last night, and the rehearsal dinner isn't until tomorrow; today was supposed to be a catch-up day, where the grandparents could commune with their friends, where Topher could run down to Wrigley for a ball game.

Here's the thing: I'm a creature of habit. I admit this freely and fully. Having a set agenda gives me a deep and abiding sense of calm. I particularly enjoy waking up on Thursday because Thursday is kettlebell day, which is my favorite workout. I have an efficient home gym set up in my basement (complete with a television) and I like knowing that on any given Thursday at 6:20 a.m., I will be in the middle of my kettlebell dead lifts, which work glutes, arms, back, and abs. Except when I tried to exercise this morning, Kelsey said the television was bothering her and I was thumping around too much and she couldn't sleep. I have no idea how she heard me from two floors away, but I stopped anyway.

Then I went up to the kitchen to make coffee and watch CNBC and Marjorie complained that the espresso coming out of my Nespresso machine smelled "too ethnic," so I had to go drink it out on the porch. Normally I like to sit on the porch, but I hoped to catch the business news as one of my clients is going through a merger.

When I tried to make my seven forty-five a.m. breakfast smoothie, Kelsey came down to complain about the noise from the Vitamix, so I was stuck with yogurt topped with chia seeds. I'm half-surprised I wasn't chewing too loudly for her.

At nine, my team has a weekly all-hands conference call. Yes, I'm technically on vacation, but I'd planned to listen in anyway. That's when Jessica had a fit over logging into our Wi-Fi, and by the time I helped her resolve the problem with her IP address, the call was over.

And now, when I should be in the eleven o'clock new-business meeting, I'm at a dog funeral. No, wait, I mean "dog memorial service." The bishop insisted that we make this distinction to the guests.

"It's a dog 'memorial service,' and no need to be snarky," I whisper back.

Patrick pinches my arm in response.

Even though today is disrupting my plans, it's a necessary evil. I reply, "Plus, if funding Barnaby's service is the price of Kelsey's clean-shaven complicity and keeps Marjorie from having kittens at said underarms? Worth it."

I mean it. Because I am nothing if not Prepared with a capital "P." Truly. For example, although Kelsey picked the wedding date, I rented both backup heaters and air conditioners for the tent, because it's June in Chicago and the weather could truly vary by fifty degrees, often within one day. Heck, sometimes one hour.

In the course of this endeavor, I budgeted for plenty of overages, even though when I started the account to save for Kelsey's nuptials, I couldn't fully envision what form said financial overages might take. (Really did not anticipate using those funds for a dog ~~funeral~~ memorial service; I will admit that.)

When Kelsey announced her engagement last year, I asked her to come home so I could sit down and review the accounts I'd set up for her. She canceled on me half a dozen times before finally showing up hours late on the agreed-upon date, with no explanation. I picked her up from the Metra station in Glencoe, where she whined about how haaaaaard it was to take the train, even though she used to have no problem taking the train downtown to use my credit card at Nordstrom.

Kelsey eased herself cross-legged on the ladder-back chair perpendicular to the desk in my home office, shaggy hair falling in her eyes and the neck of her T-shirt sliding off her shoulder. She didn't look a day over twelve years old as she sat across from me, not mature enough to be left home alone, let alone be someone's wife, but I kept this opinion to myself.

I began by showing her the sums I'd stashed away via CD, mutual fund, savings account, and a handful of investments with small but steady streams of dividends. I explained, "These will all add up to my contribution. I can't speak for your father's plans, if he wants to kick in any additional funds to maybe pay for your honeymoon, or if your grandparents intend to do anything special. They may host something at the club. Regardless, this amount is certainly enough for whatever kind of wedding you'd like, unless you're suddenly Mariah Carey, as it's well over the national average cost of a wedding."

As a natural-born saver, I'd started low-risk mutual funds for all the kids' major life expenditures—weddings, college educations, cars, orthodontia, et cetera. Chris joked that I probably even had a fund for bail. (Truthfully, my Rainy Day Reserve could be earmarked for any purpose, up to and including legal fees, heaven forfend.)

"Now, here's something to think about, Kelsey, and I wish it were a choice that had been offered to your dad and me. This money is yours to start your new life together with Milo. If you two want a steak-and-salmon wedding in a Vera Wang gown with a full orchestra on the lawn of Centennial Hills, then game on! Know that your Mimsy will die a happy woman." Considering Kelsey's proclivities, at least in her current iteration, I didn't see a formal production being her preference.

She nodded, listening intently while chewing on a ragged thumbnail. She'd uncrossed her legs and was now wedged into the seat with her chin resting on her knees, arms wrapped around her shins, as though she somehow needed to protect herself during this conversation.

Why did everything between us have to feel so oppositional? We hadn't always been like this. I remember a time when I'd be in this same office, managing the accounting portion of Chris's construction business, Kelsey right by my side, her little shoulder pressed up against me. She'd beg for simple math problems and she'd solve them while I balanced Chris's books. Yet now I couldn't recall the last time she'd even been in my office, let alone clamored to spend time with me.

Looking for something to do with my hands, I neatened the already tidy stacks of financial statements. "However," I said, "if you'd rather use this money to truly invest in your future, we can go really simple and scale back on the wedding and you could take the money and put a down payment on a condo or one of those cute little bungalows on the north side of the city. You probably wouldn't be able to afford an actual house in a trendy neighborhood, but an investment in Chicago real estate is always a good call."

Truly, a gift like this would have changed the game for Chris and me. If we'd even been granted a taste of what my parents blew on the wedding we didn't want, our early life together would have been so much less stressful. For example, we might have slept better once we brought baby Jessica home had perpetual rain in the upstairs bedrooms not been a problem due to our shoddy roof. Although we adapted, I wondered if things would have turned out differently had our paths not been set in motion back then.

I continued. "Starting off on a solid foundation can only help you in the long run. Not to sound all 'PBS,'" the name the kids call me when I cite too many statistics, partially due to my initials, but mostly because they say I'm more boring than Pledge Drive Week, especially when I start quoting figures, "but the percentage of marriages that fail due to financial stressors is immense."

Kelsey bobbed her head and then tapped a flurry of words into her phone. Ugh, really? Had I *already* lost her interest? I'm not sure what kind of reaction I'd expected from her, but I'd hoped for some elation or gratitude . . . or maybe an invitation to go dress shopping?

Instead, I got typing.

She texted back and forth for a full two minutes before responding to me, her face finally wreathed in a rare smile. She sure was a lovely girl when she wasn't scowling, pouting, or grimacing. Grimacing was more Jessica's territory, but Kelsey was known to curl her lip on occasion as well.

Patrick says Jessica's the bitch and Kelsey's the baby, but he also claims they will swap roles whenever the mood suits them. I've told him many times not to mock my offspring, to which he always replies he'll stop mocking them as soon as they stop *making* him.

She told me, "Milo and I will opt for simple so we can keep the difference to fund our new life."

"Aw, Kels, that's terrific!" I said, so pleased that Kelsey actually wanted the option that came with delayed gratification for once. I've never known Kelsey, given the choice, not to eat her ice cream first. "We can still have a wonderful party on a budget. We'll go on Pinterest to brainstorm ideas. We'll just roll up our sleeves and do a lot of it ourselves. That will save us loads of money."

She wouldn't meet my eye as she picked at a loose thread on her cutoffs. "Yeah, thing is, we don't actually want a condo. Property ownership is kind of bourgeois, you know? Who can even say if we'll be into Chicago in a couple of years, right? No, we're going to buy a second food truck with the money. We're thinking biblical-themed stuff this time, like maybe Fishes & Loaves or Garden of Eatin' if we do mostly salads? We could have, like, Easter-egg salad sandwiches or Red Sea scallops or something really decadent, like a burger with a fried egg *and* bacon *and* avocado *and* three kinds of cheese would be a Sodom and Gomorrah? We're still playing with the ideas, but I feel like this truck would be mine to run."

Sweet Caroline's, Milo's first food truck, inspired by the work of musician Neil Diamond, was currently beating the grim odds for success in a highly competitive marketplace with offerings such as the Cherry, Cherry Danish, Forever in Blue [Berry] Scone, and Girl, You'll Be a Waffle Soon. (The Madagascar vanilla–laced whipped cream really added something special to the dish, I will admit.) However, I suspected Kelsey was less interested in managing her own line of business and more interested in distancing Milo from all things "Caroline," seeing how the truck was named for his previous girlfriend, who'd come to Chicago with him from Ohio.

Of all my kids, I worry about Kelsey the most. While she's proved to be savvy and talented in many respects, graduating at the top of her class, nabbing a coveted job in public relations right after college, she's also demonstrated a tremendous lack of commitment to, well, everything and everyone.

Three months into her PR career, she decided she hated corporate America. She said that trying to sway public opinion about people and products was deceitful and underhanded. After two years of living in her sorority, she simply abandoned her sisters and her membership chairman position and moved into an apartment off campus without telling anyone, having grown tired of the whole enterprise.

When Kelsey was in high school, I was never sure what persona she would adopt from year to year, bouncing effortlessly from "soccer star" to "hip-hop fly girl" to "Lilly Pulitzer–clad class vice president," although more often than not, these phases related to her boyfriend or circle of friends du jour.

Let us never speak of the short-lived Bollywood phase, as I have no earthly idea where that originated. (*Slumdog Millionaire*, maybe? Thanks, Redbox.)

Yet remembering all those damn saris, bindis, and the chapati griddle gathering dust up in the attic is what broke me.

"Whoa, hold on," I said, with a force that surprised us both. Even Barnaby was startled, but he quickly regained his composure. You don't last eighteen-plus years by being a nervous Nelson. "No, I'm sorry, you misunderstood. Buying your fiancé a second food truck wasn't one of the options. You realize that forty-five percent of food truck businesses fail within the first year, yes? And of those on the road, forty-one percent of them currently violate sanitation standards, and they can be shut down at any time. This is not happening. You're not taking the money I've been diligently shepherding *away* from risk for twenty-three years and placing it squarely in harm's way. You can have a wedding or a down payment on a home. You're not pissing away your future on a Jesus-themed truck *when you don't even attend church anymore*. Period."

Kelsey sprang out of her seat, eyes damp with tears, arms wrapped protectively around her slight frame. "I should have known I couldn't count on you! No wonder Daddy didn't want to stick around."

I glanced over at the crystal clock on the corner of my desk, an award for managing the top-producing practice within my consulting firm for three years in a row. I thought of the weight of the crystal in my hand, the considerable heft of that leaded glass. I imagined for a moment what it might feel like to hurl the clock against the wall, watching the whole thing shatter into pieces, spraying the room with flesh-puncturing shards and bits of the very inner workings that kept the trains running on time, a satisfying burst of springs and wires and components.

Instead, I took note of the actual time and realized that I needed to make a call before I followed Kelsey down her rabbit hole of emotional blackmail. I steadied myself. "Kelsey, this is a joyful occasion and I truly don't want to argue with you. That's not what this is about. I want you to have what you want. We can work this out, but I'm supposed to call a Realtor now, so if you can give me five, then I'm yours for the rest of the afternoon for us to make plans."

This was a capitulation on my part and we both knew it, but I tried to play it off like it wasn't. I needed at least a semblance of being in charge.

She narrowed her eyes at me. "Why are you calling a Realtor?"

"To finalize details about listing the house."

Her brow furrowed. "But why?"

I explained, "Everyone's gone, and Barnaby and I certainly don't need this many square feet."

Plus, I hated being alone in such a big, empty house. I loathed the sound of my sensible heels echoing down the hallway when I'd return from work at night. I abhorred paying to heat and air-condition so many vacant bedrooms. I despised writing checks to a landscaping company to maintain a yard I used only to curb my dog. And I wanted to sell while the market was still rebounding so heartily.

More than anything, I needed to get the hell away from the scene of the crime, as I actively avoided the living room now. Given the circumstances, everyone should have been glad I was selling the place and not, say, committing arson. Every day I didn't buy a blowtorch and a gas can should have been considered a victory. I didn't care how long I lived, I'd never get the image of the open bottle of wine, those two glasses, one with lipstick on the rim, and smooth jazz in the background out of my head, walking in to Chris and That Hussy on the couch when I returned home a day early from my business trip as a surprise.

Yes, indeed, I'd say we were *all* surprised.

"Where will you go?"

"I've been looking at town houses on the north side of the city, close to Cousins Patrick and Michael. Barnaby will still have a little patch of grass with trees and birds. Or maybe I'll live farther south and finally get to walk to work for the first time in my career. Doesn't that sound great, Barnaby?"

From his bed in the sunny corner spot, old Barnaby thumped his tail. He was the kids' dog and had previously preferred the company of anyone to me. But since we'd been on our own together for the past six months, we'd formed a solid bond. We may not have been best friends for his first eighteen years, yet here at the end of his life, he'd come to value my companionship as much as I valued his.

"Then who's going to live here?"

"I guess whoever wants to buy the house. Highest bidder, I suppose." I calculated I'd have an offer on the house within a month, as the average market time in my area was sixty days. Given the amount of time it would take to close escrow, I estimated I could be living in downtown Chicago by the fall.

"What if I want to get married here?"

I picked up the Realtor's card and began to dial her number. "I'm sorry, what?"

Twin spots of color began to burn on Kelsey's fair cheeks. Oh, no, she was winding up. "I said, what if I *want* to have my wedding here? The yard is big enough for a tent with a huge dance floor. And they have those trailers with the upscale Porta-Potty bathrooms that can be wheeled in, too."

"Is having your wedding here a possibility?" I asked, hanging up the phone, when really, what I should have been doing was battening down the hatches. "You've lived in this house your entire life and you've never once mentioned you'd want to be married here. You've talked about dozens of places—from the top of the Hancock to the Botanical Garden to Coachella to Italy to Forks, Washington [let us never speak of the brief *Twilight* obsession again], to the Rainbo Club downtown. The one place you've never mentioned is *here*."

Her voice took on a shrill quality, pitched at the exact decibel that often causes spasms in my left eye. "So now I'm not *allowed* to have my wedding here? You're all, 'You can have anything you want, except everything.' Nice. Real nice. Thanks a lot, *Mom*."

I struggled to stay calm, and I could feel my head beginning to throb. My left eye began to twitch. I pinched the bridge of my nose to relieve some of the mounting pressure inside my sinuses. "Honey, I didn't say anything like that. Have your wedding where you want."

At this point, she was practically shrieking. "Fine. My wedding will be *here* next year. One year from now."

Barnaby looked at me out of the corner of his eye, his old brow wrinkled as if to say, *I do believe you've stepped in it now, Miss Penny.*

Evenly, I said, "We can do whatever you want—but are you sure you don't need to discuss anything with Milo?"

Granted, I was anxious to move downtown and to get away from the unhappy memories here, but not at the expense of ruining Kelsey's dream, even one she hadn't thought to mention *once in twenty-three years.*

I wasn't so selfish that I couldn't wait twelve months to downsize. I'd just continue to avoid the living room. I could put up one of those lovely Japanese rice-paper room dividers, perhaps. I'd simply remind myself every day that I didn't get mad—I'd gotten everything (including Barnaby), which is why the house was mine to sell in the first place. Chris had let me have it without any kind of fight.

But really, what else could he have done?

While my gut feeling was that Kelsey's decision came from a place of petulance, spite, and immaturity, I wasn't about to say that out loud.

"No, I don't. He *trusts* my decisions, unlike *some* people." Then, and I'm not sure if I imagined this or not, she stomped her foot, exactly like she used to do when Chris denied her a second Popsicle.

I sighed, rubbed my left eye, and looked at the Realtor's business card again. "Then I guess I'm going to cancel my listing appointment."

"I guess you are." With a smirk and the grace of a trained dancer (largely because she took—and subsequently quit—ballet, contemporary, ballroom, Latin, swing, popping, locking, and Masai African–style lessons), she sashayed to the doorway before turning around to say, "P.S. this house needs major refreshing before the wedding, hashtag ExtremeHomeMakeover. I'd start with the powder room."

She slammed the door on the way out, and for the first time ever, Barnaby growled at Kelsey. He rose from his bed to lick me once on the hand before lying down again, paying me his ultimate compliment.

As I heard Kelsey thump up the stairs, I viewed the account summaries again. I said to Barnaby, "I suspect this wedding is going to cost me so much more than I planned, in every possible way."

And as I stand here now in the rectory, post memorial service, writing out a check to the bishop that includes an unanticipated comma, thanks to Kanye, I find myself thinking two things: First, Monday can't come soon enough, and second, Barnaby deserved this day more than my spoiled daughter.

CHAPTER THREE

To: jessica@sinclairsartorial.com,
gabby@gabbyngretch.com

From: gretchen@gabbyngretch.com

Date: June 4th

Subject: Do the right thing

Jessica,

The new issue of *Us Weekly* is out and there are still no shots
of Mila Kunis pumping gas in the Stars—They're Just Like
Us section wearing our Gabby 'n Gretch ostrich-skin
booties. In your own words, "Those bitches at *Us* owe me,
like, so many favors I can't even. Consider this a done deal,"
but the photos have yet to materialize. It's been six months,
Jessica, and we've been beyond patient. And now per your
voice mail, you won't return the payment for our
"guaranteed placement," saying we should have gotten the
terms of the deal in writing? Jessica, *that's why we signed a
contract with you!* Don't force our hand here, okay? I told
Gabby this all has to be a misunderstanding—so please just

do the right thing, return the payment, and we can all get on with our respective businesses.

Regardless of how large the fashion world might seem, it's actually pretty insular and people talk. Make sure the story everyone has to tell about you is a good one.

Best,

Gretchen Perillo

Founder

....

Swing into a shoe-nique experience at:
GABBY 'N GRETCH
48 Jane Street
New York, New York 10014
gabbyngretch.com

BY THE NUMBERS

To: jessica@sinclairsartorial.com,
gretchen@gabbyngretch.com

From: gabby@gabbyngretch.com

Date: June 4th

Subject: WTF, SINCLAIR

Nice ostrich-skin G 'n G booties on your latest Instagram, Sinclair. Pro tip: Next time you decide to wear stolen merch, post your ill-gotten gains on a private account.

See you in court, bitch.

Gabby Perillo

P.S. Ten bucks says you don't even know Mila Kunis.

....

Swing into a shoe-nique experience at:
GABBY 'N GRETCH
48 Jane Street
New York, New York 10014
gabbyngretch.com

To: jessica@sinclairsartorial.com

From: interncassie@sinclairsartorial.com

Date: June 4th

Subject: Status check-a-roni!

Hi, Jess! Okay, you said to stay off your jock while you were with the fam, but you got this weird thingie today and I wasn't sure what to do? A crease and desist something from Mila Kunis? That's so cool—I didn't even know you knew her! *Black Swan*, I die! Anyhootie, the letter's on your desk.

Also, the guy from the building's leasing office called and he sounds hella shitty. Can't tell if he's salty 'cause he's mad or if it's just 'cause he's Eastern Euro and they all sound aggro, 'cause they spit when they talk. Anyhootie, I've got everything handled here, so zero troubs!!

XO, Cassie

. . . .

"Well, that was . . . unique," I say.

Jessica has been thumbing through videos on her phone and glances over at me in the driver's seat. "I'm glad Kelsey isn't too preoccupied with her important wedding plans to post Vines from the funeral."

"Memorial ceremony," I automatically correct.

"Memorial ceremony," she repeats. She taps the screen with a matte silver–polished nail. "I like this one where the baritone in the choir lifts Barnaby's urn all baby-Simba style during the 'Jesus Walks' chorus. Wow. How does anyone still wonder why ISIS hates us?" Then, to herself, Jessica mutters, *"Someone* needs to learn to tell that girl no."

I pretend I don't hear her. "Did you say something else, sweetie?"

"Negatory."

Jessica and I are driving down Green Bay Road. We have the great pleasure (sarcasm intended) of riding home together, as I'd been settling the bill while Jessica was outside having a phone conversation that seemed rather heated. When we'd both completed our business, everyone else had scattered and she was faced with the choice of carpooling with me or hoofing it home in those crippling little booties she's wearing. And yes, I felt terrific when she seriously considered hobbling herself on the four-mile hike home in lieu of spending ten minutes in the car with me.

After Barnaby's memorial service, the immediate family went out to lunch so we could "continue to celebrate his amazeballs life," according to Kelsey. She insisted not only on seating Barnaby's urn at the head of the table, but she also ordered him a plate, daring me to object. She said I owed it to him for all the years I didn't allow her and her siblings to feed him table scraps.

If Kelsey only knew about all the chicken, cheese, and crackers Barnaby wolfed down in the past year and a half! I'm convinced my finally playing fast and loose with the treats is why he lived so long. He and I would settle in together to watch *Homeland* or *The Good Wife* and we'd play the one-for-me, one-for-you game. If the episode was particularly riveting—Julianna Margulies, you are a national treasure—sometimes I'd accidentally skip his turn. When that happened, Barnaby wouldn't drool, bark, or nudge. Instead, he'd ever so gently lay a paw on my thigh to prompt me. I imagined him sounding exactly like an old Southern gentleman, his accent as thick, sweet, and slow as if he'd been birthed on a plantation in the middle of the Mississippi Delta. I could practically hear him saying, *Begging your pardon, Miss Penny, but I do believe you've forgotten something, if it's not too much trouble.* And then I would give him two pieces of whatever I was eating to compensate for my grievous error.

Funny, although I was never much of a dog person, once all this wedding stuff is over, I'm seriously considering going to the shelter. Of course, Patrick says I need a man. I choose to interpret his advice to mean "male dog."

Anyway, because Barnaby did not reassume his corporeal form in the canine version of Easter Sunday and join us at the table, his uneaten cheeseburger is now sitting in a Styrofoam container on the backseat. Topher will make short work of it later when he returns from the Cubs game, and he should, because it's *Kobe* beef. Honestly, we couldn't make the sacrificial gesture with the six-dollar ground-sirloin burger on the menu? We had to order the kind from a cow that received massages while listening to Bach concertos? That's not a lunch; that's a spa day. And did our beloved yet now-deceased beagle really also need Parmesan truffle-oil fries, a side kale salad, and a blood orange milk shake as part of the sacrifice? Come on!

Topher consuming the Symbolic Sandwich will likely anger Kelsey, but I'm not tossing out a gourmet lunch, especially given the waste with the wreaths. She was adamant about the Doggie Death Flowers not being reused for the wedding, despite having lilacs, hydrangeas, and peonies as part of her floral design concept. Bishop Gartner said he could bring them to a parishioner's grandmother's wake tonight, so I hope they give comfort to another family. I personally ripped off the silk banners that read BARNABY—BEST DOG EVER; no one needs to accidentally see that when they're trying to grieve for their beloved meemaw.

"I feel like I haven't talked to you at all since you've been home," I say. "Except about wedding details. How are you? How's New York?"

I expect a diatribe here as there's nothing Jessica holds in higher esteem than her city. She fell suddenly and profoundly in love with New York when she went out for her college visits before her senior year, and she's yet to stop talking about all the ways in which the Big Apple reigns supreme over the Windy City, even in areas that aren't particularly brag-worthy, such as a supposed 1:1 rat-to-person ratio.

"Fine."

Okay, we're doing one-word answers, then. How newsy and informative. I try a different tack. "Your recent blog post is very dramatic, with you balancing on the railing of the High Line in those heels with that striped Chanel skirt? Wow."

"Thanks."

Truly, her Web site is as much a paean to the city as it is to couture. If I hadn't been to New York so many times on business, I'd definitely want to visit after seeing it through Jessica's eyes.

I say, "Your Web site's more and more like a magazine every time I look at it. Is someone art directing you, or are you using a photographer or other stylists?"

"Tripod."

Around the time Chris and I split up, Jessica started a fashion blog and styling business. She'd had an internship with a famous designer after graduating from FIT but didn't last there too long. She said she could have spent years toiling behind the scenes in the industry, but this way, through social media, she's actually setting the trends instead of chasing them.

Each week, she posts artfully posed pictures of herself in various spots around Manhattan, like the recent photos on the High Line, which is an elevated park created out of an old, unused section of railway line, spanning a couple of miles across the west side of the city.

Jessica's blog is consistent in that she's always photographed in her trademark red lipstick, carrying a bag that costs as much as my first car, with her eyes obscured by some fabulous pair of sunglasses. She's a modern take on Grace Kelly in her photos, more effortlessly cool and collected at twenty-six than I could ever hope to be. I follow all of her accounts, and she certainly seems to live a beautiful life, even if she chooses to tell me about it only one word at a time.

(P.S. I believe culottes are coming back.)

"I'd never know the snapshots of you weren't straight out of *Vogue*."

"Thanks."

Okay, I'm going to get a full sentence here if it kills me. I know. I'll find common ground, discussing her interests. "Who makes the shoes with the little metal studs on them?"

"Valentino."

DAMN IT. Toss me a bone here! "Are they comfortable? You must have felt fairly steady in them to have been able to scale the railing like that."

She did not inherit her sense of balance from me, that's for sure.

"Not even remotely. But I got the stiletto lift, so they're not unbearable."

"Should I be familiar with that?" I ask.

"The stiletto lift is Botox for your feet. Basically kills all the feeling down there on a temporary basis, sort of like cosmetic cortisone. Makes wearing heels less painful."

"Whoa," I said, automatically touching my laugh lines. "I haven't even gotten Botox in my face yet."

"No kidding," she replies, but not with vitriol. No one's surprised that I'm not an early adopter, especially of anything that includes a level of risk. But I've been perusing the analysts' reports about Allergan's (Botox's parent company) stock and read about a predicted fifty percent increase in demand in the next ten years. Karin keeps insisting my time with the tiny needle is coming soon, particularly if I ever plan to pursue a man of the two-legged variety. (While I've taken fine care of myself, Father Time is kind of an unrelenting jerk.)

Until now, I've resisted invasive types of anti-aging, for fear of turning into Marjorie II, as my mother patronizes plastic surgeons like other grandmas frequent garage sales or Bingo night at St. Mary's. If it can be nipped, tucked, tightened, plumped, injected, smoothed, lasered, or sandblasted, Marjorie's had it done. I live in fear of the day someone mistakes us for sisters.

She's never been able to fix her hands, though. Her knuckles bulge with arthritis, and deep tributaries of blue veins are prominent over the ridges of her metacarpal bones, the fat deposits of youth long gone. Her hands are her own personal portraits of Dorian Gray. She figures if she wears enough diamonds, no one will notice, and she's probably right.

Because I've had so much time inside my own head over the past year and a half, I wonder if a few cc's of Botox would have made a difference. Clearly something drew Chris away from me and to a woman half my age—was it because she had so much less tread on her tires? (Or is it more tread? Chris was in charge of buying our tires, so I might have the analogy wrong.) Given that sixty percent of all spouses cheat and that fifty percent of all unions end in divorce, I guess I should have been more vigilant, more diligent, or at least less surprised that it happened to me.

Few endeavors have a higher capacity for risk than marriage. Yet we still blithely walk down the aisle on our father's arm, a vision in a poufy white dress, surrounded by everyone we know, absolutely certain that we're going to be different; we're going to be the exception to the rule. Yet the fact remains in half of all marriages, we won't. I won't even explore the path of the sixty-seven percent failure rate for the second time around or the seventy-three percent likelihood of divorce in the case of third marriages.

When I mentioned these startling statistics to Karin, I said they made me want to become a cat lady. She corrected me, telling me the term I meant to use was "cougar."

"No," I replied, "not a cougar. I don't want to date a younger man. I would rather get fifteen cats than ever go through any of this again. Can you imagine voluntarily boarding an airplane with those odds? 'Thank you for choosing Fifty Percent Chance Air today, ladies and gentlemen. Our flying time to beautiful Maui will be eight hours, unless we plummet to the ground somewhere over Sacramento with such velocity that the impact scatters debris for three square miles, which happens about half of the time. Either way, enjoy the ride!' No, thank you."

I guess my point is, if Botox leads to dating, dating might lead to a relationship, which will possibly lead to a second marriage and its sixty-seven percent failure rate, and I simply *cannot* at this point. I can't. However, I'm encouraged by Jessica's two-word response, even if said response set me off on a whole mental tangent I'd prefer to forget. I appreciate progress in any form, so I continue trying to eke conversation out of her.

I say, "How's the styling part of your business coming? Any new clients, exciting new projects? Didn't Kelsey say you had a lead with that actress from the ballet movie?"

Everyone digs talking about her job, right? Heck, I *wish* someone would ask me how my career is going. I live to discuss work! Although I don't do nearly as much hands-on analysis as I used to, which is a shame; and if I'm promoted to executive vice president (fingers crossed!), then I'll be completely removed from that part of the job. I'll miss the data analysis, because running the numbers was always my favorite challenge, but becoming an EVP is the next logical step in my career path.

As I moved up the corporate food chain over the years, my managerial duties expanded and so did my travel schedule. For a while I was a serious road warrior, gone Monday mornings until

Thursday nights. Wasn't my preference, but because of Chris's business, we didn't have a lot of choice, not with teeth to straighten, three sets of college tuition to pay, and cars to buy.

I glance over, hoping Jess gives me the inside scoop like she used to when she did photo shoots with famous people for her designer boss. I couldn't always keep every star's name straight, but I got such a kick out of recognizing them in the nail salon magazines. No one was ever who they seemed to be, from the squeaky-clean tween heartthrob who'd bang groupies in the bathroom between shoot takes, to the alleged drug-addicted punk rock queen who sent every person on the staff a handwritten thank-you note and home-made toffee.

"This town is stuck in a time warp," Jessica hisses.

No work chat, then. But maybe she wants to complain about her old hometown in front of an audience. If that means more than one word at a time, I'm all for it. Although it seems like the only thing New Yorkers enjoy more than telling you why *their* city is so great is dissecting exactly what's wrong with *yours*. Personally, I don't mind because I've never once needed to have Afghan food delivered at two o'clock in the morning and I like living without bars on my bathroom window.

Jessica gawps at a father and son on the bike trail. "My God, are those people on an actual *bicycle built for two*? I didn't know they existed except in an old-timey song! And them! Look there!"

I glance to my right to see an effervescent young family, the father clad in a pair of khakis and a pink golf shirt, being dragged along by an enormous golden retriever. The dog's mouth is comically agape with two tennis balls jammed in his maw. While I hesitate to call the dog a quitter, if pet pictures on the Internet have taught me anything, it's that he could stuff in a third one if he tried.

The mother of the group is wearing a splashy tunic covered in a sea horse print, cut in a way that makes her look almost completely asexual, as is the style around here. (We WASPs will never be accused of bringing sexy back; just ask Patrick.) The mom's paired her top with leggings and Jack Rogers sandals, and her two young daughters are wearing little dresses in the same print. They're so cute I kind of want to stop the car and hug them all.

"The McMatchingshirts are carrying a legit picnic basket, not a cooler or an insulated bag, but old-school wicker. I bet they have red-checkered napkins in there and real silverware. Holy shit, they have the same hair color as the dog! Who color coordinates with their pets? These people! Ten bucks says they have a flag in front of their house with a watermelon and the word 'summer' embroidered on it. Oh, and I can't *even* with the woman's outfit. I bet she isn't even thirty-five, yet she dresses like she's fucking *fifty*."

"To be fair, when she's eighty, she'll probably still dress that way," I reply, remembering all the octogenarians sporting big ol' hair bows in Marjorie and Max's West Palm senior living community. My parents moved there mostly full-time after my father retired and my brother, Foster, took over the company.

Jessica gives me one of her trademark grimaces. "The dog's leash matches the dad's belt. Who has time for that? Who wakes up and is all, 'What should I wear today? I dunno, lemme see what the dog's in the mood for.' Ugh. Killing self-comma-others now. What planet do these people come from?"

I focus on the road again. "Planet Glencoe, same as you."

"Then I amend my statement about Glencoe being in a time warp, because this place was never about bike rides and matching belts and family picnics for us," she says.

Oh, good. *There's* the vitriol.

I steal a glance, and her face is stony. "Come on, Jessica. We did plenty of family activities exactly like that when you were a kid."

She snorts. "Is that how you remember it?"

This again. Maybe I had to put in a few hours on the weekend here and there in the beginning when I was restarting my career, but trying to argue that point isn't worth it. Reasoning with Jessica is as impossible as it is with Marjorie. I can have all the facts and figures in the world at my disposal, and if one of them disagrees, that's it. End of story.

For example, Marjorie's primary care physician suggested she eat more protein, so I said she should add a chicken breast to her daily plate of lettuce because it's low in calories and God forbid she beef up to a size six like all the fat fatties out there. She dismissed my suggestion immediately, saying chicken contains no protein. I explained, no, in fact, each three-point-five-ounce serving contains thirty grams of protein, which is fifty percent of the recommended daily allowance, and again she explained I was wrong, which, argh! Just because she *says* I'm mistaken doesn't *mean* I'm mistaken, especially when the entire United States Department of Agriculture requires that irrefutable proof be placed on every food label.

Anyway, Marjorie came up with her own solution—now she subs out one of her beloved Gibsons for a White Russian made with Ensure each day.

Point is, as I can never win with these two, I do my best to not engage.

"Some people appreciate the consistency around here," I say, deliberately switching the topic away from Jessica's childhood, which, if you ask anyone but her, was idyllic. Maybe she didn't have two parents at every single event, but one of us was always there.

We've reached the wide, tree-lined boulevard where I live. The stately old homes here are set far back from the road and wide apart, which is apparently a tremendous selling point, according to my listing agent, who can't wait to do a walk-through with me. "I was talking to a Realtor, who tells me that even after the housing bubble burst, places on the North Shore were still selling at a twenty-two percent higher asking price than the national average. She said that people will always want access to excellent public schools, shopping and recreation, and low crime rates."

Jessica says nothing, and her silence feels oppressive. Suddenly, I long for her one-word answers.

My hometown of Glencoe is one of the sleepy suburban cities along Lake Michigan, spanning from Evanston to Lake Bluff. This area was made famous in movies from *Ordinary People* to *Mean Girls* and every John Hughes film in between. I've lived here my entire life, save for college and a couple of years after graduation when I lived downtown.

"If you're so Team Glencoe, then why are you even moving to Chicago?"

I don't explain that I'm ready to travel lighter, to start anew, to leave behind painful memories, largely because I'm far too distracted by the enormous antique claw-foot bathtub blocking the driveway to my house.

I slam on the brakes before I hit the damn thing, mom-arm automatically flying out to brace Jessica in case of impact.

A quick aside—why do I still do the nonsense with the arm? How reckless is this? Wouldn't everyone be better served in case of emergency if I kept both my hands on the steering wheel, preferably at eight and four? I'm a risk-management professional—one would imagine I'd know better, yet here we are.

"What in the *actual fuck*?" I crane my neck to the right to get a closer look as I back out of the drive.

"Whoa, language! Do you kiss your mother with that mouth, PBS?" Jessica laughs, so shocked to hear me drop an f-bomb that she momentarily forgets she's mad at me for supposedly turning her childhood into a Charles Bukowski novel.

"No, I do not, but that's mostly because she tastes like cocktail onions and Kahlúa," I reply. Jessica snorts and I'm two for two. Woo-hoo! I should drop the mic and peace-out right now because I've never had a winning streak like this before.

"Is that a . . . bathtub?" Jess asks, squinting through the windshield.

I park the Camry (an Insurance Institute for Highway Safety Top Pick Plus, Midprice Moderately Sized Division) in front of the house and hop out to take a look. "Yes. This is definitely a bathtub. I've been watching a lot of *Antiques Roadshow*, so I'd say this is a nineteenth-century double-slipper claw-foot cast-iron tub, if you want to be specific. She's a beaut. A real two-seater. I guess the question is, *why* is it here?"

"Kelsey mentioned she was looking for one to hold craft beers at the reception," Jess explains.

"Will the caterers not bring coolers?" I ask. "I can pay extra for coolers. Or is this an aesthetic thing, like the straw hats and all the burlap?"

"It's definitely for a *look*," Jessica confirms. But from her expression, I can't tell whether or not she approves of said look.

"You're a design person. Do you like what you've seen so far?" I query. "Seems like Kelsey's been pretty creative."

Personally, I've been to so many cookie-cutter-Martha-Stewart-North-Shore-country-club weddings where everyone asks for the same exact Crate and Barrel casserole dishes and Pottery Barn tablecloths that it's refreshing to encounter something offbeat, even if that offbeat item is currently obstructing my driveway like so much butter in a fat guy's artery.

"Honestly?" Jessica says. "The whole thing is ultra try-hard. Found objects are pretty 2014, you know. I feel like Kelsey Googled 'Hipster Wedding Clichés' and then started a Pinterest page. Even the whole hipster thing is passé. Yuccies are what's next."

"What's a Yuccie?"

"Young Urban Creative."

"Like the Yuppies from my generation?"

"Sort of like Yuppies, only less fun and more smug. And they use hashtags and smoke high-caliber weed."

"They're basically Sasha and Ryan?" I say, referring to Karin's self-important "social media expert" offspring who refuse to leave her house.

"Exactly. Back to Kelsey, did she even run any of this wedding nonsense past you?"

While Jessica's speaking, I attempt to lift a side of the tub, but this thing must weigh a thousand pounds. I may be strong, but I'm not moving it on my own, that's for sure. "In the beginning, yes, but she thought I was being critical when I was only trying to help, so she stopped. Now the extent of my involvement is writing checks. A lot of checks."

Jessica laughs.

Jessica laughs?

Jessica laughs!

Whoa! Look at us, having a hostility-free conversation! I love seeing Jessica's now-impeccable straight, white teeth when they're not exposed via snarling or grimacing or being bared at me. Hey, everyone on Sheridan Road—*I made Jessica laugh!*

Granted, I'm not so comfortable discussing one kid with another, but at least Jess is speaking to me in full sentences—paragraphs even, and not paragraphs about how she has to pay a therapist one hundred and thirty-five dollars an hour to repair all the damage I've caused by missing her semifinal tennis match in ninth grade, where Chris, Mimsy, Gumpy, Num-Num (Chris's mother), Uncle Foster, Aunt Judith, Topher, Kelsey, and a passel of assorted cousins all sat in the front row, cheering her on while I was on a plane coming home from Kansas City, having just run the project that allowed us to pay for the tennis camp that gave her the skills to make it to the semifinals in the first place.

Sometimes it feels like neither Jess nor Kelsey ever grew out of the surliness and drama that pits mothers and daughters against each other during their teen years. I've been waiting for us to find common ground, and this silly little conversation is a tiny life preserver in the middle of a roiling ocean. Sure, we'll probably all still drown or have our Botox-filled feet bitten off by sharks, but not right this minute. For the first time, I wonder if it's possible we could actually have a functional adult relationship someday. Dare I hope?

While Jessica speaks, her eyes keep flicking down to her phone. "Has she thanked you for anything, PBS? Like, at all?"

"Of course she has."

No. *Not at all.* Not once, with zero probability of this happening in the future.

Eyes cast down, Jessica says, "I feel like . . . this week can't be easy for you, you know? With Daddy and all? I mean, Stassi's sort of chill, and maybe under different circumstances you'd vibe with her, too. She's smart, actually. She's an interior designer with a LEED certification, which is apparently pretty tough to get. She and Dad were working on a place with a lot of environmentally friendly components; that's how they met last year. Anyway, this sitch can't be how you pictured your first kid's wedding. What I'm saying is it sucks to be you and I'm sorry."

"Jessica," I say, fighting back the welling tears, lest she sense my weakness and use it against me. "You have no idea how much it means to me that—"

Her phone *ping*s and she glances down. "Shit, I've got a crisis." She reads and shakes her head. "Everything's on fucking fire. Shit, shit, shit!" Then she stalks off in her fancy tall shoes faster than I can walk in a pair of Nikes.

I climb into the bathtub and call Karin. "You'll never guess where I am right now."

"Hiding," Karin replies.

I lean back in the tub and let the sun warm my face. "Why would I be hiding?"

"Because two-thirds of your kids are the reason tigers eat their young?"

We're both endlessly fascinated with each other's parent-child relationships because we have such different approaches. Karin tells her kids everything, and vice versa. When Sasha lost her virginity freshman year of college, Karin was the first person she called. I didn't even hear about it when Kelsey lost her bike at school.

"Ha! That's where you're wrong. Jessica was actually just nice to me. Not only did I make her laugh, but she commented that this wedding has to be really hard on me and that she's sorry. She even pointed out that she thought Kelsey was being a jerk for not saying thank you. I mean, sensitivity and everything! I'd call that a step in the right direction."

"I wouldn't."

"Then what would you call it?" I ask.

"A harbinger of evil to come."

I kick my legs out in front of me, luxuriating in the sheer size of this old tub. They don't make 'em like this anymore. A shame. "You're harshing my mellow, man."

"I liken Jessica's being decent to you to those disaster films when all the birds fly away and the rest of the animals take off for higher ground before the earthquake or tidal wave or Japanese-movie monster invasion. Any way you slice it, it's a sign of impending doom."

"I choose not to see it that way."

"That's because you're an optimist."

"Yet I'm perpetually disappointed by everyone."

"No one said you were a good optimist. Anyway, wanna come to Pilates with me? I'm going to the four o'clock group session. Bet you can sneak away since you're not on your regular schedule today."

"No, thanks." I used to practice Pilates before I started weight training. Honestly, now Pilates seems kind of silly to me. I mean, I could hold up this spindly wooden bar and try to align my sitting bones while I monitor my exhales, or I could actually bench-press serious weight, work out a lot of aggression, and push myself in five-pound increments; there's no comparison.

"Your loss. We're using the magic circle today!" She's referring to a pliable padded ring that "helps you be more connected to your center" when pressure is applied. Again, this sounds less like exercise and more like a pyramid scheme.

(FYI, there are no "magic circles" on the weight room floor. Just weights.)

"I'll pass. Today is kettlebells. Or, it was."

I hear a doorbell chime in the background. "Hey, Henny-Penny, the UPS guy is here, so I have to scoot, but you've gotta believe me. Jessica being nice is cause for concern. It's temporary. I'm telling you, you let your guard down and all of a sudden, Godzilla is going to be flattening your fishing village with his big ol' claw-tipped webbed feet. Mark my words. Okay, motoring! Love you! Bye!"

She hangs up before I ever have the chance to tell her about the bathtub, but I guess she'll see it soon, hopefully in the backyard and not still here in the driveway.

I exit the tub and collect Barnaby's urn and his uneaten lunch and head down the long, brick-paved walkway to the house, thinking about Karin's warning.

I want Karin to be mistaken. I want today to have been a first step between Jessica and me. I want to begin again with Jess. I want to have a real relationship with her. Yet I don't want to be best friends, as I find that inappropriate. The roles of mother and daughter are clearly defined. Personally, I believe that Karin's got it wrong. I'm concerned for those families who blur the lines of these relationships; if you don't have set boundaries, then what happens when you *need* to be the parent? Are the BFFamilies just a tremendous pack of pals, all roommated-up under the same roof like it's a frat house?

I feel the buddy factor is why so many kids are so comfortable living at home well into their thirties. The problem here, even though everyone may feel like they're equal because they're such great amigos, is this traps the kids in a state of arrested development that can't be healthy for anyone in the family unit. At some point the parents have to move on from just identifying themselves as moms and dads, and the kids have to define their roles beyond being someone's children. If you typecast yourself into one character, then that's the only part you're ever going to get to play. Doesn't strike me as healthy.

I clear a place on the mantel for Barnaby's urn and I'm storing the leftovers in the fridge when I hear Jessica thunder in from the backyard. She's holding one of her little booties in her hand, a busted heel in the other. She's white with rage. "What in the actual *fuck*, PBS? I just tripped over a stack of old typewriters out there. A. Stack. Of. Old. Typewriters. Which are next to a pile of bike tires. Are we hosting a wedding or a goddamned *swap meet*? Jesus! Why is everyone in this family such a fucking amateur, and *why do you keep letting it happen?*"

She storms out of the room and up the stairs, slamming her bedroom door so hard that it jostles the dishes drying in the rack by the sink.

Just like that, Godzilla appears and stomps all over my fishing boats and thatched huts, not with a massive, claw-tipped web-foot, but in a single spiked bootie. The result's the same, though— he wipes out the whole damn village.

CHAPTER FOUR

June 1988

"Chris! I love you, buddy, and I am so stoked to be your new brother-in-law. Woot-woot! In your face, Patrick! Who's the best man now, huh?" Foster flips Patrick the bird, and Patrick responds by placidly brushing imaginary lint off the shoulder of his suit jacket. Everyone's laughing, save for Marjorie. She's making the face Chris calls "cat butt" due to her three hundred and sixty degrees of quietly angry lip pucker, which only serves to make the whole scene more amusing.

Foster pulls a crumpled index card out of his tux's breast pocket. "Okay, I wrote this shit down because if I mess it up, Penny's never gonna let me hear the end of it. Here we go. On paper, you two are a terrible match. The numbers don't add up. Like, Chris is a super-fun dude, right? SO FUN! Plus a million points for you. And, Penny, you're kinda where fun goes to die, so minus ten points. I mean, I can tell 'cause we can smell our own." He gestures at me with his rocks glass, and the clear liquid sloshes over the side, dampening his cuff. He doesn't notice.

Foster is absolutely annihilated on four weak Tanqueray and tonics and half a glass of champagne. I guess neither one of us inherited Marjorie's heroic tolerance level. (Then again, we don't practice like she does.) One more drink and I guarantee he'll be wearing his bow tie around his head and gatoring on the dance floor when the band plays "Shout."

The crowd howls and Chris has to cup his hands around his mouth to be heard over everyone. "This is a really terrible wedding toast, Fos! Hey, Max, maybe it's time to close the open bar." But he's grinning when he says this, enjoying the scene as much as the rest of us, perhaps more. The crowd boos at this suggestion.

"Shhh," Foster slurs into the microphone. "I'm not done. What I'm saying here is that on paper, you two suuuuuck ballllllllllls." Marjorie places her face in her palm while my father coughs into his hand to stifle a laugh. We're all going to pay for this later, but seeing Marjorie squirm in front of all her chichi pals is sort of worth it.

He says, "I always pictured her with an accountant or a banker or, like, an IRS dealie-guy. Someone who saves his receipts, you know? He'd be all, 'I got a big deduction for you, baby,' when he was in the mood for some lovin'! Hey, remember that nimrod you dumped for Chris—what was his name? Werner? Weimaraner? No . . . Wyatt! That's it! That's a stuuuuupid name. 'Member Weimaraner liked ana-grams? He was like, 'Foster Bancroft, your anagram is Barf Cotton Serf!' Dude, no one wants to be seated next to *that* at Thanksgiving dinner for the next forty years, am I right?"

He looks out at the guests, and those who met Wyatt are nod-ding their heads. Serious, sincere Wyatt did ramble on about the hidden wisdom in anagrams. Sure, I was interested at first to learn that "the hospital ambulance" was an anagram for "a cab, I hustle to help man" and that "*New York Times*" could translate to "monkeys write," but even with my love of quoting stats, the anagram game got real boring real quick. I had a lot of trouble maintaining a straight face the day he told Patrick (Walsh) that his anagram was Watch Irk Slap, to which Patrick deadpanned, "You must be psychic, because you just predicted our future together."

Foster continues. "But you, Chris, you kinda challenge her. You make her leave her comfort zone. Because of you, she's gonna have, like, *adventures*. Her life's not gonna be all mapped out and shit. Together, the sum of your wholes adds up to more than one hundred and forty-six and a half percent. You guys prove sometimes you have to go with what's best for your heart and not what makes the most sense in your head. And that's pretty badass. So congratulations, Penny Candy, drink up, and can you introduce me to your friend Judith because she is The Hotness! Whoa, hey, don't take my mic. Oh, okay, it's your turn? S'up, Karin? If it doesn't work out with Judith, you can tell me what time it is, giiiiirl!"

Karin practically shoves Foster out of the way. "Hi, everyone! I'm Karin, the maid of honor, and, um, Miguel, we're going to need some coffee over here, please?" She points at Foster, who turns around in his chair to see if she's motioning toward someone behind him. Miguel swoops in and collects all the liquor within arm's reach so deftly that Foster doesn't realize what's happened.

Foster's almost as straitlaced as I am, which is why his performance tonight is so hilarious. Truly, I believe he's power-drinking out of empathy for me, having witnessed Marjorie's micromanagement firsthand. This week has been particularly tough after four trying months. From the moment Chris proposed, she's second-guessed every single one of my premarital decisions, to the point that I completely abdicated having preferences and simply started asking what *she* wanted.

Nothing here tonight is what I envisioned. Not a damn thing. I wanted simple and easy, intimate and personal, maybe a tea-length ivory satin gown and a corona of braids with a flower tucked behind my ear. A justice of the peace or a judge. A dinner with family and a few friends.

Instead, I got fussy and complicated and overly formal. While I can't deny I'm thrilled to be married and the reception is more fun than anticipated, I wish I'd had some control over the elements that felt important to me. Namely, I loathe my muttonchop-sleeved dress with the sheer, deep V of lace in the front that rises up into an odd sort of turtleneck with a million buttons down the back. I'm exactly as sexy as a rack of lamb right now.

I feel silly with my hair in this ridiculous Alexis-Colby-from-*Dynasty*-inspired updo, a massive pompadour of tight, sticky curls bisected with a stiff twist of tulle that juts so far out it bumped against the back window in the limo on the way over here.

I hate how the salmon with citrus aioli served on risotto makes the ballroom smell like a dirty aquarium. No one in the immediate family even *likes* salmon—we only offered it as a choice because Marjorie wanted to up the elegance factor by including a fish fork in the place settings.

Still, in the ultimate act of rebellion, I'm marrying Chris and not Marjorie's first choice of Wyatt the anagram-adoring attorney, so none of the details really matter.

While I'd love to cut loose tonight, I fear a lifetime of retribution were I to do so. Foster must have sensed this, and thus he's drinking for two. When he sobers up, I will absolutely fix him up with my college friend Judith. Come to think of it, they'd be a great match—they both feel Timothy Dalton is the best James Bond, which is madness.

"Let me set the scene for you," Karin says. "We're in tenth grade and Penny has speech class with Miss Delancey. Now, who in here went to New Trier High School?" Many of the younger guests cheer. "Cool. You guys remember Miss Delancey?" These same guests now jeer. "For those who are unfamiliar, Miss Delancey was this hag who was, like, famously unfair to her female students. She was a complete effing bee."

Marjorie's pained expression upon hearing Karin say "effing bee" takes my mind off the squirrel's nest atop my head.

Karin says, "Remember how she was so horrible to the cute girls and she'd flirt with the guys, always shoving her flabby cleavage in their faces? Pathetic. Did she need to get l-a-i-d or what?"

Our former New Trier classmates laugh and nod in encouragement while Marjorie white-knuckles her cocktail.

Chris whispers in my ear, "Look at Marjorie right now; she's *literally* turning violet."

I touch one of my offending sleeves. "These toasts almost make being dressed like crown roast worth it."

"You look delicious." He plants a kiss under my earlobe, and I feel a shiver down my spine.

I smile. "Keep it up and you might get lucky tonight."

"Yeah? What are my odds?" He takes my hand and rubs his thumb across my knuckles, a simple gesture he's been doing ever since we started dating. Years ago, his Bonpa (paternal grandfather who was Belgian) did the same after his tracheotomy. He couldn't use his words to tell Chris he loved him anymore, so this was how he communicated that thought to him.

"Easily one in four. Now, hush, we're supposed to listen."

". . . Penny had to talk about what she wanted to study in college and what she hoped to do with her degree. Pretty standard assignment in a class everyone had to take before they graduated."

My speech was on my passion for all things mathematical. I remember explaining that I adored math because it's a constant set of truths, rather than an ever-changing array of rules. I talked about how math is a way to rein in and give meaning to the abstract, whether it's the relationships between shapes or quantities or numbers. I said math allows you to solve problems and make predictions by detecting patterns and that math reveals order. I loved math because it tells you what's going to happen next and that the best part about math is that it mitigates risk.

I was proud not only of my speech, but also of my plan for the future.

In college, my friends would say, "How can you stand all those complicated calculus and statistics classes?" and I'd reply, "The numbers are easy; it's figuring out people that's hard."

I stand by this belief. I dislike that given the exact same set of circumstances, I might elicit entirely different reactions depending on location or time of day, especially where Marjorie's concerned. For example, when I was a kid, if I were to ask to sleep over at Karin's house while at the dinner table, Marjorie would shrug and tell me to do whatever I wanted. Yet if I were to inquire while she was sitting at a table full of her club cronies, she might sneer and say, "The little girl with the divorcée mother? Darling, no, she's not our kind." Which was a load of crap, because Karin lived in our fancy neighborhood long before we did. Of course, she was happy to dump me at Karin's if these same exact cronies invited her somewhere and she had no one to babysit me. I hated—and hate—never quite knowing what to expect, or when.

". . . and the whole time Penny's at the podium, Miss Delancey's sitting there with her sun-damaged rack propped up on the desk, like, rolling her eyes and shaking her head. She was *such* a jealous cow. When Penny's done, Miss Delancey goes, 'You're setting yourself up to fail, Miss Bancroft. College is far too competitive in male-dominated fields like math and science, and you're never going to make it. Please, do yourself a favor and set your sights lower.' Poor Penny is, like, shell-shocked, you know? And at the back of the room, sweet, easygoing Chris, who'd never even spoken to Penny before, totally lost it. He stands up and goes, 'Lower her expectations? To do what instead? Teach a bullshit speech class?'"

Yeah. I pretty much fell in love with Chris that day. Who wouldn't?

Karin raises her wineglass. "Cheers to the world's most romantic three-day in-school suspension and meet-cute story!"

Everyone clinks their forks against their glasses for us to kiss, save for Foster, who's climbed under the table for a quick siesta. We're happy to oblige.

Patrick takes the microphone from Karin. "First, I want to thank you two for going to different colleges and dating other people, because marrying your high school sweetheart is far too cliché. And for the record? Miss Delancey never once flirted with me, and I find that offensive because I was devastatingly handsome back then *and* still straight. I wonder if seeing those feed bags in that Forenza sweater isn't what pushed me over to the other side? People? Breasts should never be *long*." Patrick gestures like he's showing the crowd how big of a fish he caught and then he shudders, but not nearly as hard as Marjorie shudders in her champagne-colored bouclé Chanel suit.

"I've never loved your family or friends more than I do at this moment," Chris says, squeezing my arm through a yard of Irish lace and tulle.

"Me neither," I reply.

"Marjorie's going to burn the videotape of the toasts, isn't she?"

"She may well set fire to the whole Centennial Hills Club."

Chris says, "How boring were my people's toasts, right? 'We love you, Penny and Chris. Welcome to the family. We're not losing a son; we're gaining a daughter.' And I think they're all sober, too. Not one of them is napping under the head table. What's wrong with the Sinclair side? You may have made a huge mistake here. You didn't marry carny folk *at all*."

"A-*hem*," Patrick says while glowering in our direction and clearing his throat in mock indignation. "I'm about to say profound and touching things about your love, but you're not listening to me. Did you guys *want* to make today all about you? I mean, we can if you insist, but I feel like Auntie Marjorie might have a problem with the spotlight being off of her."

Fortunately, my father's drinking a sip of water when Patrick says this, so the resulting spit take is far less devastating than it would have been a moment earlier when he had a mouthful of Cabernet. Fortunately, Miguel is right here with a napkin.

"Oh, good, that got your attention," Patrick says with a wry grin. "I'll continue, then. I'm finishing up at the office on a Monday and I get a call from Penny. She's freaked-out. And our girl Penny never freaks out. Remember when I split my head open on the diving board here and everyone was losing it because of all the blood? Penny was the only calm person, and as the EMTs were loading me into the ambulance, she pokes her head in to say, 'You're probably going to want to switch your part to the other side to compensate for the scar.'"

He flips his bangs over to show the still-visible mark above his right temple.

"Anyway, the Monday in question? Black Monday." A collective groan echoes through the ballroom. No one who doesn't keep their money in a coffee can buried in the backyard was untouched by the market crash on October 19th last year.

"She was still in the training program at Smith Barney then, but did what she could to help the other brokers try to stanch the bleeding—we noticing a trend here with our girl? Of course the day was a train wreck that started in Hong Kong and worked its way around the globe, and, really, what could she have done? The Dow dropped five hundred points. Penny said her Reuters screen was like an altimeter on a plane plummeting to the earth. The numbers just kept going down and down and down. I've never heard her like that on the phone before. I said, 'Get your skinny ass in a cab and meet me at the Burwood.' That was the bar in her neighborhood. 'You need a drink right now.'"

Patrick was a champ that night, helping me realize exactly how much I despised my job. For as much as I loved analyzing the data, I hated the inherent risks that came along with being directly responsible for anyone's fortune. I wasn't a daredevil. I didn't have the intestinal fortitude to be a stockbroker, and I definitely lacked the people skills. He convinced me that, with my degree and GPA, I'd have no trouble finding other work.

Patrick says, "The Cuervo's flowing, and the more we talk, the more Penny realizes she's in the wrong job and she starts to get happy. Real happy. The night actually turns into a celebration. I want you all to picture Penny in her pin-striped suit and her floppy silk bow, suntan panty hose, sensible shoes missing at this point, one tequila, two tequila, three tequila, floor, standing on the bar, belting out the lyrics to 'It's Raining Men.' And *that* is when Chris walks in. He doesn't even live in the city. He was just meeting a friend down there. Well, she spots him because it's a Monday and the bar's not too crowded. She jumps directly into his arms and she says, 'I never should have let you go!' Then she lays the biggest kiss on him you have ever seen."

I blush and shrug and the ballroom erupts into laughter. Marjorie clenches her eyes shut and shakes her head ever so slightly.

"The best part?" Patrick says. "Chris just looks at her in his arms like he can't believe she landed there and then looks at me and then looks back at her, and then he *takes off running out the front door with her*, all *Officer and a Gentleman* style, and I didn't see them for the rest of the night."

"Thanks again, Miss Delancey!" Chris shouts, before re-creating our epic Burwood reunion kiss.

Once the applause finally dies down, Marjorie rises to give her toast. The room becomes unnaturally quiet. She holds the stem of her martini glass so tightly that I'm shocked it doesn't snap. She takes a couple of measured breaths before finally speaking. Her fury isn't evident to anyone who doesn't know her intimately, but trust me, it's there, lurking just under the surface. My drunken wedding party has broken her one cardinal rule, which is to not embarrass her.

Too bad I'm only getting married once. Maybe next time she'll listen to me when I say I want something small and informal because I was crystal clear on who would be here and how they might behave.

"Penelope, Christopher . . . may your lives together be as long as they are happy."

Okay, that actually seems like a pleasant wish, all things considered. Sure, one could interpret it to mean she hoped our lives were both short and fraught with unhappiness, but who would say something like that? She's not a monster so much as she's just high maintenance.

Chris leans in to whisper, "I was expecting a lot worse."

I smile and nod, not breaking eye contact with Marjorie. I have a feeling she's not yet made her point.

"May you both be blessed with more laughter than tears. May your troubles be few and your prospects infinite. May you end each day with sweet dreams."

"This is actually kind of nice," he says.

"Wait for it," I reply.

"May you build your lives together on a solid foundation of faith, trust, and love, with the sun on your face and the wind at your back."

Marjorie pauses to take a sip of her Gibson, and then she focuses solely on me as she finishes her toast. "And may all your children be daughters."

And there we have it.

We raise our glasses. Through clenched teeth, I say, "Was I wrong?"

Chris replies, "I'll never doubt you again . . . Mrs. Sinclair."

CHAPTER FIVE

To: penelopesinclair@colbyaustinwaterstone.com

From: adrienneaugust@colbyaustinwaterstone.com

Date: June 4th

Subject: Your calendar

Penny,

Potentially big, big news . . . Carrie from Mr. Waterstone's office just e-mailed me about your availability. She wants to put you on his schedule July 1st! This date is not a coincidence. They want to make you executive vice president on the day the third quarter begins. I am sure of it. The position is yours! So there, Vanessa!

Best,

Adrienne

P.S. My apologies about the Vanessa remark. That was unprofessional. Not undeserved, just unprofessional.

. . . .

"Penny, are you aware the bathtub is still sitting in your driveway?" Marjorie says by way of greeting as she enters the kitchen. She makes a beeline for the fridge, where she pulls out a jar of cocktail onions and begins to assemble the makings of a Gibson.

"Yes, Marjorie."

After selling their old house in Glencoe and relocating to Florida full-time, my folks bought a condo up here, which they rarely use. However, they had some water damage while they were gone, so they're staying with me this week. (Somehow Judith and Foster weaseled out of hosting them. Not sure how, especially as Marjorie loves to remind me that Foster's house is bigger, newer, and nicer than mine.) Fortunately, my folks have spent the majority of their time with friends at the club, so they've mostly been out of my hair. I still can't fathom why they'd keep their membership at Centennial Hills active given the amount of time they're here, but that's none of my business. I feel that when you ask someone about their finances, you're telling them you'd like to participate in paying their bills and that's not okay.

"Are you going to *do* something about the tub? Or at this point are you planning to sell it along with the house? Mayhaps you can call it a water feature?" Marjorie cracks herself up. I suspect the gin is helping her humor.

"Yes, Marjorie. I'm in the process of taking care of it as we speak."

Marjorie finally notices I'm not alone at the table in the breakfast nook and comes to stand over the two of us, waiting to be introduced.

"Marjorie, please meet Adrienne August, my executive assistant. Adrienne, this is Marjorie Bancroft, my mother."

Adrienne rises to shake Marjorie's hand. "Hello, so nice to meet you! Wait, did I hear you right? Do you actually call your mother by her first name?"

I explain. "Marjorie started having my brother and me call her that when we were junior high aged. She didn't think she looked old enough to have kids who were teenagers."

Adrienne takes in Marjorie's features, admiring her plump, taut skin and bright eyes. "May I be frank? You are stunning, Mrs. Bancroft. The two of you could probably pass for sisters."

Marjorie claps her bejeweled hands together. "Love this girl. Give her a raise."

Great. Now I have to get Botox.

As for giving Adrienne a raise, not an issue. She's already the highest paid executive assistant in my whole division. Trust me; I've done the math, and it's more cost effective to pay Adrienne any extra dollars per hour she requests than it would be to find, train, and retain someone else of her caliber. Nine years ago, she walked into my office with her associate's degree and level of dedication forged from years of pitching in at her family's dairy farm in Kenosha. She won me over ten minutes into our interview, when she answered the standard question about describing a difficult circumstance and what she'd done to overcome it. I'd already talked to an endless parade of millennials that day, each snowflake more special than the previous, all of whom assumed they deserved a coveted entry-level position at my firm just for having shown up.

One young woman told me about the trauma of not getting into Dartmouth and toughing it out on the mean streets at Bennington College. *Vermont!* she cried. *They don't even have a Target up there!* Another applicant described the abject humiliation of giving the salutatory speech despite a perfect GPA, since the valedictorian had taken advanced placement chemistry instead of honors chemistry. His parents tried to sue the school district, but to no avail.

As for Adrienne? She walked me through the afternoon when her parents were stuck in town with an overheated radiator, so she had to assist a dairy cow in distress with a breech birth. Without hesitation, she'd reached into that heifer, turned the calf, and saved both animals' lives. Yes, she was frightened, she admitted, but life on a farm was all about doing what needed to be done.

By the way, she was *eleven*.

At eleven, my daughter Kelsey couldn't even fix her own Froot Loops. In fact, Chris made her breakfast every day until she left for college. I was so impressed that I hired Adrienne over all the Ivy League grads. My rationale was, the kids from Harvard and Princeton hoped for a stepping-stone into my firm, while Adrienne actually wanted to *do* the job.

I've never regretted my decision, especially because Adrienne's essentially the Karl Rove of office politics. For example, I work with a woman named Vanessa, whom I used to quite like. I found her professional and courteous, capable of producing top-notch work. Adrienne was only with me a week before she came into my office with a grim expression on her face.

"That Vanessa woman who just left?" she said, pointing at Vanessa's retreating form. "What's her deal?"

I glanced up from my monitor. "What do you mean?"

"Were the two of you up for the same job recently?"

"Funny you should ask that, but yes. I was promoted over her.

That's why I'm in this office with an actual door. I got the position, and that's why I was able to hire you."

"Huh." She chewed on her lip and made no motion to leave.

"Is there something on your mind, Adrienne?"

Adrienne pulled out her steno pad. "I've been making some notes—in my opinion, she's trying to undermine you, trying to make you look bad."

I gave her my full attention. "How so?"

Adrienne tabbed through her pad. "Are the two of you friends?"

I shrugged. I was not normally one to mix business with my personal life, but I wasn't opposed to being friendly when the opportunity arose. The research indicates that people who have friends at work report higher levels of job satisfaction. "More like colleagues. I don't see her socially, no. We don't have lunch together very often, as I'm usually eating at my desk. I think we might have had coffee? We do say hello in the hallway, and she's quite personable. I like her."

Adrienne nodded. "Uh-huh. Has she ever met anyone in your family? Or, does she have any children, especially around your kids' ages?"

"No. She's never met anyone in my family, and she doesn't have any children. I'm not even sure if she's married, actually."

Adrienne chewed her lip some more. "Yeah. That was my concern. You don't ask her personal questions, so the exchange is kind of one-sided. She seemed really interested in questioning you about your kids in the staff meeting with all the EVPs. Specifically, she wanted to know about Jessica's college visits and all that these visits might entail. If she doesn't have a child doing the same thing, and if you're not buddies, doesn't it seem kind of odd that she'd want to take time out of the middle of a meeting to parse out your schedule like that? Particularly when you're trying to figure out who's going to run that gigantic new project in New York? To me, seems like she's trying to plant seeds of doubt about your availability and your focus."

"Hmm," I said, letting that tidbit sink in. Generally, the child-free aren't much into hearing what we breeders have on the horizon, especially once the kids aren't cute anymore, but I assumed Vanessa was being polite.

"That's not the only time," she added. "She said something about Kelsey's recital on the conference call with the New York clients yesterday. Later, in the elevator with Mr. Waterstone, she wanted to know if you were leaving early to see Topher's hockey game. Then she brought up the college visit thing, too. It's not a coincidence."

"You're right. It's not a coincidence; it's a pattern," I said.

"She's gunning for your job. She's trying to make you look like you're too busy being a mommy to do your job."

"But that's not true!" I protested. "I always put the firm first."

Just ask Chris, I thought, recalling a recent argument.

"I know. That's why you're going to shut her down the next time she gets nosy, particularly in front of decision makers. As far as she's concerned, you live with ten cats. Share nothing with her, okay? Loose lips sink ships."

Thanks to Adrienne, I saw for myself exactly how Vanessa was jockeying for my position. I'm still polite, but I never let down my guard around her, and I redoubled my efforts in the office, which is why I couldn't stop myself from replying to Adrienne's e-mail this morning about getting a little work done. The Vanessa threat is always on my horizon.

Marjorie has been hovering behind us as we review our paperwork. I ask, "Marjorie, do you need something? If so, can I have ten minutes? Let me finish up, and then I'm all yours."

Adrienne offers, "I've never seen anyone as devoted to her job as your daughter. I can't believe she's even taking any vacation this week. She's never not working. Truly, she's the first one in every day and the last one to leave. You have how many more vacation days banked now, Penny? At least forty? You could abscond for the rest of the summer if you wanted. Anyway, there's a project that's ready to roll as soon as she signs off on it. Instead of making the client wait, she's carving out time to double-check it right now. Who does that? I had this sixth sense she was antsy, so I e-mailed this morning, and I was right. She asked me to bring everything here, telling me she'll enjoy the wedding weekend more if she could just check this task off her list. How dedicated is that?"

"Hmm," is Marjorie's response.

"Okay, then, Marjorie, I'll be with you in a few," I say, and I literally turn my back to her. I hear her splash some more gin in her glass, which means that everything will be "brilliant, darling" very soon. I plan to hustle Adrienne out of the house before that happens.

"What's the situation with the bathtub?" Adrienne asks. "You mentioned it's been here since yesterday?"

"Uh-huh. The guys from the scrap yard weren't sure where to leave it, so they dumped it at the end of the drive. Interesting approach to problem solving. It's too heavy for us to move on our own, even with all of Topher's friends helping, so I'm trying to get the crew here again to relocate it into the backyard. The damn thing is really throwing off the caterers and the people from the party-rental place, since it's cutting off the main artery to the house and backyard."

Adrienne frowns. "Why am I not managing this process?"

"Because it's not your responsibility."

I've never allowed Adrienne to handle my home life because I feel this crosses a line. Asking an assistant to pick up dry cleaning, schedule a haircut, or buy a present for a loved one does free up the exec to focus on more pressing corporate business, but the act inadvertently creates intimacy, a glimpse behind the curtain of one's real life.

To me, it's important that Adrienne never feel like she's an ad hoc extension of my family by having to manage my personal affairs. The more private matters run over the course of a business relationship, the more muddled the lines between professional and personal become between boss and assistant.

And we've all seen how that worked out for Chris.

Adrienne asks, "Have you tried threats and recrimination?"

"I have, but I feel like my home run swing is bribery. I've put out a number of calls, so we'll see who responds first."

Adrienne does not seem satisfied with this answer. "If you change your mind, I'm here to help."

"Thanks. Let's power through this so I can get back to dialing for dollars." I don my reading glasses for the final document review and everything seems to be in order. I'm almost done initialing all the forms when the doorbell rings, but I don't make any motion to get up.

"Do you need to get that? Or shall I?"

"No. I'm sure it's a neighbor telling me there's a tub in the driveway."

"Ha. Okay."

I keep reading and initialing and thirty seconds later Topher appears in the kitchen doorway. "Hey, Mom, Nancy from down the street stopped by. She wanted to let us know that—"

"Tub."

"Yep. What are we up to so far?"

"Fifty-six percent of all households in a two-block radius. We have one hell of a neighborhood watch program, if the crime in question were marauding vintage plumbing fixtures."

"Right? Like that's not getting old." Topher walks farther into the kitchen to grab a soda. "Oh, hey, Adrienne. What's up?"

"Your mom's crossing her t's and dotting her i's."

Face shrouded in concern, Topher glances back over his shoulder. "Really? You're working? You'd better finish up before Kelsey catches you doing anything not wedding related, Mom. She will shit kittens. I'm not kidding."

He's right, too. Kelsey isn't my most rational child on her best day, and the stress of this week has taken a toll on her already delicate constitution.

Last night we all endured a half-hour crying jag, not because of Barnaby, but because Kelsey's friend Hannah isn't coming to the wedding.

Her friend Hannah who isn't even invited to the wedding.

Her friend Hannah she hasn't spoken to since fourth grade when her family moved to Salt Lake City.

I quickly initial the last document and almost have Adrienne out the front door when Kelsey comes bounding down the stairs with yet another Cherry, Cherry Danish from Milo's truck. Does she have a secret stash of those somewhere? I've been finding the wrappers all over the house. At first I thought Barnaby was picking them out of the trash, because I keep forgetting he's gone. (Sniff.)

But when he was alive, he was far too gracious and proper to dig through the garbage. I imagine his only regret in life was a lack of opposable thumbs and the ability to operate a knife and fork. He always seemed vaguely embarrassed having to eat from a bowl on the floor, like an animal.

"Who's this?" Kelsey demands, narrowing her eyes at Adrienne. Kelsey should consider becoming an eye-narrowing professional; truly, she sets the standard.

Also? Uh-oh.

"This is . . . This is . . ." I try to come up with something that won't set off Kelsey like so many atomic bombs.

Adrienne shifts her weight from one clunky Dansko to the other. "I am definitely not here in a professional capacity."

Kelsey's eyes turn to slits. "What?"

"Isn't she funny? This is Adrienne. We've been seeing each other," Topher says, slipping his arm around her waist. "Totally caj, haven't really mentioned her." He plants a kiss on Adrienne's cheek, and she plays along beautifully, resting her head against his. "So glad you stopped by, Ades. Missed you much. Catch you on the flip side, bae." Topher begins to guide her out the front door, his hand on the small of her back, but Kelsey blocks her exit.

Oh, boy, here it comes.

I brace myself. *Of course* Kelsey's not going to buy Topher dating a conservative former farm girl almost nine years his senior, especially with her messy bun and big plastic glasses, dressed in a cardigan with too-long sleeves, because she looks . . . well, actually, a lot like Kelsey's friends.

Wait, when did Kelsey's peer group start dressing like harried executive assistants from America's dairy land?

Kelsey begins shrieking and dancing around the entry hall.

"Topher is seeing someone? How is this possible? You have a GIRLFRIEND and you didn't tell me? No way! Ohmigod! Adrienne! You have to come to the wedding tomorrow! You HAVE to come! Say yes!"

Stricken, Adrienne pivots her gaze back and forth from me to Topher. "I have, um, a . . ."

"A date! With my baby brother! For my wedding! This is so great! I'm always so worried because he's *such* a gaylord! He never makes time for girls, but here you are, without any of us even knowing. At this point we all thought he was smooth like a Ken doll down there, right? Like practically neutered."

In a heroic act of self-restraint, Topher says nothing. He's dated plenty of nice girls in the past few years, just none of them seriously enough to subject them to his sisters' scrutiny. And who could blame him?

Kelsey squeals, "This changes everything! I'm *so* happy. So you'll be there. Of course you will. Everything starts at six o'clock. See you then. This is going to be amazeballs!" With that, Kelsey gives Adrienne a squeeze and stomps back up the stairs. "Jessica! Jessica! You'll never guess who's not a eunuch!"

A stray Cherry, Cherry Danish wrapper floats down in her wake.

"Kelsey's not my favorite person right now," Topher says. "Any chance she can just stay over there in Italy after her honeymoon? Like, forever?"

"We can always pray for an international incident," I reply. To Adrienne, I say, "Please don't feel like you have to come."

"Heck, I'm kind of afraid not to. Plus, I'm now invested in what happens with the tub," she replies, hoisting her cross-body bag over her shoulder. "What should I wear? I have a black cocktail dress that's cut pretty low in the back. You think that's okay, or will it be too much?"

"Sounds wonderful," I reply.

Topher snorts. "Don't look at me. *I'm* a gelding, according to my sisters. Wait, you lived on a farm—what's a bull called when you castrate him?"

Adrienne replies, "A steer."

"Then I'm a *steer*. Apparently you can show up naked and that would have no impact on me."

Adrienne giggles. "Don't worry. I'll cover the R-rated parts at a minimum. I guess you've got yourself a date, Topher. I hope you know how to do the Wobble. Anyway, take it easy today, Penny, and please know I'll keep Vanessa from unlawfully entering your office. She did try yesterday, but I busted her. Pfft, like she doesn't have her own Scotch tape dispenser. See you tomorrow night." She exits and makes her way down the long drive, pausing to chat with Patrick, who has just arrived and is staring at the tub.

At some point in the conversation, Marjorie materialized behind us. "You have a date with that clever girl?" She ruffles Topher's hair. "Bloody well-done, lad."

· · · ·

"Twirl."

I oblige.

"Love. Love, love, *love*."

"Really?" I ask, turning to inspect my reflection in profile. "You're not just blowing sunshine up my skirt?"

"When have I *ever* done that?" Patrick asks.

"Excellent point."

We're up in the master bedroom, and I'm taking a break from the Great Immovable Tub Crisis to model my mother-of-the-bride dresses for Patrick. Jessica's been busy wrangling bridesmaids and Kelsey's too wrapped up in being Kelsey, but even if they weren't both preoccupied, I'm not sure either would much care what I wore.

Patrick, on the other hand, hasn't stopped agonizing over my options since the moment Milo and Kelsey Instagrammed their engagement announcement from the Mumford & Sons show.

Patrick lounges on my puffy white duvet, nestled between all eighteen of my artfully arranged throw pillows, which is one of the few upsides to now being single. I can keep as many goddamned pillows on the bed as I'd like.

"Take the compliment, bitch. You look phenomenal in *both* the dresses you picked out. No one's more surprised than me about this. But the tickets to the gun show?" he says, referring to my newly toned arms. "That's just *beyond*. You look like a less ropy Madge. I knew you'd been working out but did not know you'd gotten so cut."

Ever since I stopped monkeying around with Pilates and started pumping iron, I've seen a change in my body for the better. My shoulders are square and my muscles tightly defined for the first time since I used to swim all those summers ago. Apparently I still had triceps and biceps hiding underneath all that middle-aged skin; who knew?

"Did you just compare my upper body to Madonna's?"

Patrick nods and fiddles with a tassel on one of the smaller, tufted, down-filled models. Chris did not understand the feminine fascination with multiple pillows. He claimed no one ever needed more than two pillows, because that's enough to prop yourself up to read or watch *SportsCenter* in bed. Anything past that is just egregious. "I did. Your shoulders and back, too. Oh! I know! Remember when Kate was doing the rowing machine before the royal wedding? That's what you remind me of—that shot of her on the boat in the black tank top and those leggings. Bravo. Mean it."

Full confession? I sort of don't love the pillows now, either, and I see what Chris meant. Yes, I cackled with glee as I sped down the aisles of Bed Bath & Beyond, tossing in cushions with abandon. I must have looked like a lunatic, careening past all the candles and wineglasses and towers of towels, filling three whole shopping carts in my zeal. Then I came home and shouted expletives as I placed every single goddamned, ass-reaming, shit-snacking, goat-sucking one of the bastards on top of the new duvet cover and *it felt good*. Not Terry-McMillan-*Waiting-to-Exhale*-set-his-car-ablaze good, but still supremely satisfying. But now? Now it's like playing a never-ending game of Tetris every morning when I make the make the bed and each evening when I strip it.

"Did you know your triceps are actually a three-headed muscle—hence the 'tri' prefix—and they comprise about two-thirds of the overall mass of the upper arm? I see people in the gym only hitting their biceps and I think, 'You're never going to achieve proper definition without compound movement. No mass for you.'" I flex in demonstration, pointing out the brachii lateral, medius, and longus. "See?"

He tosses a (cursed) pillow at me. "Only you could nerd-up pumping iron."

I duck, but he still pegs me. "It's a gift."

Patrick says, "Remember Gam-Gam's arms?" referring to Marjorie and Auntie Marilyn's mother. Our maternal grandmother was a true victim of the times. As a teenager during Prohibition, she made a small fortune brewing, bottling, and distributing her own beer here in Chicago, only for our grandfather to gamble away her whole nest egg once they were married. She never forgave him, but she never left him, either. If the world were different back then, I have no doubt she'd have kicked his butt to the curb and then gone off to run a Fortune 500 company. Instead, she had seven children to whom she showed nothing but indifference and an occasional flash of contempt. The whole story makes me sad.

"Gam-Gam's arms were like a couple of kimono sleeves made out of flesh. Kind of glad she wasn't a hugger."

"Talking about Gam-Gam always puts our mothers into perspective, doesn't she? Marilyn and Marjorie may be obnoxious and controlling, but at least they want to be involved in our lives, you know?" Patrick refluffs the bolster behind his back.

"Lucky us."

I ran the numbers on the damn pillows, by the way. I spend about four minutes each morning putting the pillows on the bed, which means it takes me four minutes to clear them off the bed. I may be under the weather a few times a year and I don't make my bed those days. If you factor in time I'm traveling, let's say I go through this ritual twice a day, three hundred and fifty times each year. That works out to twenty-eight hours. If I live another thirty years—and the actuarial tables do favor this outcome—that works out to eight hundred and forty hours moving pillows. That is *thirty-five full days*. More than one full month of my life. I will spend *more than one month of my life* engaged in the Sisyphean task of arranging feather-filled discs on this bed, only to move them around again twelve hours later because I have the pathological need to prove something to the one person who I can guarantee will never actually sleep in this bed again.

Of course, every one of these pillows is a metaphorical way of saying, "Bite me, Chris Sinclair," so you can see my dilemma.

Patrick says, "Anyway, let's not speak too ill of the dead. I don't trust that bitch not to haunt us. Back to you and your new guns. Let me say this—the Divorce Diet may have destroyed your psyche, but, girl, it's done wonders for your physique."

"Tell me more about how fab I look. Please spare no detail," I say, but I can't hear his response, what with all the screaming.

For a second I wonder if the specter of Gam-Gam has found a way to break through from the spiritual realm and we've somehow accidentally summoned her à la *Beetlejuice*, but then I recognize the familiar timbre.

Ah, yes—that's pure Kelsey we're hearing.

We both take off down the hallway, our instincts kicking in— mine propelling me toward my child, who sounds to be in pain, in danger, in trouble of the worst sort, and Patrick, who's automatically drawn to anything smacking of drama or intrigue. Our sock-clad feet slip and skid on the hardwood, and we both end up inadvertently *Risky Business*–ing into Kelsey's room.

"Quite the entrance," Jessica remarks as Kelsey draws a breath to howl again. Jessica's perched in the window seat across the room from Kelsey's bridesmaids, who are clad in their dresses and forming a protective semicircle formation around the bride. Then I realize that Kelsey's trying on her gown, too. I try not to feel bothered that I was excluded from this moment.

"What on earth is the matter? What happened?" I ask, noticing the splotches on Kelsey's chest. "Are you hurt? Are you bruised? Were you *hit?* Wait, are those . . . birds?"

Kelsey begins to wail in earnest. While she's a striking girl, fair-skinned and symmetrical, with high cheekbones and bow-shaped lips, she is not a pretty crier. I'm talking a veiny-headed, red-rimmed, pinchy-pinchy, snot-bubbled fish mouth here. Jessica, on the other hand? Cries like a movie star, and tears simply make her lashes look thicker and her eyes bluer. (Of course, Jessica would never deign to allow anyone to see her so vulnerable.)

"Are you upset about your tattoos, sweetie? Do you have buyer's remorse? We can get some Dermablend and cover them right up. You know, thirty-six percent of your peer group has ink, so it's not a big deal either way," I offer by way of comfort.

"Noooooooo," she sobs. "I love my sparrows."

That's when I notice all the bridesmaids have a matching sparrow tattooed on their collarbones as well, save for her friend Zara, who has a duck in flight in the same spot instead. A mallard, I believe.

"Then what is it? Honey, I can't help you if you don't tell me what's wrong."

From behind me, Patrick leans in and quietly says, "Girl, you'll be a waffle soon. *Real* soon."

Bella, her maid of honor, with a heavy fringe of bangs poking out from under a crocheted cap reminiscent of what Gam-Gam used to cover the spare roll of toilet paper, steps aside, and I spot the problem. Kelsey's dress won't zip.

At all.

"When was your last fitting?" I ask.

"I'd guess it was before she was elected mayor of Carb Town," Jessica offers with a smirk.

"Not helpful!" I say. "Where's the dressmaker?" I try to recall the name on the check I'd written, having never been invited to the shop. Was it in the city? The suburbs? I don't actually know. "We'll go there now and have a seam let out. This is easy. This isn't hardball; this is softball. Wiffle ball, no problem."

"The lady's out of town," Bella says. "She's making the dresses for a destination wedding and she's there doing the final alterations. That's why we had to pick up the gown early."

"Then on to Plan B. Jessica, you can sew, right? You took classes."

She shakes her head vigorously. "Not under these circumstances, I can't, not for this goat rodeo. I'm not going to be held responsible for her happiness."

Probably not the worst choice on her part.

"Fine, then who do you know in fashion in Chicago that can help her, Jessica?"

"'Chicago fashion' is kind of an oxymoron," she replies.

"Surely you have a contact or a designer friend here. We have thirty-three hours until this wedding and we will find a fix for this."

Jessica glances at her phone and begins to scroll through her contacts. "Hmm . . . Who to call? Who to call? You know what? I'd probably talk to the tent rental people. They're used to dealing with large swaths of fabric."

Kelsey's friends gawp openmouthed at Jessica, and Kelsey's cries assume a fresh urgency.

Even Patrick, Patron Saint of Snark, is appalled by the casual cruelty of her remark. "You do not throw that kind of shade at your *sister*. Get on your broomstick and fly away, Jessica. Now."

She saunters out of the room with deliberate slowness, while Bella mutters, "At least her dress is paid for," but I don't have the time to deconstruct that sentence and find the hidden meaning. I have a situation to resolve. I am Ed Harris's character in a vest, and this dress is my busted oxygen tank on the *Apollo 13*. Failure is not an option.

"We are going to divide and conquer," I say. I point to the girl with the pale blue bobbed hair. "Delilah, you help with the zipper. Bella, you go to Twitter. Get recommendations on local tailors, dressmakers, even dry cleaners who are open late."

I gesture toward Zara with the duck tattoo and whose plastic, lens-free glasses take up most of the real estate on her face. "Zara, you handle Instagram, but DO NOT take a picture of this dress, because I'll tell everyone you still love Justin Bieber and not because he's ironic. That's right, I ride the train with your mom; you'd better *belieber* it. Now post a selfie or something. Start the conversation."

I turn to the tall one with the messy red bun. "Brianna, you scour Yelp. Nothing under four stars."

And to the girl with the pierced cheekbone—pierced cheekbone, oh, your poor parents—and Katniss Everdeen braid, "Gemma, you're on Facebook."

"Ugh," Gemma says, "no one's on Facebook anymore."

"Would you rather man the phones?" I ask. "You're welcome to make calls."

"I'm down with Facebook," she quickly replies.

Recently I heard on NPR that eighty-five percent of millennials have smartphones and this surprised me—honestly, that figure seems low, as does the stat that they touch their phones an average of forty-five times per day. Perhaps I only know the ones who skew toward heavier use?

Everyone busies themselves with their tasks/smartphones while Patrick, Delilah, and I see what we can do with the dress. Kelsey bawls, but who can blame her?

My father, clad in an exceptionally loud pair of plaid knickers and a set of golf spikes, clacks into the room. I shudder to think of what the cleats are doing to the hardwood, but a few dings in floors

I won't own for much longer seem minor in comparison. "Don't worry; it's all under control. I took care of it."

"What's that, Uncle Max?" Patrick asks. He has his hands on Kelsey's zipper, attempting to force it up while Delilah and I hold either side of the dress. Patrick's fingertips are white with the effort and my palms are cramping. A thin sheen of sweat dampens Delilah's brow. We can possibly do this. Maybe with a corset and some Spanx and a second corset and more Spanx . . . With Kelsey inhaling on cue, we're making slow but steady progress. We're not past the point of no return. (One more scone and we would be.) I estimate a seventy percent likelihood we can get this dress zipped, and once it's zipped, the fabric will give and this won't be so much of a struggle tomorrow. We'll give her lots of lemon water tonight and restrict her sodium intake and I believe we'll be okay.

"The junk dealers. I sent them away. They tried to leave a bunch of garbage here, but I said, 'No way, José.' Ironically, I believe his name was José. Or are they all named José? Anyway, I said, 'You're not leaving those disgusting old birdcages here. My granddaughter wants *new* birdcages, and you're not going to pass off rusty bits of tin as long as I'm around. Listen, this isn't the *Sanford and Son* set.' This is *Glencoe*, not a Dust Bowl–era garage sale. Oh, and I tried to get him to take the tub. Unfortunately, it was too heavy. Or they might have just been lazy; you never know with *those people*. No need to thank me."

When Kelsey screams—and believe me, she does scream—the force of air being expelled from her lungs is such that the zipper separates violently and entirely from the dress.

Everyone in the room gasps, except for Max.

Without missing a beat, he says, "Okay, then. I'm meeting

Bunky Cushman for a quick nine holes before the rehearsal dinner. If you see Marjorie, tell her I'm leaving. And, Penelope? Is that what you're wearing tomorrow? Don't love it on you, nope, nope, nope. You remind me a bit of that handsome octoroon in those car movies your mother won't admit she enjoys. Muscly fellow with all the big white teeth? What's his name, the Stone? Not a fan."

My father seems absolutely immune to Kelsey's shrieking. Then again, he's been tuning out Marjorie for more than five decades.

"I do not enjoy the Rock; that is balderdash," Marjorie says, shoving her way past Max in the doorway, holding an empty bottle. "He practically ruined *San Andreas*. Didn't even take off his shirt . . ."

"What's an octoroon?" says Bella, glancing up from her phone.

Zara answers, "A French cookie, made with coconut. They're super-delish."

Marjorie clucks. "And don't get me started on what that half-blood behemoth has done to the *Fast and the Furious* franchise. A travesty. He fancies smiling and flashing his pectorals as a substitute for acting; well, it isn't."

Kelsey's wailing continues, unabated.

Max taps his cleated foot, upset that I may have missed his earlier point. "I'm just saying with your dress, Penny, you can do better. You have too many muscles to look pretty. Can't get a man if you look like a man. No offense, Patrick. Alrighty, I'm off."

"Penelope, love, we have a major problem," Marjorie says.

"Yes, thank you for recognizing that," I say, gesturing toward Kelsey. "Anyone? Any luck yet?" The bridesmaids all shake their heads no. "Marjorie, who's *your* tailor up here? Or, who do you know who can get here quickly and can help us?"

She waves me off. "Oh, darling, everyone I knew has retired.

I have no bloody idea where the good help is now. All the Mexicans have taken their jobs anyway. When is *someone* going to build that wall?"

"*Damn*, your Mimsy and Gumpy are bigots, Kels," Bella remarks. "What's up with that?"

"Racism is *not* okay," Delilah agrees. "One world, one love."

"But what if it's a British thing? Like a cultural difference?" Zara suggests.

"Don't defend her, Zara. You don't even know the difference between a duck and a swallow," Bella retorts.

"Wait, were you British earlier, Mrs. Bancroft?" Gemma asks.

Marjorie snaps her fingers to get my attention. "Penelope, focus, please. I need you to be a love and pop over to the shop. We're out of Boodles gin. I can't make a proper Gibson without Boodles."

This inspires a fresh round of yowling from Kelsey. I'm tempted to join in with her.

"Is this real life?" Patrick asks, still holding Kelsey's now detached zipper.

"Anyone? Does anyone have anything?" I ask, feeling a rising sense of anxiety, filled with dread, then wrapped in trepidation, like a gordita, only made out of panic instead of taco shells, ground beef, and flatbread.

"I do!" squeals Zara, holding up her iPhone. "I have fifteen likes so far on my selfie, and that fly bartender from Violet Hour thinks my brow game is on fleek."

"Anything *useful* for *Kelsey*," I clarify.

"It's useful if she wants to start seeing my brow girl," Zara says. "I feel like the place she gets threaded is leaving her way too Demi Lovato up there, you know?"

So. Much. Crying.

The force of this round of caterwauling splits another seam.

"Was this the wrong time to tell her that?" Zara asks.

"You think?" Patrick spits.

Uncle.

I give up.

I am beaten.

This is my Waterloo. I have officially reached my capacity for dealing with this situation. I'm swinging outside of my weight class and I cannot hold out until the bell ends the round. I'm punch-drunk; I'm tapping out.

"I was afraid it was going to come to this," I say to myself more than to anyone else.

Patrick blanches. "Penny, don't. You can't. You've come too far."

"I'm at DEFCON ONE," I reply, pitching my voice to be heard over Kelsey's sobs. "I have no choice. I have to go nuclear. I swore I would never do it, but it's what has to be done."

Patrick lays his hand on my newly squared shoulder. He's still holding the zipper. Stray bits of white thread dangle from it. "God-speed, Penny Arcade. You're the bravest, most selfless person I've ever known."

I march down the hallway to the master bedroom to retrieve my cell phone, about to make one of the hardest calls of my life-time. I punch in the number and pray for voice mail.

But the odds are not in my favor.

He answers on the first ring.

"Chris, please pack a bag and come to Glencoe. Yes, right now. Plan to stay here tonight. I can't do this alone. I need your help."

CHAPTER SIX

October 2002

"You sure you can handle the next few days all on your own? They can be a lot to take. They're good kids; you know that. Topher's a dream, but the girls take some finesse. Plus, Jessica's got play practice, tennis, and French club this week, and Kelsey's doing soccer and dance. There's a lot of coordination involved, many, many moving pieces."

"Of course I'm sure. I'm not some random stranger off the street; these are my *children*."

"There's no shame in bringing in a babysitter to help you. No shame at all."

"We're not going to need a *babysitter*. I'm not incompetent."

"No judgment if you did need one."

"If you don't leave soon, you're going to miss your flight. You have to budget at least two hours for security at O'Hare. They're really taking safety seriously since 9/11; it's a different world now."

"Listen, I don't have to go to this convention. I can cancel if you need me to cancel. Should I stay here? I should probably stay here."

"Go."

"Are you sure?"

"Yes."

"Okay, but at a minimum, don't concern yourself with making dinner. You cooking? That's the last thing anyone needs. There's cash in the cookie jar. Tonight, get some pizzas from Barnaby's in Northbrook. It's Jessica's all-time favorite."

"I know. I've met her *and* the dog she named after the place."

"Right. Everyone will eat salad, too, as long as no tomatoes touch Topher's portion."

"Salad, yes, tomatoes, no. Easy-peasy."

"Avoid peas. No one will eat peas. Serve peas and you'll have a riot on your hands."

"Just an expression, not a dinner plan."

"Also, order one plain cheese—Kelsey's a vegetarian this week."

"That is news. That I did not know."

"And *please* make sure all of her leggings are clean. She says she's 'not into' wearing jeans right now. I suspect she's feeling self-conscious because she's in a growth spurt. Eleven is so awkward, right? Fifth grade is hard. Anyway, she doesn't remember to toss her leggings in the laundry basket, so she leaves them wadded up by the side of the bed when she puts on her pajamas at night. She'll freak out when she can't find the ones she wants in the morning. After she goes to sleep, I make a point of picking them all up and running them through the wash, even if I'm not sure they're dirty. Sometimes she'll try on three or four pairs before she figures out what she wants to wear, so it's best if all her options are available. Trust me, your morning will go one hundred and fifty percent more smoothly if you do this."

"Sounds a lot like you're negotiating with the terrorists, and I thought we didn't do that as a nation or as a family."

"No. This is a pick-your-battles situation. Don't fight this fight. You will lose. She's not trying to be difficult with the pants; it's legitimately hard for her to make decisions about what to wear, so I'm taking one of her stressors off the table. You realize that's why I fix her cereal, too. The kid doesn't know her own mind yet. That's why she's so easily swayed, always jumping from one trend to another. She's not mature enough to trust her own judgment. That's why in cases like the pants and breakfast—*and only those cases*—I help her. Again, I pick my battles."

"Sounds like capitulation."

"It's not."

"Agree to disagree."

"So, your plan is to . . ."

"Wash leggings, got it."

"Do you want to write this down? I feel like you should write this down."

"And *I* feel like you should get going or you'll miss your flight."

"Okay, okay. I'm going. You've got the hotel's info and I'll have my phone and pager with me at all times. If you need anything, anything at all, call, please. Remember, there are no stupid questions."

"Understood," I say. I steer Chris toward the door because if he doesn't leave now, he really will miss his flight. Those security lines are no joke. I should know. I've been in them every week lately because of my consulting engagement in Omaha. "One more thing—which kid goes to which school, again?"

All the color drains from his face. "I should stay."

"I'm kidding! Chris, I'm their *mom*. I've got this, okay? I did this myself for a long time, remember? We're going to be great. Love you! Have a great time at your boring builders' convention in tedious old Las Vegas!"

He kisses me and says good-bye, glancing over his shoulder so many times on his way down the walk that I start to feel insulted.

Granted, he's morphed into more of the custodial parent because he's self-employed. He's arranged his schedule so that he's home once the kids finish school for the day. Yet that doesn't mean I'm not involved or am less invested in their lives, just because I'm not there to make their snacks.

Because I'm the primary breadwinner now, I'm not able to attend every soccer practice or dance recital. We fought hard to stay in this school district, knowing the opportunity the education would afford our kids later in life. If the cost of admission is that *I'm* not always there, but Chris is, and we can still give them all that they need to be successful? Well, *I'd* be the selfish one if that were a price I wasn't willing to pay.

Anyway, I don't know why Chris is so concerned that I'm not going to be able to handle the next few days as a full-time mom. Given the complexity of what I do in the office, coordinating carpool and slicing oranges seems more like a vacation to me.

• • • •

"She won't stop crying. She's eleven. Why is she crying? Isn't eleven kind of old for crying? Is this a hormonal thing? She says I humiliated her with the oranges. How could I humiliate her with *oranges?*"

"How'd you slice them?" Chris asks.

"I don't know—I guess in slices, like when Marjorie makes an old-fashioned?"

"There you go. You're supposed to quarter them so when the girls bite into them, they look like mouth guards."

"How could I have possibly known that?"

The slot machines chime merrily in the background as we speak. Chris hasn't even been in Vegas a day and I've already gone off the rails here at home. He tells me, "I'm going to say this as gently as I can, but I did suggest you write everything down."

"You did not tell me how to cut oranges."

"I did. You said we'd use fewer bags if they were sliced thinner. Something about wasting less negative space if you cut them your way."

Oh, yeah. "Shit. How do I make this right?"

"Are you able to turn into Superman, reverse the earth's orbit, and go back in time to before you cut the oranges wrong? If not, say you're sorry and move on. You can't fixate on this mistake because that will make it worse. You have to trust me here. Acknowledge and proceed. If you wallow in how bad you feel about this, you're going to give Kelsey all the power. Don't do that. You're the adult; be in charge. Tell me something, Penny—is this the hill you want to die on?"

"No, but she's making me feel terrible!"

Chris laughs. "She's making you feel terrible because she's a manipulative little shit. That's what she does. She's eleven, and it's how her brain is wired. Acknowledge and proceed. Don't give in. Pick your battles."

"I will," I say, but I sound about as confident as I feel.

He laughs. "You are a terrible liar. The girls are like sharks, Penny. The minute they smell a drop of blood in the water, well, then, Chief Brody, you're going to need a bigger boat."

"I have no idea what that means."

"That means you're the only person in the world who's never seen *Jaws*. And it means don't give in. Do we have a deal?"

Why do I want to disagree with Chris? He's right. I'm crazy to even consider allowing an eleven-year-old to call the shots. *I'm* the adult here. I make the rules and the onus is on me to enforce said rules. I'm going to pick my battles. I shall acknowledge and proceed and that's all there is to it.

"We have a deal."

· · · ·

"Why does Kelsey get an iPod?" Jessica fumes from the backseat. "What'd she do that's so damn special? It's not her birthday. She didn't ace her report card. She can't even feed herself breakfast, and all of a sudden cool electronics are raining down from the sky for her? This is so unfair, so unbelievably unfair. Play favorites much?"

Well, Kelsey gets an iPod because she could force secrets out of the Taliban with her ability to whine. Honestly, I didn't know the human voice could be so shrill. Fifteen minutes in Gitmo listening to her and every single one of those POWs would turn on everyone and everything they hold holy, I guarantee.

The bitching and moaning about the damn oranges was like audible waterboarding. I was in pain; I mean it, actual physical discomfort. Her voice reverberated inside my ears in such a way that I could actually *taste* her whining.

I *literally* couldn't take another minute of her histrionics, and I was so desperate for something to shut her up that the iPod seemed like the most expedient solution, especially as she'd been hinting so hard about wanting one.

So, yes, I snapped, but I can't say any of this to Jessica because it would be the equivalent of pouring a whole bucket of blood into shark-infested waters. Instead, I ask her, "Does your father know you use the word 'damn'?"

"Obviously," she replies. I'm going to have to double-check that. I can't tell if this is one of Chris's pick-your-battles instances or not.

Jessica rages on. "Let's not change the subject here, *Mother.*" How is she able to make "Mother" sound like a curse word? "Not only does Kelsey get an iPod for doing nothing, but *you're late*. I'm standing out here in the rain by myself where any variety of pervert could abduct me. Look at me! I'm a pretty blond girl with big blue eyes and skinny legs, just the kind the weirdos like. It's never the uggos who get snatched. You never see a homely kid on a milk carton. Fact. And you're late picking me up because Princess Kelsey couldn't decide if she wanted the iPod or the MP3 player. But do *I* get an iPod? No. I get almost abducted. *Then,* I can't even sit in the front seat like a normal person. I have to cram back here with the rest of the cootie platoon."

"I don't have cooties, Jessie," Topher says. "I was sprayed for them at recess. Want me to give you a squirt?" He holds out a pretend can, his finger on the pretend trigger. Jessica pushes away his hand.

Kelsey says nothing, as she's busy playing with her iPod. I realize having bribed her makes me a terrible, terrible parent, but every minute she isn't sobbing is a minute I'm not losing my will to live, so I stand behind this decision.

"Jess, until you're fourteen, the safest place for you to sit is in the backseat. You know that. You are precious cargo, and I'm not taking unnecessary risks," I say. "The American Academy of Pediatrics says that—"

"The American Academy of Pediatrics didn't say *dick* about you trading in our big, comfortable van with the swivel captain chairs and three rows of seats for a hideous little Honda where we all have to be squished together like a bunch of veal calves in that PETA video Kelsey made us watch."

"Language, Jessica!"

(And where is Kelsey finding PETA videos? Is this why she's abandoned her beloved cheeseburgers? Does she actually care about the cows, or is this another cool-kid thing?)

"It's like you bought the Honda to punish us."

With the rise in gas prices because of everything happening in the Middle East, and with Topher having graduated out of his booster seat, I thought it was time to upgrade to a proper car I could drive to client meetings instead of the nightmare of a minivan I've been stuck in for the past decade. No matter how many times I had that thing detailed, I was never able to lift the fug of chicken nuggets and kid farts that permeated the upholstery. And the Cheerios. My God, the Cheerios. No one even ate a Cheerio in there for at least five years, yet they'd still magically appeared every few days, just seeping out from somewhere, like the salty efflorescence leaching out of an untreated brick wall.

"I love the Honda," Topher says. "It's got that new-car smell and there are no footprints on the ceiling yet."

"Kiss-ass." Jessica deliberately knocks off Topher's Cubs hat, which he retrieves with his feet and repositions on his head.

"Jessica!" I admonish. "Apologize to your brother."

Jessica crosses her arms over her chest. "Why? I'm not sorry. Everyone gets everything except for me."

I look at her in the rearview mirror and try to catch her eye. "Is this really about the Honda, Jessica?"

"Whatever." She turns her head and begins to stare out the window with an expression that seems more introspective than sullen.

"Jess, is something else going on?"

"She's not Maria," Topher volunteers. "She's only a *girl*. I heard her tell her friend she's only a *girl*."

Jessica tightens her arms around herself. "I lost the lead in *West Side Story*, okay? I'm playing one of stupid Maria's stupid girls. Serena Oberlin got the lead because she went to the theater camp *you* said was too expensive."

"Sweetie, the camp cost more than a semester of my college tuition."

Jessica pounds a fist on her knee. "*That's because it's a really good camp!* I'm just tired of everyone having everything cool and I have nothing. It sucks, okay?"

I look back at her again. "'Everyone' and 'everybody' are absolute terms. Can you be specific? What do you need that you don't have? Your dad and I aren't unreasonable, Jessica; your life isn't *Oliver Twist*."

"You want a list? Fine. Serena just had backstage passes at an Avril Lavigne show, Casey went to a Linkin Park concert, and Kathryn saw Eminem."

I can't stifle my snort of derision. "You're too young for a concert, especially Eminem. What is wrong with Kathryn's parents? An Eminem show? At thirteen? What, no reservations available at the crack den?"

"This is why I don't tell you things." Jessica pinches her lips together.

Shoot. I need to apologize and proceed. How does Karin get her kids to tell her everything? "I'm sorry. That wasn't very empathetic listening on my part. What else do your friends have that you don't?"

Jessica begins to tick off items on her fingertips. "Ashley has an iBook, Bethany has her own horse, and Patrice's parents take her on cool vacations *all the time*. They went to Turks and Caicos for Easter, Hawaii over the summer, and the Winter Olympics in February this year. She and her parents sat in the first row behind the judges at the ladies' singles figure-skating finals and afterward they met Sarah Hughes. She won the gold medal, you know. And Bode Miller was on the plane on the way home with them. He signed Patrice's shirt. Where'd we go for vacation again this year? Oh, yeah, *nowhere* because Princess Kelsey needed braces. I'm tired of being the only poor people in town."

How do I explain to my kid that just because we happen to be in a Honda in a parking lot full of Range Rovers, we're not poor? In fact, we're doing better than many of her peers, because we live within our means. We're not leveraged to the hilt or surviving on credit, and before we spend a cent of my salary, I immediately allocate a portion to various savings and retirement accounts.

Speaking of which, I slow down to let a Range Rover pass in front of me, largely because the driver was going to cut me off anyway. Early on I learned that math is really the science of patterns. A pattern I've noticed again and again is the more expensive the car, the less courteous the driver. I pretty much pull over whenever I see a Bentley; it's just easier.

I say, "Listen, Jess, I grew up here, too. I know what it's like to be from a town where there's an abundance of wealth. You'll always run into kids who have more than you. There was a girl a year behind me who lived in that one gigantic house on Rockgate Lane? With the big iron gate? Her dad had a private jet. John Cougar played at her graduation party before he was Mellencamp."

She rolls her eyes. "Am I supposed to know what that means?"

"John Cougar Mellencamp was my generation's Eminem. Sort of. Honey, I'm saying if you constantly compare yourself to others, you'll never be satisfied. The trick is to find a way to be happy with what you have."

"Whatever."

The car is quiet as we turn down the street to Barnaby's, save for ambient bits of sound escaping from Kelsey's headphones. Now and then Topher tries to catch the tune and hum along. Topher's a perfect example of what I'm trying to illustrate—I could buy both the girls new bikes and Topher would be thrilled to play with the boxes the bikes came in, never once demanding to know where *his* new ride might be.

I break the silence by saying, "Your father and I are working really hard to balance everything, Jess. Do you want to grow up in a family like so many of your classmates, being raised by nannies? A lot of your friends have all those toys because their folks feel so guilty for never being around. I mean, do you really want a horse, or do want your dad with you every day after school to help you with your homework?"

She perks up. "Is a horse an option?"

"Jess, we made the choice to be parents first," I say. "Your father takes smaller projects so he can be there after school. For me, I'd make significantly more if I were to travel like the firm wants me to; my career would be fast-tracked. I hate how much I've been away because of the Omaha project, and I'm so glad it's over. You don't want me gone Monday morning until Thursday night, right? I mean, didn't you guys miss me as much as I missed you?"

"Yes!" Topher offers. Jessica pokes him, which makes him giggle. See? He even likes when his sister is being mean to him.

"We were fine," Jessica says. "More than fine. Dad knows what he's doing. We get to ride in his SUV, and he's way better at a lot of stuff than you, especially cooking."

"You guys like my omelets."

"Yeah, once in a while, not, like, every day. When you were around all the time, you messed us up by doing everything wrong. No offense, but Dad's a better mom than you are."

Huh.

I'm torn between feeling hurt and feeling . . . a tiny bit exhilarated by having Jessica confirm my suspicions. The whole time I was a stay-at-home mom I felt as though I was failing in some respect, although maybe that's because my focus was split between child-rearing and preparing for my series of actuarial exams, and later, a part-time job. Staying at home with the kids was isolating and, honestly, kind of dull and repetitive, so diving into my prep material was needed intellectual stimulation. Often, kid duty and studying overlapped, and I'm sure somewhere in their synapses, these three recall stories of *Snow White and the Seven Life Contingent Risks* and *James and the Giant Exposure Rating*.

Chris was a champion in those days, always stepping in to assist with the kids in one way or another, much like I'd jump in to help him balance his books or manage his subcontractors. I was always seeking a problem to solve more complex than, "Who's got your nose?" because, spoiler alert, it's me; it's *always* me who's got your nose.

Am I somehow disloyal to admit that I much prefer having a

career outside of the house? I was so excited to have a few days of vacation, but I found I missed going to work today. Is that awful to say? I revel in the predictability of what I do for a living, knowing that if I apply the rules consistently within, say, financial modeling, I will always produce the same outcomes. Try that with an eleven-year-old girl. Go ahead, I dare you.

I derive such satisfaction from my work, yet a part of me feels guilty for enjoying that at which I excel. Of course I love my family a million times more than I could care for a profession, but in some ways I feel like I'm actually better at solving problems for clients than I ever was at running my household, if the past twenty-four hours are any indication.

Is it wrong to derive more satisfaction from research and analysis than I ever did from domestic duties? That's not to belittle anyone who excels at homemaking, because it's such an important job. In fact, it's too important a position for *me* to hold. Honestly, I'm as awkward with some household stuff as I used to be on the tennis court; it's just not the best fit for our family. I am so fortunate to have an outstanding doubles partner. As that's the case, why not have the Boris Becker of the home returning the domestic serves, if that's what he wants to do, too?

Now Jessica has me thinking—what if I *did* take on more responsibilities at work? A lot of consultants have stepped back their travel in the past year, unwilling to be away from their families for any amount of time given the state of the world. While I understand their reticence, would I be foolish to pass up the opportunity to leapfrog ahead? In a few years of being a road warrior, I could double or triple my salary. That's not insignificant. With everything I'm stashing into savings right now, we have little left over at the end of the month for frivolity.

With four solid walls, clean drinking water, and plenty of food, our standard of living is practically criminal, given the state of every other country in the world, and, of course, material goods are no indicator of satisfaction. (See: *Bancroft, Marjorie*.) Yet being an adolescent in this particular town is hard, and Jess doesn't have access to the extravagances that Foster and I took for granted as children. In fact, I used to look at whiling away the summer at the club as an obligation and not the tremendous luxury that it was. I was so fortunate back then and I didn't even realize how blessed I was. More than anything, I was annoyed to be a pawn in my parents' status-seeking game.

Things were particularly easy for me, and I realize that now. When I was Jessica's age, I didn't want for any material trappings. More important, I had math, which was the great equalizer for entirely different reasons. Math taught me how to fit in. And at Jessica's age, fitting in is generally just a matter of not standing out.

For example, neither Karin nor I had sisters, so we were clueless about wearing makeup once we hit high school. (Patrick had distinct ideas about what we should do, but we didn't yet know to listen to him.) I told Karin we should spend the first week watching what everyone else did, so we tracked the patterns of data we observed. We noticed that sixty-eight percent of the girls in our classes wore four types of cosmetics or fewer (lip gloss, mascara or eyeliner [not both], pressed powder, blush or eye shadow) on a daily basis.

In addition, I noted that the girls who wore more than five types of cosmetics were more likely to be catcalled in the hallways by boys on the football team, be yelled at more severely by teachers for the same offenses as girls in less makeup, and be shunned by groups of girls in the lunchroom, especially when wearing a skirt cut above the knee. What was so ironic is that these young women thought they were doing something to make themselves more attractive, but instead, with every brushstroke, they were singling themselves out for negative attention.

But because I was fourteen and didn't know any better, I didn't befriend those girls who'd done nothing wrong. Instead, I bought Maybelline Great Lash, Clinique Black Honey lip gloss, and Covergirl pressed power and simply blended in with everyone else.

But how do I explain any of this to Jessica?

If our family had more financial breathing room now, if we weren't quite so tightly budgeted, would Jess have an easier time navigating middle school? And if middle school is a challenge because she feels inadequate, like she's being left behind, then how difficult will high school be for her if we don't make some changes?

Will these kids grow up to be well-adjusted adults who make the best choices if I don't provide them every opportunity? What if the theater camps or the French-club trips or the photography classes or the voice lessons or the private tennis coaching or any of the myriad requests I've rejected due to cost are the key to these kids being happy and successful later in life?

I feel like I owe it to them to find out.

Obviously, I'll run any professional changes past Chris before making irreversible decisions, but if we were to start making adjustments, now seems like the time to do it.

"Hey, Mom?"

"Yes, Jessica?"

"Did you see that sign?"

"Which one?"

"To the right. That Toyota dealership over there is having a Mini-van Madness event. Looks like they're taking huge markdowns on the 2002s before the 2003s come on the lot. Thought you'd want to know."

I find myself clenching the steering wheel. "Why would I want to know?"

"Just in case."

"Jessica, we're not buying a new car."

"But there's no harm in stopping in."

The kid could use a win today, and this feels a lot like a pick-your-battle situation. Plus, I bet the dealer would give Topher a balloon, and that would delight him to no end. I loosen my grip on the wheel. "Fine. We'll take a look after dinner. But we're not buying anything, and that is final."

• • • •

"You hated the minivan," Chris says.

"I didn't *hate* it," I reply.

"Yeah, you did. You quoted the Reverend Martin Luther King, Jr., word for word when we signed the trade-in paperwork. 'Free at last, free at last, thank God almighty, we are free at last,' you said. You hugged strangers in the parking lot of the Honda dealership. You cried hot, salty tears of joy. You rolled down the window and shouted, 'See you in hell!' as we drove away, much to the confusion of Steve, our salesman. He thought you were talking to him. When we got home, you and Patrick christened the Honda by breaking a bottle of champagne over the bumper."

"I feel like you're exaggerating. Also, the payments are the same, and I got a lower APR."

"Pen, I'm not saying a word about the finances; that's your department. If you say we can afford a 2002 Toyota Sienna, then

I trust you. If you say we can afford a 2002 turbocharged BMW 3 Series with spoilers and a sunroof, then I *really* trust you."

"We can't."

"Damn. Too bad. I would look *fine* in that car. Anyway, my concern is you're rewriting history and I'm trying to understand why. You were unhappy with the minivan but you stuck it out until it made sense to trade it in, and I was proud of your self-restraint. Now we don't need a van, but we got another one anyway. I suspect you let the kids bully you into it, and I'm worried you're going to be unhappy again. I don't want that."

"Point taken." I'm not offering much by way of counterargument in the hope that he'll drop the conversation.

"I don't want to set a precedent. The girls are both at an age where they're starting to push their boundaries. If they see you're an easy mark, we're going to have trouble with discipline down the line. If they find they can push you around, they aren't going to respect you."

I'm starting to feel like Chris is disciplining *me*. He's given me a fair amount of grief since he came home, first over the van, then over the iPods and all of Jessica's new clothes, and also Kelsey's, and the whole Harry Potter Lego setup I bought for Topher. Technically, he didn't ask for anything, but I wanted to be fair.

"Chris, you do things for them all the time, especially Kelsey, like with the cereal and the leggings!" I argue.

Chris runs his hands through his hair, like he always does when he's trying to maintain an even keel. "Yes, to *help* them. I also require each of them to either do chores around the house or earn good grades before they receive any rewards. If we just hand them whatever they want for no reason, they won't appreciate what they have. They'll grow up to be spoiled. We promised ourselves we weren't going to be *those people*. There are too many of them around here. We agreed we weren't going to be the overindulgent absentee parents with the obnoxious kids who can't function as adults."

"No Veruca Salts," I say, referring to the promise we made back when I was pregnant for the first time and we'd watched *Willy Wonka & the Chocolate Factory*. We'd both freaked out a little bit after Veruca launched into her "I want it now" business. We'd seen the movie a dozen times, but never with one on the way before, and we'd both panicked.

"Do you get it? Are we on the same page? Are we cool?"

"You're right," I say, nodding. "I get it. I do. We are cool. I lost my head, but I've located it again. Here, it's right on my shoulders where it belongs."

He hugs me and kisses me squarely on the forehead. "Thank you. Then I'm gonna check in on the boy, help him out with his Hogwarts building project. Can you see how Jessica's doing on her pre-algebra? I suspect it's going slowly. She really didn't inherit your genes there, did she?"

"You've got it."

I climb the stairs and walk down the hallway to Jessica's room. Her door is closed, as usual, so I give it a tentative knock.

"Come in."

Jessica's not solving for X—instead she's standing in front of her full-length mirror, trying to copy Hilary Duff's *Lizzie McGuire* style from a recent *People* magazine. From the bangs to the floppy hat to the gummy bracelets, she's pretty much nailed the whole look. Barnaby is lying on her pillow, watching her intently. He's rarely more than a few steps away from Jessica. He eyes me suspiciously as I enter her room.

"Are you Hilary Duff or Jessica Sinclair, because I can't tell," I say.

"Really?" she says. She tries to fight her urge to smile, and ultimately loses. She looks so young when she turns on the full wattage of a genuine grin.

Sure, I put more on the credit card than I meant to at Old Orchard Mall, but Jessica and Kelsey were so thrilled at their new things and their attitudes have greatly improved over the past few days. I realize they've been behind the curve with their peers in terms of wardrobe, and I hope what I bought them helps them blend in, too.

Chris is not keen on the idea of me stepping up my work schedule *at all*, so if I want more activities for the kids, I'll have to implement austerity measures around the house. I'm sure I can paint my own nails. And how hard can it be to trim my own bangs? Everyone can wear an extra sweater in the winter, too. We can do this. We'll figure it out.

"Really," I confirm.

"Yeah, but . . ." She trails off, and the smile disappears.

"But?"

"See that necklace?" She points to Hilary's silver Return to Tiffany heart dangling from thick links, fastened with a round toggle. "I wish I had one like that. The heart would so complete the look, and I really, really love it. . . ."

I begin to say, "You can certainly have one—"

She squeals and throws her skinny arms around me. I can feel her heart beating through her chest. Barnaby wags his tail in approval as well. "Oh, my God, I love you the most, Mommy! You're the best mother in the whole world! Bethany is gonna be sooooo jealous! Finally! I finally win! I finally have something that will be better than her! Thank you, thank you!"

This all happens so fast that I'm not able to complete the rest of my sentence, where I planned to say, "as soon as the Walt Disney Corporation gives *you* a TV show, too."

Shit.

Now I'm obligated to buy the stupid necklace.

There's no take-backsies here, not after that over-the-top reaction. I'd rather cough up the hundred bucks (two hundred?) (*three hundred?*) than have her mad at me for the next six months. And I walked right into it, too; this is one hundred percent my own doing.

So I guess the new austerity measures will start as soon as I get back from Tiffany. Do I have to pick up something for Kelsey, too? Yeah, I bet I do. Damn it.

I will not be mentioning *any* of this to Chris.

I mean, one more tiny set of unearned presents isn't going to be what Veruca Salts the girls . . . right?

CHAPTER SEVEN

To: jessica@sinclairsartorial.com

From: collections@empireartsupplynyc.com

Date: June 5th

Subject: PAST DUE: THIRD NOTICE

Invoice #46129978

Account #9893342

Amount Due: $3,296.51

Date Due: March 1st

Dear Miss Sinclair:

Your account is now ninety days past due. Immediate action is required to bring your account current. If we do not receive payment within the next five business days, this debt will be turned over to our legal team for collection, which may adversely affect your credit rating. Please mail a check to us at once.

Thank you,

Harold Rochester

Collections Specialist

Empire Art Supply, NYC

To: jessica@sinclairsartorial.com

From: service@chelseabankofnyc.com

Date: June 5th

Subject: Credit Limit Reached

Dear MISS/MRS./MR. JESSICA SINCLAIR:

Our records indicate that you have exceeded your $25,000 VISA CREDIT CARD LIMIT. No further credit will be available until you make a payment, which you can do at your local branch of CHELSEA BANK OF NYC, online at CHELSEABANKOFNYC.COM, or at any one of the two million STAR interbank networked ATMs across the United States.

Thanks,

The Friendly Bankers at CHELSEA BANK OF NYC

BY THE NUMBERS

To: jessica@sinclairsartorial.com

From: interncassie@sinclairsartorial.com

Date: June 5th

Subject: Status check-a-roni, part dos!

Hi, Jess! Um ... should the lights be off in your apartment? I feel like the lights shouldn't be off. Should I call Con Edison? I feel like I should call Con Edison. Can I eat the caviar in your fridge? I feel like I should eat the caviar in your fridge because it's gonna go stink-a-roni soon, and who wants to come home to hot, bad fish eggs, right? I feel like I should drink the champagne, too. Same reason.

I feel like I should probs work from home because I'm not sure what else to do without electricity and it's kinda stuff-a-roni in here. Anyhootie, have a totes kewl weekend!

XO, Cassie

. . . .

"You brought Stassi," I say, opening the front door. I watch as Stassi gathers assorted bags from Chris's car, feeling like I've been sucker punched. "You brought Stassi *to stay at my house*."

"Yes," Chris replies. "She packed her sewing machine and the material she needs to fix our daughter's dress."

"Your girlfriend is going to sleep in the house where you and I lived when we were married. To each other. Until we weren't because you started dating your secretary."

Chris sighs. "She also has an iPhone full of all of her interior designer contacts so we can track down more birdcages to replace the ones Max sent away. And she's already called her uncle with the forklift, who's on his way here to move the tub."

What he's telling me isn't registering. I can't see past the idea that That New Hussy is going to sleep here. "You and your girlfriend are going to have a slumber party. Together. In my house. Where we raised our babies. Where we mourned your parents' passing. Where we supervised homework. I don't remember growing older— when did they? Seedlings turn overnight to sunflowers, blossoming even as we gaze."

Why am I suddenly quoting lines from *Fiddler on the Roof*? Am I having a rage stroke?

Chris shifts his weight from one foot to the other. "Do you want to see the string of texts I received from you after we talked? You outlined all the problems up here, and I went through them one by one. Stassi is the key to the solutions. She took the rest of the day off of work for us. She canceled her client appointments."

"Slumber party at Penny's house, woo-hoo!"

I might be having a rage stroke.

"What's going on right now with Kelsey? A new iPod can't fix. Math can't fix. Bribes can't fix. But Stassi can; you just have to *let* her. Please don't let your pride and anger ruin your daughter's day."

"Has Stassi been to a slumber party recently? I'll give you five-to-one odds that she has in the past ten years. Because she's, what, twenty? Do they still freeze bras? Wait, she doesn't wear one, so I bet she doesn't know."

Twin spots of color begin to rise on Chris's cheeks while the rest of his face turns white. "Number one, she's in her thirties, and number two, you can't allow my mistakes to ruin our daughter's wedding day, especially when Stassi didn't do anything wrong. Penny, be reasonable. You're better than this."

"What, will you both sleep on the pullout sofa in the den, or will one of you take the living room couch? I'm just curious. How will this work? Ooh, brainstorm, let's all have breakfast together in the morning! I'll make omelets. Does Stassi like goat cheese? How does she feel about fresh chives?"

He braces himself against the doorjamb. "I understand how difficult this is, Penny, believe me. You think this is easy for me? That this is what I envisioned? This should be joyful, and I'm so goddamned stressed I want to throw up in that fern over there," he says, pointing at a potted plant on the corner of the porch.

I'm not helping the situation, and yet I can't stop myself. The bitterness spews out of me like lava from Mount Vesuvius, which we were supposed to see on the anniversary trip to Italy we didn't take, what with Chris's active social life and newfound love of smooth jazz.

I fucking *hate* smooth jazz now, by the way.

I query, "In terms of sleepwear, do you two go all old Doris Day film, with her in the big plaid jammie top and you in the matching bottoms? 'The pajama game is lots of fun; two can sleep as cheap as one!'"

Chris's eyes are pleading. "Penny, please. I'm not asking for me. I'm asking for Kelsey."

Yet I am relentless.

"Or is she more of a boxer-shorts-and-tank-top kind of a girl? What about lingerie? Does she trend more La Perla or Fredericks of Hollywood? Inquiring minds want to know, but I have my suspicions."

Chris runs his hands through his hair. "Jesus, Penny, this is already hard enough."

"Penelope Bancroft Sinclair, come here this instant."

I slowly turn to face Marjorie. I swear to God I'm going to buy a bell to place around her neck because I've had it with her sneaking up on everyone with her little cat's feet. You'd think we'd at least hear all the gin and onions sloshing around inside of her, but no.

Marjorie says, "I have an amethyst choker that would be brilliant with your dress. Come along, pet. You'll try it on posthaste." And before I even realize what's happening, she whisks me up into the guest room and closes the door behind her. She points to the bed. "Be seated."

I sit. I feel like I have no choice. I notice that she and Max have practically moved in, which is no surprise. Marjorie was never one to travel light. Once on a family trip to Yellowstone, she brought eleven suitcases. Why she thought she might need her choice of ball gowns in a national park, I have no clue, but she was prepared for any eventuality. Perhaps I get my deep and abiding love of contingency plans from her?

"My dear, I have walked this earth more than sixty years," she begins.

I interrupt. "You realize who you're talking to, right? I know how old you are. You weren't nine when I was born. Lying about your age insults us all."

She glances at herself in the vanity mirror and applies a loose dusting of powder with a fat mink brush. "Not a lie, darling. I *have* walked the earth for more than sixty years."

"*Considerably* more."

"To-mah-to, po-tah-to," she replies. "My point is this—today you have to eat what is inelegantly known as a *shit sandwich*. Unfortunate, but true. But you have a choice—you can swallow it whole and be done, or you can take a dozen small bites, chewing each one thoroughly and for no good reason. Right now you're taking one small bite after another. Stop it. Swallow the bloody thing and move on. I promise, when you look down at the empty plate, you will feel better."

I consider her statement—either way, I still have to consume everything today's delivering to me on said plate, and there's no getting around it. But if I heed Marjorie's advice, at least I won't have to prolong the most unpleasant parts.

"Marjorie, that's the least terrible advice you've ever given me," I say. I hesitate to use the word "best," especially with the woman who once advised me that only homely girls finish college.

"Oh, good! Well-done, me," she replies. Instead of hugging me, she makes more of a shooing motion. "Okay, then, off you go."

"That's it?" I ask.

"Yes."

"We're done? Didn't you want me to try on a necklace?" I ask.

"A ruse, my dear. I wanted to save you from yourself. Amethysts? Really? What are we, *Italians?*"

I stand up and walk to the doorway. "Well, sound advice anyway. Thank you."

"Penelope, darling?"

I turn to look back at her. "Yes, Mo—" I stop myself. For a second I almost called her Mom. Damn. This has been a crazy day. "Yes, Marjorie?"

"We're still out of Boodles."

• • • •

Confident in my inability to harness my fat yap around Stassi, I've been tacitly avoiding finding reasons to enter Kelsey's room. Yet I keep walking past Kelsey's door, waiting for the invitation that never comes.

Kelsey quit wailing quite a while ago. Now the buzz coming from her end of the hallway is upbeat and celebratory, so I sense that Stassi has the situation well in hand. I'm catching threads of conversation here and there. Earlier Stassi mentioned being able to sew curtains in her sleep. *Really?* I wanted to shout. *Because I can do calculus in* my *sleep!* But I didn't.

The last time I passed, Kelsey had her shoulder pressed against Stassi's as she mended the dress and saved the day. That felt like a knife in the heart. Now I hear Zara say something about Arctic Foxes and Fleet Monkeys, to which Stassi replies, "You mean, like, Vampire Weekday?" and everyone dies laughing. Another joke I'm not in on.

I feel old and useless and painfully unwanted.

I should be grateful for Stassi's assistance, and to an extent, I am. Yet I still want to kick a lung out of someone. Probably Chris.

I'm not sure what to do with myself. I'm at such loose ends. I've been wandering around here aimlessly for the past couple of hours now. I'd work off some steam in the basement gym, but the room's all staged with Mason jars and flatware for tomorrow, so there's not a square inch of floor space left.

I'd be happy to supervise some of the crews, but the bathtub has already been relocated, thus unplugging the main artery to the backyard, so caterers, florists, and party-rental reps are scurrying around getting everything ready for tomorrow, under Bella's watchful eye. I'd simply be redundant if I were to volunteer. Topher and Patrick are already gone, having taken Marjorie out to the rehearsal-dinner site, luring her away with the promise of an unlimited supply of Boodles.

Chris spoke with Stassi's friend about borrowing a few vintage pieces. With instructions to load up on "anything rusty" at a local storage facility, he returned with a moving truck full of items flaking off all over the place, and he's currently arranging them in the yard, so I prefer to stay inside. Kelsey shrieked—the good kind—when she saw the decrepit swing set and the oxidized tricycles. And the corroded teeter-totter? She said she simply "couldn't even." Naturally, Kelsey thinks her daddy is some kind of hero right now.

I watch from the window on the second floor as Chris attempts to string burlap banners across the sad old pieces of playground equipment.

"It's like the set of *The Walking Dead* out there," Jessica says, coming up behind me.

Seriously, I am buying bells for *everyone*. Or is it that I'm losing my sense of hearing? Terrific. First I need Botox; now I need Miracle-Ear.

"We should give out tetanus shots as party favors instead of Mason jars full of Jordan almonds," I reply. I don't even attempt to mask my contempt at this point.

"Wow. That was utterly and profoundly bitchy," Jessica replies. Before I can apologize or explain myself, she adds, "There may be hope for you yet."

. . . .

"What's our plan? Smother them both while they sleep? Together? In your house? Like, what in the actual *fuck*?" Karin glowers at Stassi and Chris, seated on the other side of the restaurant from us at the rehearsal dinner. I'm pleased that she's able to express the outrage that I have to suppress in the name of familial harmony.

"Wouldn't Kelsey notice she was walking down the aisle alone tomorrow?" I reply.

"Shit. We can't *Weekend at Bernie's* him?"

"I feel like you can only animate a dead body realistically in the movies."

She shrugs. "Then I'm fresh out of ideas."

Patrick and Michael, who are sitting with us, exchange glances with each other. Patrick rolls his eyes but says, "Go ahead."

Michael clears his throat and then says, "Penny, I love you; you know this. But your anger concerns me. I'm worried it's eating you up. I'd like to see you channel your energy into something more positive."

Under his breath, Patrick coughs and says, "Pollyanna."

Michael continues. "Instead of despising Chris for being with Stassi, why not find your own Stassi? You could be happy with someone else. I think it's time. Wouldn't it be nice to have a plus-one who isn't Karin for once?"

Karin says, "But, Michael, sweetie, where's Penny going to meet her own Stassi? All the middle schoolers are currently at camp for the summer."

Everyone laughs, save for Michael. I've never quite understood how someone as biting and acerbic as Patrick could wind up with a guy who always says "please" and "thank you" to the telemarketers who call during dinner.

"You can be bitter or you can be better. Which would you prefer?" Michael asks.

At the same time, both Patrick and Karin say, "Bitter!"

"I wouldn't even know how to meet someone," I protest. "Do I just go to bars? I haven't had a date since 1987, when only doctors had car phones and long-distance calls cost twenty-five cents a minute."

"Technology, honey. You let technology do all the work," Michael says. "Sign up for a dating site. There are so many out there. There's eHarmony, Match, PlentyOfFish, OkCupid, ChristianMingle—"

"There's Tinder," Karin says, "if you just want to hook up. You know, make sure all the equipment is still working before you actually get back in the game. Swipe right for yes and left for no, or vice versa. Actually, I'm not sure; might be the other way. Sasha's on it *all the time*. I'll have to ask which way to swipe because it seems important."

"Every single thing you've just said disturbs me!" I say.

"What about Ashley Madison or Grindr?" Patrick asks, with a wicked grin.

"Not funny," Michael admonishes. "Oh, and there's OurTime and SeniorPeopleMeet if you're looking for someone more mature."

"Please," Karin says. "Those sites are for geezers or for girls hunting for sugar daddies. Penny doesn't want any of that."

The three of them argue about which site might be the most appropriate for me, but I've stopped paying attention. Instead, I'm distracted watching as Kelsey calls Stassi over to her table. She proceeds to give Stassi a tremendous hug before introducing her to a group of her friends. All the girls at the table then bound up and take turns hugging Stassi before she returns to casually fling one arm over Kelsey's shoulder. They stand there, side by side, arm in arm, best of friends, whereas Kelsey hasn't even acknowledged me since Stassi showed up, let alone introduced me to anyone.

Yep, this is a real shit sandwich all right.

But chewing every bite is entirely my decision.

• • • •

I'm standing in the front row when Chris walks Kelsey down the aisle to Regina Spektor's "Us." Honestly, I'm glad she didn't pick a more traditional song here. If she'd gone with Pachelbel's Canon in D, I might have been overcome. Sure, I've heard the tune at dozens of weddings since mine, but this is the first time since our day that I'll have had the perspective of being on the other end of the aisle from Chris. I feel a lump in my throat noting that the reflection of pride and love on his face is almost exactly the same as it was on our day, too.

As Kelsey proceeds toward him, Milo weeps openly, and Topher, who has already conveniently lost his straw boater, hands him a handkerchief.

Kelsey is luminous and beatific, like none of the chaos of the past couple of days ever transpired. Her dress is divine, as Stassi made it better than new. She added in a few elastic panels and draped them with swaths of vintage tulle, thus improving on the original design. Kelsey says now she'll actually be able to eat and dance at the reception. The few extra pounds actually fill her out nicely, as I always thought she was too thin. The wreath of flowers nested in her wild hair makes her seem like a nymph from a fairy tale. For all my quiet skepticism, I cannot imagine her ever being more beautiful than she is at this moment. I don't even hate the sparrow tattoos.

Okay, I do hate the sparrows, but in a benign way, like how I hate fennel seeds or the idea of Ben Affleck playing Batman.

Chris hands Kelsey over to Milo and then comes over to stand by me.

I exchange a look with Patrick, who's on the other side of me, as if to say, *Why is he standing* here? *Where is Stassi? Shouldn't he be with his date?* Patrick gives me a shrug, equally confused.

As though Chris can hear my racing thoughts, he leans over and says, "This is family time." His familiar scent of cloves and citrus and cinnamon hits me at such a visceral level that I suddenly can't imagine him *not* here at this moment.

Bishop Gartner invites us to sit, and we all take our seats in the gold bamboo chairs lined up in neat rows in front of the lattice arbor, which is woven with blush-colored New Dawn roses. I had the arbor built next to the old apple tree, now strung with vintage chandeliers. Spring came late this year, so the last of the apple blossoms are still in bloom, filling the air with their sweet perfume. Pale pink petals spill down around the couple when the wind blows. The scene looks so much like the inside of a snow globe that the guests collectively gasp with delight.

"You did good, kid," Chris whispers.

"All I did was write checks."

"Wrong. All you did was make this happen."

I look from Kelsey to Jessica in the middle of the bridesmaids and then over to Topher. I have to fight the urge to put my head on Chris's shoulder, not because I'm overcome with emotion for him, but because regardless of where he and I are, this is what we created.

We made this happen.

The ceremony is short, and I'm surprised at exactly how traditional the vows Kelsey and Milo exchange are; in fact, they're almost exactly the same ones Chris and I pledged to each other once upon a time, with the better or worse, sickness and health, richer and poorer, and the loving and cherishing. Maybe the lesson here is that it's fine to be offbeat and indie in all areas of the wedding, save for the ones that count in the long run.

Like forsaking all others.

The bishop pronounces them husband and wife, they kiss, Milo thrusts a fist in the air and cheers, everyone applauds, and then it's over. As they head back down the aisle, we all turn to watch them, and that's when I spot Stassi standing in the back row. She gives me a small wave and mouths, *So beautiful!*

Damn it. If I'm not careful, I might accidentally end up liking her. She could have come up here and been so officious, so smug at having righted all that went wrong, but instead she simply stood by herself and let me have this moment with my daughter's father. Even if I hate him right now—and the jury's still out on that—I will never forget having had the opportunity.

Stassi had better lose her top on the dance floor or hit on my dad or barf in the punch bowl at the reception, because her being a good person does not fit my narrative.

• • • •

"Yes, I like you, Stassi. No, I'm not kidding."

Stassi's laugh is like a musical instrument, and her eyes sparkle in the ambient lighting of the tent. I want so badly to despise her right now, but at some point I had to give that up. Was it when she gave the Heimlich maneuver to Mrs. Bunky Cushman because her salmon went down the wrong pipe? Perhaps when she administered the EpiPen to Zara, who didn't realize the crab puffs contained crab? Or maybe it was just watching her kick off her shoes and scuttle up the apple tree like a goddamned rhesus monkey to relight the chandelier that finally won me over, but she did, and now I can't legitimately hate her.

(I might hate myself, however.)

Truly, we'd have crumbled without her. For example, who'd have guessed all the rusty crap would have turned the backyard into something so magical and otherworldly?

Even the bathtub seems appropriate in this setting.

Sensing that this day might be too much for Jessica, it was Stassi and not me who thought to have her father ask Jess to dance. They were laughing the whole time they spun around the floor to "Sweet Child o' Mine." Kelsey was testy that someone diverged from her hipster playlist, but Stassi distracted her with fake mustaches long enough for them to have their moment. That was the first time all day I saw Jessica smile.

As for the slumber party? Stassi called her friend who lives in

Kenilworth and camped out there so we didn't have to worry about sleeping arrangements. P.S. She even wore a bra today. What more could I want? Under different circumstances, I suspect Stassi and I might have even been friends.

"Don't tell Chris, but I like you, too. If he knows, he'll get nervous and worry we're plotting against him," Stassi says.

"Then we'll keep it between us. Seriously, thanks for everything. Now I'm going to go somewhere that isn't here because this is so awkward that I can't even stand it," I say.

"I wish we could have been friends, Penny," she replies before merging back into the thick of the party. She stops to chat with Topher, who's doing a fine job of perpetuating the fiction that Adrienne is his date. The two of them have been dancing up a storm all night. If I didn't know better, I'd actually believe they were a couple. I like how they're holding hands—really helps sell the lie.

I head in the opposite direction, to the corner of the yard where it's dark and quiet. Years ago, Chris built a playhouse for the girls, and after they outgrew it, it morphed into a storage shed. Right now I'm planning to hide behind it and smoke a cigarette I bummed from one of the groomsmen.

I know. *I know.*

I'm not normally a smoker for so many reasons, but mainly because tobacco usage is the leading cause of preventable death in the United States, plus it's gross and expensive and I could go on and on. Really, there's no good reason to smoke except in this moment it's the only thing in the world that I want to do.

I slip behind the playhouse and find an old book of matches under a terra-cotta pot. I sit on one of the tree-stump benches and light my cigarette. I draw in the smoke, letting it fill my lungs, reveling in the sheer wrongness of it all. I do this maybe once a year, and I refuse to feel guilty for these five minutes of unadulterated bliss.

I shut my eyes and listen to the band playing in the distance. Everyone sounds like they're having a wonderful time. I'm glad I stuck it out here for another year; I would hate to have missed this night or denied the family this one last time here together.

"I can't believe you held out until ten thirty to smoke. I'd have laid four-to-one odds on it being no later than nine o'clock." Chris sits next to me on one of the stumps.

"I'm a woman of infinite mystery," I reply.

"You are at that," he says.

I pass him the cigarette. "You want in on this?"

"Like you've ever been able to finish a whole one by yourself," he says.

"The mind is willing; the flesh is weak."

He laughs. "The flesh never learned to inhale."

"Hey, the flesh has delicate little lungs. The flesh can't help it."

"So, how was it?"

"The cigarette? Weird. The kids are smoking American Spirits these days. They're organic with no nicotine. If I'm going to smoke one per year, it may as well be a cowboy killer, you know? Marlboro Reds? Ooh, or Lucky Strikes? Now, *they* were cigarettes."

"I mean the wedding. How was the wedding for you?"

"The wedding was great and I loved it. At the same time, I wish I felt more relevant and connected to the kids. This week wasn't about me, yet I'm hurt by the extent to which it wasn't about me. Is that horrible to admit?"

"You are perfectly justified, and your secret's safe with me."

"Thanks."

"So . . . now what? What's next?" He hands the cigarette back to me.

I take my final drag and exhale slowly, letting the smoke out in one long plume that curls and disappears into the darkness. I lean back against the playhouse and look up at the stars. "I don't know. I don't have a plan. I wonder if not knowing isn't the worst thing in the world?"

"That's always been my philosophy."

We're quiet for a full minute.

"Hell is the truth discovered too late," I finally respond.

"Hey, Pen?" He leans companionably against my shoulder.

"Yeah?" I breathe in the cloves, cinnamon, and citrus.

"Are we cool?" He takes my hand and rubs his thumb over my knuckle.

I offer him a wry smile while I look down at our hands together. "No, Chris. We are not cool. But I'm willing to give you two-to-one odds that we could be someday." I take my hand back.

"Then it's a good thing I'm a bettin' man."

We spend another couple of minutes in companionable silence. The whole world stands still, and I feel like we're at peace. We've reached some kind of truce. While this moment feels familiar, it's no longer imbued with all the pain of the past few years.

Perhaps this is our new reality.

Maybe there's some middle ground between perfection and the proverbial shit sandwich. Possibly . . . friendship?

He rises and brushes the dust from his tuxedo pants. "I'm going to head back to the party. You coming?"

"I'm going to enjoy the quiet for another minute or two."

"Cool."

He begins to walk away.

"Hey, Chris?"

He turns around. "Yeah?"

"Stassi says you guys are leaving for an ecotour of Costa Rica soon? You're going to zip-line through the jungles? That sounds exciting. Do me a favor, though, and double-check your life-insurance rider to see if—"

"Henny-Penny," he says, "it's not your job to worry about me anymore." If I didn't know him better, I'd say he sounded melancholy about this.

"Sorry. Have fun."

I wave as he walks away, but he doesn't see me in the dark.

So . . . I did it. I got through this whole wedding relatively unscathed. Kelsey's married, Jessica and I had a moment, and Topher, well, he's still Topher. I feel like I've been able to let something crucial go with Chris. Maybe by releasing some of my rage, I'll have time to process other thoughts and that will make room to grow.

I feel ready to get on with the next phase of my life. And damn it, I'm actually kind of excited. I want to see what's next for me. I need a new role to replace what I've lost. I can't just be what I do; that's unhealthy. I need balance. To achieve equilibrium, I need to move on, to a new house, a new city, maybe a new pet, and, if Karin has her way, a new face. (Or, a new and improved old face.) And if Michael has his way, a new man.

I'm ready to start over.

I'm ready to embrace whatever comes next.

I might even be ready to defy the odds and love again. Sure, sixty-seven percent of second marriages fail—but what about the thirty-three percent that make it?

I'm a mathematician; I could make those numbers work. I

could be a thirty-three percenter. I'd just have to pay attention to the patterns and I could figure it out. I'm sure of it.

"Penelope, darling, *do* come out from behind that shed!" Marjorie calls, British accent out in full force. "There's a lorry parked in front of the house! And the bloody barkeep says we have no more Boodles! Put out your fag and fix this posthaste!"

But before my new life begins, before I can start over, before I can embrace what's next, I need to get all these people out of my damn house.

CHAPTER EIGHT

Wait, what's that noise?

I listen more closely.

Oh, yes, it's . . . nothing! Ha-ha! Because there is *no* noise! None whatsoever! The house is utterly and completely silent! No one's demanding gin with a British accent that cuts in and out like a distant radio station during a thunderstorm. No one's suggesting we wall off Mexico, all of it, and what the hell, New Mexico, too, while we're at it. No one's crying for a friend we last saw during W's administration, and no one's slamming doors and stomping upstairs simply because it's Tuesday.

This is bliss. Utter and complete bliss.

The caterers and party-rental folks had the backyard torn down and put to rights by Sunday night, and the fancy trailer full of Porta-Potties was hauled away at some point yesterday. I have no clue what happened to the bathtub or the Playground of the Damned; I just know they aren't here anymore, and that's all I care about.

The house finally emptied yesterday; everyone had vacated the premises by the time I came home from work. It's almost like last week never even happened. The only difference is that Barnaby is now on the mantel and not waiting for me by the front door. Okay, that part makes me want to cry (note to self: serve less cheese and crackers going forward), but the rest of it is a cause for celebration! Nothing could delight me more than getting back to my routine.

On Mondays my alarm goes off at 4:45 a.m. and I'm at the gym no later than 5:00 a.m. for fifty minutes of full-body work on the strength machines. I shower at the gym, where I grab a protein-packed smoothie and Quest Bar for breakfast, and take the 6:47 a.m. train into the city. I prefer to arrive particularly early on Mondays to jump-start my week. I could get to the office a few minutes earlier were I to take a taxi from the station, but I always hoof it, as new studies have shown that twenty-five minutes of brisk walking a day can add up to seven years to your life span. (Unless I were to be hit by one of the lunatic bicycle messengers in the Loop, in which case, I would be pissed.)

Because I concentrate on major muscle groups on Monday, Tuesday's my rest day. Depending on my energy level, I'll spend some time on the basement elliptical either before or after work. I still catch the 6:47 train whenever possible, but on these days I either go with steel-cut oats and fruit or cold-pressed juice and hard-boiled eggs.

Wednesday mornings are all about the treadmill, which I find dreadfully boring, so I have to pull out the big guns—that's right, the Hallmark Movie Channel, my secret shame. If it's wrong to want to see a cheesy Christmas movie starring Jennifer Love Hewitt in July, then I don't want to be right. Sometimes a gal just wants a happy ending.

Thursday starts off with kettlebells and homemade smoothies

in the Vitamix, and on Fridays I work with my trainer, Lars, first thing in the morning. I generally drive downtown on Fridays because I don't get out of the gym early enough to catch an express train. Plus, I like the ride downtown. Instead of using the expressway, I take the back route down Sheridan Road. A few miles south of me, my street jogs and begins to wind past the lakefront. From there on, houses morph into mansions all the way into the city, and the scenery is spectacular. The speed limit's only thirty miles an hour, but traffic often moves faster on this road than it does on the Edens, and I can still make it to the office by 8:10. Long ago, Vanessa gave up on trying to beat me in to work, so now she shows up sometime between eight thirty and nine o'clock, like everyone else.

My weekends are a bit more flexible. Sometimes I'll go to a yoga class on Saturdays or I'll meet Karin for a walk around the lakefront. And at some point I'll hit Starbucks for a skim latte. On Sunday I go to church, and afterward, I'll meet up with Michael and Patrick for brunch, or maybe Judith and Foster.

Truth? I'm not entirely sure what to do with myself on the weekends. If there's ever a time I'm going to ruminate or reflect on what's not right in my life, this is when it will be. But maybe with a change in venue, this won't be the case.

I spend an entire week after the wedding getting back into my daily routine, as I don't want to be too impulsive, but today I'm ready to pull the trigger; Penny 2.0 starts right now. I leave the office early because I'm having the listing agent come here for a walk-through before I sign an agreement.

At exactly 4:59 p.m., Kathy Kormandy pulls into the drive that's lined on either side with hearty hostas and daylilies. I'm sure it's her because she's in a black S-Class Mercedes, which is what every Realtor on the North Shore drives. On Open House Sundays, I wonder if they don't all get confused as to which car belongs to whom. Or if it even matters.

Kathy bounces out of the car and practically skips up the brick walkway, which is bordered with black-eyed Susans, sprays of fountain grass, and wispy lavender Russian sage. She's casually chic with her swinging black bob and sleeveless white blouse, tucked into satin ankle pants. Jessica would definitely know what kind of purse she's carrying—but I believe the quilting indicates Chanel. I greet her at the base of the porch steps, and she pumps my hand so hard I sort of want to yell, "Ow!" As we greet each other, a black Maserati cruises past. The driver, who looks a bit like Miguel, honks and waves. Must be Kathy's friend, because I don't know anyone with a car like that.

"Love everything I'm seeing already!" Kathy exclaims. "These fab Queen Annes never come on the market. Especially not this close to the beach. We're going to sell this place in five minutes, not kidding. Okay, I parked in the drive—is there a garage?"

I reply, "Yes, if you follow the driveway, there's a three-car garage around back with a little bonus room above it. There's a bathroom in there, too, but it's pretty dated. We never did get around to renovating it."

She claps her hands, and her enamel bracelets clack together. "Four minutes. We'll have this place sold in four minutes."

"I appreciate your confidence."

"Tell me about this gorgeous property." We climb the stairs and cross the threshold of the wraparound porch, which spans the whole front of the house. For the wedding, I bought a ton of Boston ferns, arranged in heavy urns. Hot-pink geraniums with flowers the size of softballs spill from oversized pots, framed by verdant ivy and violet-hued lobelia. The plants are so lush and full they almost don't look real. The wide wooden planks on the porch's floor sport a fresh coat of dove-gray paint, and there are six new white rocking chairs beckoning for someone to "set a spell." Everything is crisp and pristine, and the whole scene is reminiscent of an old inn on Mackinac Island. "The porch is *to die*. Can you feel the lake breezes from here?"

"Yes." So why don't I ever sit out here to enjoy them? I wonder.

"Let's see . . . The place is about a hundred years old, and it was built by a Chicago lumber magnate as a summerhouse. There's a book about the family inside."

"Oooh, a home with history! We're down to three minutes. Did you do much renovation?"

"Ha!" I bark, and then I catch myself. "I mean, yes. Extensive. Everything, top to bottom. That was the only reason we were able to buy here. The previous owner intended to do a total rehab. They gutted it, all right, but they lost so much in the market in 1987 that they eventually defaulted on their loan before they could start rebuilding. This place was basically a shell; it was down to the studs. The house was so far gone it wasn't a 'tear-down' so much as it was a 'fall-down.'"

Kathy scans the intricate ornamentation on the home's facade, each exterior bracket, spindle, molding, and gable sanded and refinished in shades of cream and goldenrod and forest green. "You'd never know now."

"Thank you. The neighbors were days away from having the place condemned before we bought it. But my ex owns a contracting company and my dad a custom cabinet company, so we made it work. The neighborhood came around because they were glad we were keeping the integrity of the architecture instead of erecting a

McMansion. Trust me, though, the first few years in this house were not easy. You know the expression the cobbler's children have no shoes? Well, the contractor's children had very few toilets and a roof that leaked."

Kathy asks what we paid, and she howls at my response.

"You didn't *buy* this house; you stole it," she says. "You should be in jail."

"You wouldn't feel that way waking up to a thick blanket of snow on Christmas Day—in the family room," I reply. "Come on, let me show you around the inside."

We step into an open and welcoming entryway, which technically could be a sitting room, but I always liked the drama of the airy and unadorned space, letting the grand oak staircase with hand-carved spindles and one simple table that holds the mail take all the focus.

"Fabulous! Oh! And that living room! So bright! That must be your favorite room!" Kathy exclaims.

I grit my teeth in an approximation of a smile and continue the tour. I show her the newly renovated powder room and the freshly beadboard-covered family room walls, having finally done away with the hideous old ducks-in-flight-print wallpaper, per Kelsey's request. Sure, we started from scratch back in 1988, but a lot of our work became quite dated (the mauve! the peach! the plaid! the chrome!) so there's not a square foot that hasn't either been rebuilt, rebrightened, rebleached, rescraped, repainted, or re-powerwashed in the past year. Patrick says the place looks like a Restoration Hardware catalog exploded all over it; I choose to take this as a compliment.

The great irony is everything's now completely done to my taste and I finally live in the house of my dreams . . . which I'm leaving. While I realize this is a great house, I have no business staying here on my own. This home is meant for a family. Kids need to live here. Grandkids ought to spend their holidays here. I'm never going to climb the old apple tree or huddle with a comic book in the cupola on a rainy day. I'm not going to play an ad hoc game of kickball in the elementary school parking lot down the street. Plus, I still want to set the living room on fire because of the unhappy memories, so you can see my dilemma.

Kathy coos with delight when she spots the fireplace in the master bedroom, having no concept of when Chris and I slept huddled in front of it as it was our only source of heat that first fall. She exclaims over the third-floor bonus area, clueless as to the summer the two of us spent playing mixed doubles up there, only instead of running after tennis balls, we were shooing bats. She snaps copious shots of our Bancroft Custom Kitchen without ever once inquiring about all the years that dinners came from a hot plate or the microwave before this gourmet kitchen with warming drawers and a second dishwasher came to be.

After the tour, we sit in my office to discuss a proposed asking price. I had an idea of where this number should be when I planned to list before Kelsey got engaged. Given the state of the housing market, I estimate our asking price to be within five percent of this figure.

Kathy has been making notes on a pad, in addition to snapping pictures. She writes down a sum. "Here's what I'm thinking." She tears out the sheet of paper and slides it over to me.

Is it me, or is this exercise a tad ridiculous?

Don't do the slide-y paper business like we're some kind of mafia kings. We're here, having a conversation. Just say the number. I'm sitting right across from you. All alone. No one will overhear us.

I'm not writing a check, so I don't need to see the figure written out. Just say it, for crying out loud. I find these theatrics a little silly and somewhat—

HOLY MERCIFUL MOTHER OF CRAP!

"This can't be right," I say, looking up from the sheet.

"Oh, yes, it can," Kathy assures me. "This is exactly what the comps for Queen Annes by the lake are selling for; plus this place is immaculate."

"This is three times what I expected."

Kathy beams. "Terrific."

"I'm not sure you understand. Remember what I told you we paid for this house? This number is that number *plus two zeros on the end*."

"Yes, but you poured a ton of capital into the place."

I feel like I can't wrap my head around this. "True, but not two zeros on the end's worth."

Kathy crosses her legs and sits back in the chair holding up a single finger. "One minute. We are going to sell this place in one flipping minute. And this is what I'm estimating for an asking price. You get buyers in a competitive bidding situation and you could get well over your ask. The house is great, granted, but the land? The old-growth trees? The walkability? The schools? Location, squared? Please. You could not have made a better investment back in the eighties. Microsoft, Target, Home Depot? Nope. Nothing would have paid off like this."

"I feel overwhelmed," I admit.

"I understand," Kathy says. "It's a lot to process. What I'm going to do is leave the listing agreement here. You look it over, you think about it, and if you're comfortable, you sign. If you're not, you call me, we talk, and we figure out what you need to be comfortable. This is your home; this is your life. I'm not going to push you into anything. But know that if you do sign, I will sell this place in, like, thirty seconds. Really, just like that." She snaps her fingers to illustrate her point.

Kathy gathers up her pad and her phone, placing them in her big quilted bag. "I'm going to head off and leave you with your thoughts. You, Penny, imagine what you might do with that kind of windfall. Travel, invest, maybe a little nip, perhaps a small tuck, so many options! Anyway, thank you for showing me your beautiful home, and I will be in touch!" She gets up, and I show her to the door, and when she exits, the scent of gardenias, vanilla, and myrrh lingers for a moment in her wake.

I should be celebrating right now, but I can't stop fixating on Chris. Specifically, on what he gave up, having now seen what our home is worth. He was so specific that the house should go to me and me alone, to the point that his attorney yanked him out of the room by his collar. As angry as I was back then, I didn't set out to "get even, get everything," yet that's exactly what happened.

He let me have it all without a fight.

Was he so anxious to be done, to be away from me, that he was willing to forgo a small fortune? Or was he so racked with guilt that he felt he deserved nothing? For the past year and a half, I've been assuming the former.

But seeing how he behaved at the wedding, how he rose to the occasion, now I'm wondering if his actions were based on the latter.

If so, then truly he worked his whole adult life for nothing, and that seems patently unfair.

Damn it, why is this house so quiet?

I don't want to be alone with my thoughts as this is not a

subject I'd like to contemplate. I'm literally willing to do anything to avoid rehashing this in my mind right now.

Anything.

I text: You may create a Match.com profile for me if we can meet for dinner—offer good tonight only.

I type in "Patrick," "Michael," "Judith," and "Karin" and click send.

Within thirty seconds, I have confirmed dinner plans with three of my four best buddies.

So there's that.

. . . .

Karin says, "Let's get started and find you a date!"

"Whoa, hold up," I say, throwing my hands up in front of me in a protective gesture. This was a mistake. A huge mistake. A blunder. A slipup. A terrible gaffe. I should have just been subject to my own thoughts. They couldn't have been that bad, right? I begin to twist my napkin into a rope as I verbally process exactly what a terrible idea this was.

I yelp, "A date? I don't want to date yet! Too soon! Can I test out his writing skills first, before we ever get to the spoken word? I mean, what if he's the kind of guy who doesn't know 'y-o-u-r' from 'y-o-u apostrophe r-e'? 'Y-o-u-r the apple of my eye'? I can't live with that. I can't receive a love note I want to edit with a red pen!"

Karin, Michael, and Patrick say nothing as I twist and fret. Or maybe it's that I don't give them a chance to interject before I continue. "And then we'd *definitely* need to chat on the phone first, or Skype or FaceTime long before a date, long before I worry about what to wear or, oh God, what kind of underwear to buy, or how high I should shave. I don't want to imagine how stringent the standards of grooming are now. When we were in college? Sexy was shaving below the knee. Sexy was baggy Bermuda shorts and a flipped collar. Sexy was powder-blue eye shadow. Shoulder pads were sexy. Cybill Shepherd was sexy. Spiral perms were sexy."

"Penny—," Karin starts to say, but I plow right over her.

"Like, what if he has a weird verbal tic? I worked with another consultant once, heck of a guy, but he ended almost every sentence saying ''n 'at,' which was somehow short for 'and that.' He was from Pittsburgh; I believe it's a bit of regional dialect."

"Penny, it's just—"

"Anyway, I liked him plenty, as I said, and he was exceptionally competent, but I can't build a life with that, or ''n 'at.' I couldn't do it. I couldn't. I guess I'd like to take a time-out here and catch my breath for a minute before I go on an actual date."

Karin stops me by holding up her iPad and pointing to the screen. "This is *literally* the first line on the screen on Match after we enter your e-mail address. I was reading what it says. You're already fighting this process."

I stop twisting my napkin.

"She is *absolutely* fighting this process," Patrick confirms, nodding in a manner I find smug.

"Mmmf mmmf mmmf mmmf," Michael replies.

"Beg your pardon?" Karin says, leaning forward.

Michael finishes chewing his slice of bread, which he'd drenched in olive oil before sprinkling it with Parmesan cheese. He brushes the crumbs off of his mouth and his shirt. "No, I'm sorry. I said, 'Give her a chance.'"

Patrick says, "How are you eating from the breadbasket in front of us? That's just mean-spirited."

Michael places a loving hand on Patrick's shoulder. "I disagree. You're being mean-spirited to yourself by trying to maintain your thirty-one-inch waistline. You're fifty-two, Patrick. What's the worst thing that will happen if you have to size up? That I would love you less? Never in this or any other lifetime. So have some focaccia—it's delicious."

With some impatience, Karin says, "Yes, yes, we're all super-concerned about Patrick's manorexia. You two have been repeating this conversation for twenty years. At this point, I'm sure this is foreplay for you, like those people who have to get dressed in mascot costumes to become aroused."

"The Furries," Patrick confirms.

"That's a *thing* and there's a *name* for it?" I ask.

"Yes," says Karin. "Ryan dated a girl who was a Furry."

"I wish I could unknow that," I say.

She ignores me. "But with the two of you, it's all, 'I can't eat the ziti!' and 'You must eat the ziti!' and if that's what you're into, if that's what gets you off, if that's what keeps it hot and fresh for you both, outstanding and God bless. You wanna be Carbies, go ahead, but *not right now.* We have what's probably a once-in-a-lifetime opportunity to get Penny on this site, so let's focus and do this and you guys can get back to your erotic eating disorders next time, capisce?"

Michael and Patrick glance at each other and both nod. "Capisce."

"Super. So, you are a *woman* seeking a *man* aged what to what?" Karin asks.

"What if I give myself a ten-year buffer in either direction?"

I say. "Is that too much or too little? Would we still have the same cultural references that way?"

Michael says, "Yes, for the most part. You don't want to go too young because then they don't know that Bill Clinton was someone other than Hillary's husband."

"Definitely," Karin says. "Also, you can probably expect the interested men to skew a little older. A forty-one-year-old guy will be trolling for a chick in her thirties."

"Ha! Try twenties," Patrick says.

I grab Michael's butter knife and make pretend slashing motions across my wrists. "Killing myself, thanks."

"Remember to go *with* the grain," Patrick tells me, repositioning the knife. "Vertical, never horizontal. Horizontal is a rookie mistake."

Michael *tsk-tsk*s him and takes the knife from me. "Not funny. Either of you."

"Was a little funny," Patrick mutters.

"Search radius—shall we say within fifty miles of your place?" Karin asks.

"No!" Patrick insists. "Too far. Do twenty-five miles. That will include the city but none of the grotesque suburbs. Bolingbrook? Ugh. I think not."

"What's wrong with Bolingbrook?" Michael asks. "There's an IKEA there."

"What's right with it should be your question," he replies.

"Let's see," she says, scanning the screen. "'Relationship Status' is 'Divorced' and under 'Have Kids,' we'll put 'Grown and out of the house.'"

"Add 'Thank you, baby Jesus,'" Patrick suggests.

"Don't add that," I say.

"Under 'Wants Kids,' 'No,'" she says.

"Or, 'No, thank you, baby Jesus,'" Patrick says.

"I feel like Match is no place to joke about the Christ child," Michael says.

"Unless you're looking for someone who finds that funny, too," Karin suggests.

"I don't," I verify.

"Then we won't add it. Okay, 'Ethnicity.'"

"Is 'mayonnaise on Wonder Bread' an option?" Patrick asks.

"'WASP' doesn't seem like the worst drop-down menu choice," Michael admits.

"'Caucasian,'" I say, with some finality.

"'Faith.' Do you want me to put 'Episcopalian,' or are you willing to walk on the wild side if you were to meet, say, a hot Lutheran?"

"Can you put 'Christian, but open to all faiths'? Religion isn't a deal-breaker for me."

"Well, look at you, embracing ecumenical dick!" Patrick exclaims, which makes Michael snort. I glower at both of them.

Michael shoots me an apologetic look and says, "I'm sorry, but that *was* funny."

Karin begins tapping away as she finishes up the profile. "Alrighty, you're five foot six, you have brownish hair, maybe a bit more gray than I'd like to see—"

"We should work on that," Patrick says. "Highlights would not kill you."

"Hush," I reply.

"Hazel eyes, athletic build—"

"Don't write that. Athletic implies I'm good at sports with balls," I say.

"No, hon," Patrick says. "That's the thing with these dating profiles. A lot of times what you say has an entirely differing meaning in a profile. Like in a real estate listing? 'Motivated seller' means 'owner losing his shirt.' Saying you're athletic doesn't mean you play sports—it means you're not a fat chick."

I reply, "Then definitely don't write that I'm athletic. I don't want to date someone who'd be so discriminatory! I want a man who'd care more about someone's heart than her hips! Actually, I'd probably look better if I put on a few pounds. The weight would fill in some of my fine lines."

"So would Juvéderm," Patrick says. "As would Restylane or Perlane. P.S. I am not opposed to going on a trip across the pond to see what's up over there, because they're a good three years ahead of us in terms of injectables. Do you know they have more than seventy-seven different types of hyaluronic acid fillers in the EU? Europe has a very simple approval process because they don't have to mess with the FDA like we do here."

"How do you know this?" Michael asks.

"Marjorie was educating me at the wedding. She's kind of an anti-aging expert. She's like the Stephen Hawking of cosmeceuticals. Did you know she uses a skin cream made out of foreskin?"

"She does not!" Karin exclaims.

"She does!" Patrick says.

"Wow, just when I think she can't be more Cruella De Vil, there she goes," Karin says.

Patrick says, "She says the serum works miracles—and you've seen her skin. The problem is the lotion is so expensive. You know, I always thought since I wasn't having any kids, the whole circumcision debate was not my business, but now I have an opinion. Off with their heads! Bring those prices down! Baby wants his college complexion back."

I start twisting my napkin again. "Do I just look old and worn-out? Is it that I'm hideous and no one thought to mention it to my face? Because my face is too hideous? Is that what you people have been keeping from me all these years?" I take a healthy slug of my wine.

"Pen, sweetie, you're fab. This procedure is horrible. Imagine the online dating profile like a mortgage application—you have to check all the boxes to start the process. Once you get the house, you live in it however you damn well please, but these are the hoops you have to jump through to begin," Michael says.

Karin says, "Anyway, 'athletic build,' you drink socially, and one cigarette a year behind your shed doesn't count toward making you a smoker. Now, for the creative part, tell me about *you* in your own words for the 'About Me' section."

I ponder this, taking another sip of my Chianti to buy some time. "Hmm. My own words . . . my own words . . . umm . . . I guess. Wow. Tough one."

"Why don't you let me write it?" Karin says. "My communication degree's gotta be good for something, right?"

I snap, "No! I mean, I can do this. I guess I'd say . . . I'm an actuary."

"Really, it's no problem. Let me write this part for you."

"How about—I'm an actuary *and* I like math."

Karin gives me a blank stare while Patrick pretends to hang himself.

"Sweetie," Michael says, pity practically emanating out of him. "No."

Our dinners arrive before anyone can mock me further. A

waitress, not our waiter, sets down the tray and begins to distribute our meals. "Baked eggplant?" she asks.

I raise my hand. "Hello!"

Mind you, I wanted the spinach gnocchi tossed in the gorgonzola sauce for my first course, followed by the filet of beef topped with sun-dried tomato butter and caramelized shallot and port wine reduction, served with horseradish mashed potatoes for my main, but since someone other than Chris or my ob-gyn may see me in my underwear for the first time since 1987, I figured now is not the time to eat my feelings, even if it would fill in a laugh line or two.

"Orecchiette with sausage, brown butter, and sage?"

"Present!" says Michael. The runner passes him the plate with a smile. Michael has that effect on people.

The waitress scans what's left on the tray. "Saltimbocca?" She holds up a luscious-looking plate of veal, wrapped in prosciutto and fresh mozzarella, topped with a brandy and sage sauce.

"Over here!" Patrick says, waving both hands.

"No. You got the roasted radicchio salad, dry, with a side of chicken," Karin says. "The veal is *mine*."

Patrick practically eye-rapes Karin's veal as it's placed in front of her.

"Nope," she says. "Do not give me sad face. You could have had this. You could easily have had this. You tried to steal it, but if you'd been successful, you wouldn't have even eaten it. You'd have just looked at it and sighed and touched it with your fork. You'd have forked it, you motherforker. Again, we're not playing your Carbie reindeer games today, Mary Chapin Carpenter."

I whisper, "You mean Karen Carpenter. Mary Chapin is alive and well and singing on tour."

Patrick takes an angry bite of grilled lettuce and chews with great discontent. Karin ignores him. "Hey," she asks, "where's Judith?"

"She texted back and just said, 'family here, major chaos, pray for me.' I believe all the kids are home from college for the summer and it's too much so she couldn't make it," I say.

"Bummer," she replies.

The eight of us—Karin and her husband, Tom; Chris and me; Patrick and Michael; and my brother, Foster, and his wife/my college friend Judith—used to go out together all the time. Although everyone in the group is Team Penny, it's still like the band has somehow broken up, because without Chris, neither Tom nor Foster wants to hang out nearly as much. Judith's and Karin's husbands lobbied for Chris's attention, and he was a terrific sport, spending hours debating Tom's fantasy-football lineup while still showing equal enthusiasm for Foster's endless indecision over whether Callaway or TaylorMade was the better golf club manufacturer. Now we're much more splintered, and I don't believe the seven of us have been together more than a handful of times in the past year and a half. And when we are en masse, it's like our spiritual center is missing. Foster and Tom were beside themselves at the wedding, finally getting to see Chris again without having to feel somehow disloyal to me.

I hope that if and when I meet someone new, he'll be able to mesh with our group and we can regain a little bit of what we lost. Divorce doesn't just divide man and wife—it splits up the whole damn ecosystem.

"Hey, for my 'About Me' section, why don't I say something about being a single woman looking for a kind, considerate, mature man to make our group whole again?" I suggest.

Karin stops chewing mid-bite and Michael drops his fork. Patrick's laughter begins as a sputter, but the more he tries to suppress it, the more it spurts out. After a couple of seconds, he is full-on guffawing, slapping the table, and dabbing his eyes with his napkin. Karin and Michael have joined in, too.

"What is so damned funny?" I ask.

Karin clears her throat. "Penny Candy, when you phrase it like that, you're basically asking an old man to have group sex with you and your friends."

I consider what she's telling me.

"Maybe you should just write this section for me."

· · · ·

Men are winking at me!

Ha!

I'm unclear what winking means, but I assume it's positive and nonthreatening, and it's not like someone flashing his genitals at me on the train. (Karin assured me it's not that kind of Web site, so I consider this a win.) (And yes, her 'About Me' section turned out nicely. She made me sound intelligent without being overbearing or closed off to having fun. Also, in no way would someone interpret my description as an orgy invitation, so that's a bonus.)

I wonder if I should hone my religion answer a tiny bit because I've already received an e-mail and apparently I'm not as ecumenical as I imagined. Should I specify "No Wiccans" going forward, or have I just heard from all of the fifty-year-old White Witches in the Skokie area?

Anyway, today was big. I made major strides. I have a live

dating profile on Match.com. Maybe I'll go on an actual date. Maybe soon my weekends will turn into something I actually look forward to?

Plus, I signed my listing agreement and faxed it back to Kathy, so my house is about to go on the market.

HA-HA, IT'S ALL UP FOR SALE NOW, BABY!

No, I'm not drunk—I only had two glasses of wine, but I did take an Uber to and from the city, just in case. (Tipsy, perhaps.)

If this is what moving on feels like, then . . . bring it on! I feel lighter and less encumbered than I have in a very long time. I feel like I'm about to start my second act in life and that there's this whole new world of possibilities out there for me. Probably not with a Wiccan, though. But best of luck casting your circles, Rowan Sage-river. I wish you really symmetrical pentacles, or whatever it is you're into, my magickal suitor.

I can't express how pleasant it is to lie here in bed and not be enraged. I wonder if some of my calm is because of the pillows. When I cleared them off the bed last Saturday night after the wedding, I never put them back. They've just been stacked on the window seat ever since. For the past week, every time I've gotten into bed without delay, I've thought, *Bonus month of my life back!*

Before the wedding, I was holding on to everything so tightly— who knew that in letting go, I'd release all that built-up pressure? All that anger? I'm moving along with the stream now, literally going with the flow, instead of being lashed again and again by the water rushing past me as I cling tenuously to a limb.

I'm coming to accept that I can't change the past; I can only look to what's ahead of me.

And so far? That horizon is wide-open.

So, I'm alone and I've always hated to be alone, but I've found there's a real peace that comes with the solitude. I've come to appreciate the stillness. Reflection is possible only in quiet like this. I should welcome the quiet now. I bet good times—boisterous times—are right around the bend, so I should appreciate the momentary tranquillity.

As I reflect on what I've accomplished today, I feel gratified. I feel content.

I feel . . . so sleepy.

· · · ·

"*. . . marmalade.*"

The Chianti is making me dream that Marjorie's standing over me, demanding to know where I keep my marmalade. Only she's pronouncing it mar-ma-LAHD. Yikes.

"*Penelope.* Where do you keep your thick-cut marmalade? I can't have my toast without my thick-cut marmalade."

More of a nightmare, then.

Wasn't I dreaming about doing an audit with Daniel Craig a few minutes ago? I should get back to that dream. I will audit you anytime, second-best James Bond. I snuggle deeper under the covers, only to feel them being pulled back off of me.

I crack open one eye. Marjorie is indeed standing over me in the bright morning light of early summer. "Oh, good, you're awake. I can't find your marmalade anywhere. Thick-cut, Baxters if you've got it, but it must be orange. God help you if it's not orange. Where do you keep it?"

I blink and reach for my reading glasses. "Marjorie?"

Then I take off my glasses and rub my eyes.

"Which cabinet is your pantry? Couldn't find any in the icebox."

"Marjorie?" I pinch myself. Nope. I'm definitely awake. "Why are you here? Wait, am *I* here?"

"Oh, darling, it's too early for existential questions. I can't possibly ponder something like that until I have my toast, and I can't have my toast until I find the marmalade."

"Did you look in the fridge door? That's the last place I saw it. Again, why are you here?"

She breezes out of the room. "Because Foster's wife is a *harridan.*"

Judith?

A *harridan?*

Judith is an accountant.

I hop out of bed and throw on my bathrobe, following Marjorie out the door. I pause in front of the guest room, which is now full to the rafters with my parents' things again. Questions race through my mind: Why aren't they in Florida? When did they get here? How did I not hear them come in? And what exactly is going on?

I hustle down the back stairway to the kitchen, where I find Marjorie spreading a microscopic layer of mar-ma-LAHD on her multigrain toast.

She holds up the almost-empty jar of Baxters. "Order some more, darling. We're going to be here for a while."

CHAPTER NINE

October 1987

've made a huge mistake.

Massive. Colossal. Monumental. If errors were racehorses, mine would be the Secretariat of all blunders. What seemed like the best idea ever last night looks awfully different in the pale light of dawn.

Let's go through the checklist, shall we? I am now:

Unemployed.

Unemployable in my field after having quit in such an unprofessional manner, namely leaving a rambling, drunken message on my boss's answering machine.

Cheating on my lovely boyfriend.

My God, I am the Triple Crown of fuckups.

What was I thinking?

Sure, yesterday was a bad day, a terrible day, the worst day. And each day before that was no great shakes either.

Fine, I hated what I was doing and I could not see myself with Smith Barney for the long haul. But to be so flighty, so impulsive, to simply take my ball and go home? Max is going to *murder* me. He can't stop "casually" mentioning to everyone that his kid's a stockbroker, even though I've yet to execute a single trade on my own.

Max is so cagey about his own past that all of his country club cohorts assume he made his money the same way they did— inheritance. They haven't a clue that he didn't finish high school, having lied about his age to start a union carpentry apprenticeship. (And a union member to boot? Bunky Cushman would die!) So having a child with a legitimately blue-blooded career is doubly important to him. Appearances are everything to him and Marjorie. But at some point last night, the tequila convinced me that my happiness takes precedence over his pride.

Oh, boy, Thanksgiving is going to be fun this year.

My head is killing me but not as much as my liver. I'm sure it's broken. My spleen, too. Is it possible to sprain your kidneys? My throat feels like sandpaper. Was I singing? I vaguely remember singing. I want to take a bath in Gatorade and then brush my teeth with an entire tube of Crest. Possibly some bleach.

Now my question is, what do I do next? I'm sure I can explain away not wanting to be a broker, and I'm certainly employable, given my grades and the various internships I've held, but doing what instead?

In the bed next to me, Chris stirs. I look down. I see pajamas were not an option. I wrap the sheet around me like a toga. This was definitely not a garden-variety slumber party. With an ever-so-slight curl of his lip, he appears to be smiling in his sleep.

Damn it, why does he have to be so masculine? So good-looking? He's still tan, so he's obviously been working on projects outside. His hair's been lightened by the sun, and the contrast between the downy blond hair on the nape of his neck and the tawny skin is making me break into a sweat. His back is broader than the last time I saw him, and he has all these new muscles in his arms and shoulders and his obliques and lower . . .

Oh God, oh God, oh God.

I'm both sweating and freezing at the same time.

Once I shower and have some coffee—a lot of coffee, so much coffee—I can likely figure out the next professional steps. I will run the numbers and determine the best course of action.

I guess my larger issue is *what am I supposed to do with this naked man in my bed?*

I need to get a grip here. Chris and I broke up for a reason. Sure, we had a nice run, but we were never a logical fit in the long term. When he went off to Southern Illinois, it didn't make sense for him to have to worry about some girl still finishing her senior year of high school, so we parted as friends. I'd read an article in *Seventeen* about how only fifteen percent of relationships started in high school make it through college. Truth was, there was nothing unique about us/our love to defy those odds, so I figured why fight them?

We did get back together the summer after his freshman year, but called it quits before I went to the University of Illinois three months later. We dated again after my freshman year, and it was like nothing had ever changed between us, only to end it again before the fall semester began.

However, after my sophomore year, everything changed. I think Chris expected us to pick up on our whole summer thing, and maybe I did, too. But instead of the cushy lifeguarding job I'd previously held for so many years, that summer I had an internship at an insurance company in the city. He spent the summer bartending and doing odd jobs for a roofing crew.

Our schedules no longer meshed, and our time together was all too brief. We found ourselves with less and less in common, and by the time the Fourth of July rolled around, we knew that was it for us. Or, *I* knew that was it for us. He still wanted to make us work.

Here's the thing: Chris is the fifth kid of five. His family is great, but he's the baby. Because of that, no one has particularly high expectations of him and I think he's taken this to heart. Ultimately, I can't see myself with a man who isn't always pushing himself to overachieve. So, regardless of how pleasant our time together was, how comfortable, how right it felt in the moment, why pursue that which would ultimately fail?

I missed him once we were done, though. I dated other guys, and none of them possessed Chris's natural affability. No one else has had his ability to put others at ease or to just make them laugh with one of his goofy impressions. My brother, Foster, who's two years my senior, was devastated when we broke up. He insists that Chris is the only "cool" guy I've ever brought home. More than once, I've noticed him rolling his eyes when Wyatt speaks.

I glance down at Chris's sleeping figure.

Shit, Wyatt, I'm so sorry. You don't deserve this.

I met Wyatt a year ago at a Young Urban Professionals mixer held on the top floor of the Hancock Tower. Did he take my breath away with his rumpled suit and Heat Miser hairdo? Has he ever once resembled a sleeping Adonis covered in a crocheted afghan when he's stayed here? Definitely not. He's a whole lot more pale and hairless, kind of like a baby mole.

Still, he charmed me in his own quiet way.

"Shrimp toast?" he said, frowning as he gestured toward the

trays of dubious-looking appetizers the waiters were circulating. "You realize the anagram for those is Mishap Trots."

"I was unaware," I said.

"Terrible habit, the anagrams, my apologies. Wyatt Chapin, hello. I'm an attorney with Drake Headley—which is Redhead Leaky. Try not to read anything into *that*," he said, pointing at his ginger hair. "I almost didn't take the job there because of it. Anyway, pleased to meet you."

I grinned and held out my hand. His shake was firmer than I expected, which was a pleasant surprise. "Hi, I'm Penny Bancroft. I'm in the training program with Smith Barney."

"Ah, Math by Siren," he said.

I laughed. "Some days it feels like that."

"Are you enjoying the view?" he asked.

This time, I actually snorted. The whole tower was socked in with fog. Each window of the ninety-fifth floor, which normally affords an unfettered vista of the lakefront and the Loop, looked to be covered in pale gray cotton batting.

"I've never seen anything like it," I replied.

We ended up chatting most of the evening. Did I fall instantly, irreparably in love like when Chris defended me to our heinous speech teacher? No, but I wasn't sixteen years old, either. Instead, our relationship slowly progressed from quick lunches to casual drinks after work to lingering over dinner. Eventually, we found ourselves in a committed relationship, spending weekends together with the *Times* crossword puzzle, which he always completed in pen.

Wyatt checked every one of my boxes with his position in contract law. He has a retirement account to which he makes the full contribution each month and an ironclad ten-year plan that

includes purchasing a home in the best school district and bud-
geting for vacations on foreign soil. He also wants a family, and
we've discussed every parameter we'd need to satisfy before even
considering taking any sort of step toward that goal.

He's arranged every aspect of his life by the numbers, and
there's absolutely no margin for error. He's ideal and outstanding
in every way.

What's wrong with me? Why can't I be satisfied with the best
man for me? On paper, the two of us are an outstanding match. We
have so much in common—even esoteric things, like believing that
ham salad should always include relish and eggs. (These ingredi-
ents are both low in cost and high in protein. As an added bonus,
the preservatives in the relish extend the shelf life and the eggs
double the volume without negatively impacting the flavor. Everything about this combination is a win, and yet the few times Chris
found relish mingling with his ham salad, you'd have thought he'd
found a finger in his lunch.)

The kicker here? Chris doesn't even have his own apartment!
He's still living at home in Glencoe! Who does that? Granted, we,
um . . . didn't do a ton of talking last night, so I don't know his
rationale, but it's weird. People our age are not meant to live with
our families; we're meant to be on our own. What am I supposed
to do? Ring the doorbell at his house and say, "Hi, Mr. and Mrs.
Sinclair; I'm going upstairs to Chris's room to get freaky with him
on his Chicago Bears bedding'?"

I can't.

This is so messed up.

Somehow this is Patrick's fault. He goaded me into this. Like
a double-dog dare. That man is a terrible influence. The bad angel

on my shoulder. I will have words with him later, that's for damn sure. (I'm surprised he's not already calling me to dish. Is he in a meeting?) Regardless, I have to extricate myself from this bed, I have to wash every single one of last night's missteps off of me, and I have to figure out what I'm supposed to do with the rest of my life.

First up, I have to get Chris out of my apartment.

With the sheet wrapped around me so tightly I'm cutting off most of my circulation, I poke him in the shoulder. "Hey." He shifts but doesn't wake. I poke him again. "Hey. You have to *go*. This was a mistake."

He opens one of his denim-blue eyes, fringed in black lashes. "This was not a mistake. You. Come here. Right now." Then he pulls me to him.

Well.

I can probably give him five minutes to state his case.

Not like I have to go to work today.

. . . .

"You're dumping Wyatt? No! He's supposed to fix me up with his friend next week!" Judith wails. "Can't you break up with him after I meet his buddy? Maybe in a few weeks? A month, at the most. Give us some time to get to know each other. Come on! I never went out with a lawyer!"

Karin comes up behind me and grips my head in her hands. "Do you see this shit-eating grin, Jude?"

With some petulance, Judith says, "Yes."

We're hanging out in the Lincoln Park apartment I share

with Karin. Judith is here, ostensibly to help me figure out what I should be doing with my life. She and I met at U of I in a stats class freshman year and we bonded in our study group. Eventually we lived together on campus and I convinced her to leave her hometown of Cleveland and settle in Chicago permanently after graduation.

However, no one's into résumé chat today. All anyone, including me—especially me—wants to discuss is what's happening with Chris. Karin says, "This is the grin of someone who is done with Wyatt and his anagrams. Sorry, Jude. I'm sure she'll find a way to make it up to you." Karin does not let go of my head. Instead she turns my face toward her and looks at me. "This isn't even the face of someone who wants to hang out with us right now. In fact, she's just watching the clock, waiting for him to get here so she can go in her room and shut the door and turn on her Al Green cassette really loud. FYI? *Not loud enough.*"

"No!" I protest, albeit weakly. "Chris and I will totally want to hang out with you guys."

"Peddle your lies elsewhere, Pinocchio. Your nose is already so long you can't turn your head without scraping it on the wall," Karin replies, finally releasing me. I shake out my hair, trying to smooth it back into place.

"Plus, I didn't ask Jude over here to discuss some guy," I start to say.

"Some stud," Karin interjects.

Do not squeal. Do *not* squeal. Do not *squeal.* Compose yourself.

Ahem.

I take a deep breath and try to keep the shit-eating grin from returning. I do legitimately need Judith's advice. "You know where I've interned and what classes I've taken—what seems like my logical next step?" I ask.

Judith taps her index finger over her lip as she thinks. "What about teaching?"

I reply, "If I shift from stockbroking to teaching, I really will be disowned."

"Do you want to go the CPA route?" Judith asks, as that's what she's pursuing.

"The idea of combing through box after box of strangers' receipts for the rest of my life makes me want to die," I say. "At tax time, my parents bring every piece of paper in the house to the CPA because someone once told them to save everything. The poor guy ends up having to sort through postcards and their old shopping lists to try to make sense of their finances. No, thanks."

"I don't think every client is like that," Judith says.

"No offense, but your parents are kind of jerks," Karin adds.

"None taken," I reply. She's not wrong. Every time Karin sees my mother, Marjorie asks her if her mother is still divorced.

"If you want to stay in the world of finance, you could always be an analyst. Although, if you want to have a family eventually? Consider being an actuary. That's one of those jobs you always hear about having a decent work-life balance, as long as you don't go the consulting route. You liked our actuarial classes, right? And you interned at that insurance company after sophomore year. So you're aware there's a fairly steep barrier to entry with a hell of a lot of qualifying exams and—"

Before Judith can finish her explanation, there's a knock on the door. Chris is here early!

"Actuary, yeah. That sounds good," I say, rocketing up from where I've been sitting to answer the door. "I'll be one of those."

. . . .

"Thank you for inviting me, Mr. and Mrs. Bancroft," Chris says. He pulls out my chair and waits for me to be settled before he sits down himself. Once he's in his seat, he unfolds his napkin and places it on his lap.

"*Did* we invite you, Christopher? When Penelope said she was bringing her boyfriend, we assumed she meant Wyatt, that nice attorney she's so serious with," Marjorie says. She acts as though I haven't been telling her about Chris for months and months now. Argh.

"This"—she points back and forth between the two of us—"is new."

No, it isn't, and she damn well knows it.

"Tell me, darling, are we just repeating *everything* from high school now? Are you going to start layering your alligator shirts again and listening to Bruce Springfield?"

I say, "Do you mean Rick Springfield?" I'm trying to keep my equanimity, but she's definitely making it a challenge.

"Or Bruce Springsteen?" Chris adds.

Marjorie takes a measured sip of her Gibson. "Does it really matter?"

"To a fourteen-year-old girl, I imagine it matters substantially," Chris replies with great cheer.

Ha, I forgot about this. I forgot how Chris always maintained an even keel and a sunny attitude, no matter how hard my parents tried to intimidate him.

"How is Wyatt these days?" Marjorie asks. "He's an attorney, you know. Lovely young man. So focused. So polite. Such purpose."

Dude. *Harsh.*

"I can't say," I reply. "As I've mentioned multiple times, we no longer see each other. I haven't spoken with him since last fall, and now it's March."

Our breakup was easier than I feared, largely because Wyatt is such a decent person . . . or possibly because he's a bit of a wuss. But I felt I owed it to him to be honest, so I was, to an extent. I spared him *graphic* details (I saved those for Jude, Karin, and Patrick over a bottle of white zinfandel—so much squealing), but I was frank. I explained that even though he and I were perfect on paper, there was something about Chris that made me abandon all logic. He seemed to understand and alluded to someone in his past who'd had a similar impact on him. I encouraged him to find her again. Who knows; maybe he made a new love connection, too?

Chris and I have been back together for four months now. In that time, I've secured an entry-level actuarial job with an insurance company, and I'm studying for the first in a series of accreditations. Actuarial science is an ideal fit, as it plays to all my strengths—the only downside is how long it will take to be fully accredited. But at least I'm not wasting time pursuing an option that's wrong for me.

Yes, I decided on said career on an impulse, but thus far, my impulsive actions are the ones that are paying off. Quitting Smith Barney? Brilliant. Jumping into Chris's arms? Best idea ever. To think that I could be here with Wyatt and his anagrams right now? Unimaginable. (Mania Lube Gin.)

Chris and I are different together this time around and I can't put my finger on exactly why. Is it that I'm less rigid? Or is it that

Chris has finally stepped up? His dad had a health scare last year (he's okay now), and Chris said that made him much more cognizant about the future. That's when he began to make plans. While he's still working for his family, on his off time, he bought and renovated a tiny house and sold it for a small profit. His goal is to do more of these renovations, on a larger scale, with the intention to spin off his own company.

Chris has an actual business plan written up and secured in a three-ring binder. Not to be indelicate, but a three-ring binder for me? Total panty-dropper.

His act is together in all the ways I'd wished for back when we were in college, and he did it all without me standing over his shoulder, telling him what to do. Again, a man with self-direction? Pretty much the *Kama Sutra* for me. So, given our history together and seeing how there're no longer any barriers to entry, we're rapidly progressing to the next level.

Miguel appears at our table, and his whole face lights up when he sees Chris. "Mr. Chris! Hello, hello! Welcome! So good to see you here again!" He goes to shake Chris's hand, but Chris pulls him down into a one-armed hug, and Marjorie practically chokes on her cocktail onion.

"I will get water for you right away," Miguel says, rushing off.

"You and your family, you're not members here," Marjorie says, more as a statement instead of a question. Marjorie flaunts her Centennial Hills belonging like the newly affianced flashes a diamond.

"We are not," Chris confirms.

"Hmmm. Do you need me to put in a word?" Marjorie offers with an insincere crinkle of her eyes.

"No, but thanks anyway."

"It's no trouble," Marjorie says. "We know everyone; we have sway."

"I appreciate the offer. But when we moved down from Lake Forest in the late seventies, my parents just held on to their membership at Onwentsia," he replies, mentioning the name of the most exclusive club on the North Shore. "It's only fifteen minutes away, and it's a Charles Blair Macdonald–designed golf course, so they weren't about to give that up."

Max, who'd been completely taciturn to this point, suddenly comes to life. "Chris, my boy, what have you been up to? So good to see you!" He claps Chris on the back for good measure. Miguel arrives to drop off Marjorie's glass of water. "Miguel! Bring my man a Dewar's rocks!"

"I don't recall Wyatt being a golfer," Marjorie says. "I imagine his caseload was simply too heavy. What is it you do again, dear? Construction worker?"

This is so like her to try to minimize what Chris does for a living.

"Wait, was Wyatt an attorney?" Chris asks, the picture of innocence. "I didn't realize."

Max cups his face in his hand and gazes dreamily into the distance. "Bunky Cushman says the bent grass on that course is exceptional. Plays so smooth. Especially with the long drive off the first tee."

"Maybe you'd want to hit the links with my father sometime? You're in the custom cabinet business, right? Seems like you and he should finally meet. You two probably have a lot in common. Our family owns a construction business, some commercial, but mostly residential. I work for the family business, and I have a degree in building trade construction," Chris says.

And just like that, my dad becomes Team Wyatt Who?

Marjorie is none too pleased with Max's sudden defection. Finding herself without an ally, she concentrates on her drink.

"Do you live in the city, Chris? Or are you somewhere up here?" Max asks.

"Actually, most of our jobs are North Shore, so it never made sense to move downtown and do the big reverse commute," he replies. "I'm actually still with the folks, if you can believe that."

"Afraid of cooking and cleaning for yourself?" Marjorie asks. She doesn't think we can hear her mutter, "Mama's boy," to herself, or maybe she does and simply doesn't care.

I can feel myself tense up, but Chris puts his hand over mine. With one touch, he assures me he's got this covered. "Just the opposite, actually. I take care of all the household chores in exchange for free room and board, which gives Mom more time to take care of her parents, who live down the street. This way, I save every cent of my salary to invest in my business. Way I see it, real estate's always a solid bet and home prices are never going to be this low again."

Max nods. He made it from the streets of the south side of Chicago to a country club on the North Shore in one generation, predicated on the strength of the housing market.

Chris continues. "There are a few places in Glencoe I have my eye on. I'm talking real fixer-uppers. I've already flipped one farther south. If I can pick up one of the places here in town, live there while I put in the sweat equity, I can triple my investment in a couple of years. Or maybe I can even hold on to one with an eye toward having a family in the future. I mean, this *is* one of the best public school districts in all of America."

Max holds up his scotch glass. "Very enterprising! You sound like a young man with a bright future."

"Thank you. The future is important to me," Chris says. "Exceptionally important. Actually, the future is why I asked Penny to arrange this dinner tonight." He breaks into a massive smile. "We have some news. Your daughter has agreed to marry me, and I feel like I won the lottery."

Last weekend Chris was down at my apartment and acting rather strangely. I chalked it up to spring fever, as the weather was unseasonably warm. We'd made plans to meet up for dinner with some of our friends. I decided we should swing by the Burwood for a drink because he was clearly too hyper to continue to sit around the apartment. Not even March Madness basketball could hold his interest, which was shocking. Chris made a big deal out of me calling everyone to tell them to come to the bar first. I didn't understand why, but as he doesn't ask for much, I complied.

We settled at the bar and ordered our drinks, and then he got up. I noticed him having a word with Jimmy, our usual bartender. The Van Morrison song that was on stopped mid-verse and "It's Raining Men" began to play. I looked over at Chris, who'd returned with a basket of popcorn.

"You're never going to let me forget that, are you?" I asked.

"No," he said. "I'm not. Listen, if I had to choose the perfect tune to represent 'our song,' this would not be my first choice. Not even close. Top of mind, I'd suggest Flesh for Lulu's 'I Go Crazy' or U2's 'With or Without You.' Or maybe some Peter Gabriel and 'In Your Eyes.' We could get our classic rock on with 'Something' by the Beatles or the Beach Boys' 'God Only Knows.' But this?" He pointed to a speaker. "*This* is what I have to work with. *This* is the sound track to our great, rekindled romance. Not Bono's haunting lyrics about how on a bed of nails you make me wait. Not Peter Gabriel's sweet, soulful groove about your eyes giving me the resolution to all the fruitless searches. Instead, we're gonna get absolutely soaking wet because it's gonna start raining men."

"Hallelujah?"

He slid a basket of popcorn over to me. "Have some."

I pushed it away. "No, thanks."

He pushed it back toward me. "Take a few bites."

"I don't want to wreck my dinner."

He slid the basket over to me again. "This popcorn will not wreck your dinner, I promise."

"I don't want it."

"Yeah, you will."

I noticed the velvet box tucked amid the salted kernels about the same time I realized Chris had gotten down on one knee.

By the time Mother Nature took over heaven in the song, I was no longer a single woman. Proposal accepted, our friends came screaming out of the back where they'd been hiding.

We'd been back together only since October, so marriage wasn't on my radar, but as soon as he asked, I knew this was absolutely right for us. I didn't need two more years of dinner and a movie to be sure I wanted my future with him to begin immediately. What's ironic is no one else thought we were rushing into anything. Rather, those closest to us, like Karin and Patrick and Foster, wondered what had taken us so damn long to figure out what they'd already seen. (Foster is already lobbying to be Chris's best man.)

"No."

"I beg your pardon?" Chris says.

"No," Marjorie says. "You do not have my permission to marry my daughter. This is not what I want for her."

Chris's slow, sweet grin never falters; nor does his confidence.

"My gosh, I guess you must have misunderstood us. We weren't asking your permission; we were sharing our good news. We'd hoped this night would be a celebration. I'm sorry to hear about your disapproval because family is so important to us, but if this is how you feel, no one will try to dissuade you. Please know we'll miss having you as part of the wedding."

For once, Marjorie is speechless.

Because it can't be said enough when it comes to Chris: Not all heroes wear capes.

CHAPTER TEN

"She sent me a friend request. She's on her stupid eco-tour in stupid Costa Rica and she still has time to send me a Facebook friend request. Must not be a very good vacation if she's messing around on stupid social media," I huff.

"You said you liked her," Karin replies. "Why do you sound out of breath?"

"Because I'm on the treadmill."

"You don't use the treadmill after work. It's Wednesday. You walk on the treadmill in the morning."

"I walk on it at night now whenever Max claims the television in the family room and Marjorie the one in the den. Neither one of them can hear, so between his war show on the History Channel and her film with the Rock on full blast, it sounds like Jalalabad up there."

"When are they leaving?"

"I'd like to get a straight answer on that myself. According to Max, their place is being renovated. But Marjorie said something about putting their condo on the market. When I ask them when they're together, they both change the subject and begin to criticize *me*."

"I'm sorry they're such a handful, but that's nothing new. Remember when Marjorie grounded you for a month that one time Chris didn't ring the doorbell when he was picking you up? 'Darling, only slatterns jump in boys' cars. Whatever will the Cushmans think?' No wonder you're basically Sheldon Cooper. Back to Stassi—she sent you a friend request? Why are you mad about that? You said you kind of liked her. A friend request seems appropriate."

"I did kind of like her! For a minute, in the moment, because she saved our butts. Not enough to have her pop up unsolicited in my friend feed, though. Not enough to view a million selfies of her in a tiny, unlined yellow-and-white-striped bikini that leaves zero to the imagination. Not enough to see her and Chris frolicking in crystal clear waterfalls or riding palominos bareback on the beach or feeding each other conch fritters with mango dipping sauce in a restaurant with a thatched roof."

"Those sound like really specific images; did you accept her request?"

"No! It's still pending."

"Then how do you know what flavor the dipping sauce was?"

I have to be honest with her. "Because I was *stalking* her page, okay?"

Karin says nothing for a couple of seconds and then finally exhales. "Oh, Penny."

My pace quickens as I explain my rationale. "I *know*. Listen, it's easy to pledge to yourself that you're moving on and you can really mean it this time. You can engage in all the right activities that will help you propel yourself forward, too, like listing your house on the market and signing up for Match.com. You can even fully participate, winking at men who may or may not be appropriate, exchanging e-mails with Wiccans with poor punctuation, and you can feel good about it. Yet a moment will come, maybe after a glass of wine, or maybe while you're on the elliptical, or maybe while you're in the middle of a staff meeting talking about Q4 projections, but the urge to know what is happening in your ex's life will strike and it will become all-consuming, and there's almost nothing you can do to stop it except to satisfy that urge. So you take a peek. You feed the beast. And it's not a big deal. You look, and then you get on with your day. Maybe you see an unlined, striped bikini; maybe you see tempura-battered conch with mango dipping sauce. The point is, you get that quick rush of dopamine from the instant gratification and a tiny bit of closure, and that's what helps you live the rest of your life like a normal person."

By the time I finish my explanation, I'm practically running and I'm panting fairly hard.

"Penny, I'm telling you this as a friend. You're too old for this nonsense. Stop it. This is junior-high-school-level stuff. You're essentially riding your bike past their houses. If you're already looking at her status updates, just approve her as a friend."

"But—"

Her voice is stern. "Click 'accept friend request.' This is what a mature person does. I mean it. You can't just spy on her page like you're twelve years old. I want you to do this now. I'm going to log onto your page and look at your group of friends, and I'll be pissed if I don't see her listed. Do it. Immediately. I know you have your iPad within arm's reach."

She's right, of course. I open my iPad, pull up Facebook, and stab the button before I can change my mind. Without a glance at Stassi's newly friended page, I snap shut the case.

"Done. Are you happy?"

"Blissfully so. You don't realize it yet, but this is more forward motion for you. Keep making strides like this and maybe soon you won't have to hide in the basement from your mommy and daddy."

I stop in my tracks. "That was mean, Karin."

"Intentionally so. You don't accomplish anything until you get mad. I don't understand why they're at your house and you don't, either. Correct me if I'm wrong, but they were cagey with Judith and Foster, too, right? They either need to give you some straight answers or GTFO."

"Get the Florida out?"

"Close enough."

"This is all I can do today. We've reached the limits of my capability."

"Then you've probably earned yourself a plate of cheese and crackers and a Candace Cameron Bure movie. I'm gonna locomote. Something downstairs is burning. My kids are probably smoking something. I don't know what it is, but I'll be damned if they're not sharing. Later, bitch."

I hop off the treadmill and collapse onto the old love seat where Barnaby used to watch me exercise. As I sit, I catch a whiff of cedar and leather and I'm overwhelmed with missing him. Any other dog would have reeked of dander or dust mites or Fritos, but somehow Barnaby managed to smell like something out of a Ralph Lauren showroom. He was even elegant in an olfactory sense. They broke the mold with him, that's for sure.

I do indulge myself with a Hallmark film where the actress

from *Revenge* teaches a group of homeless children in a makeshift classroom with the help of Treat Williams. I follow this one up with a Lori Loughlin flick. I swear this programming is like visual Prozac, and it always evens me out. Chris was one of the few people who never mocked my quiet love of these movies—he said if people didn't embrace a happy ending, then it was their loss.

By the time I climb the stairs to the first floor, I'm mellow again. I'll probably have a glass of wine and maybe a quick bath. Then I'll hit the sheets to be nice and fresh for Kettlebell Thursday.

"Where have *you* been? Stassi has been trying to get ahold of you all night."

A scowling Jessica stands in front of me in the kitchen with her arms crossed tightly over her chest, blocking my access to both the wine and the cheese.

"Jessica?"

Jessica, my daughter who lives in New York, the greatest city on earth, Jessica? Here in my kitchen?

"How do you not have your cell phone on you in case people need to reach you?" she asks.

"Jessica?"

"Like, I can't *even* with how inconsiderate that is. How were we supposed to know where you were? We were trying to find you and we couldn't. That's a problem, okay? Big, fat, huge, hairy problem."

I'm somewhat dumbfounded. "I'm sorry, but I was here . . . in my house. And the landline didn't ring. Where are Mimsy and Gumpy? Didn't they tell you I was in the basement?"

"Obviously not."

Because I don't wish to simply stand here while my child admonishes me for spending time in my basement while she lives one thousand miles away from me in the cultural center of the universe, I tidy up my parents' dinner dishes. They've left them in a precarious stack on the kitchen island in between the two dishwashers, both of which are empty. Apparently ours are not those self-loading models they'd come to expect from having watched *The Jetsons* forty years ago. "Jess, what's going on?"

"Dad had an accident."

I stop in the middle of rinsing petrified arugula off a salad plate. "What? Oh, no. Sweetie, what happened? Is he okay?"

"He was zip-lining in Costa Rica and he fell when the cable broke. Luckily he was at the very end of the run when it happened and he wasn't up that high."

"When did this happen?"

"This afternoon."

Shit, shit, shit. This must be why Stassi was trying to get ahold of me on Facebook. I don't think anyone can message me if we aren't friends. *Damn it.*

Why did he have to go on the stupid zip line? Didn't I specifically warn him about those? They're already so dodgy, especially in a country where safety isn't as stringently enforced as in the United States. Say what you will about our overly litigious American society, but frivolous lawsuits do keep us protected in so many ways. For example, we went to Cancún for spring break the year after I started working and I vowed we'd never go there again. Every activity was fraught with danger, from boats without life vests to beaches without lifeguards to elevator doors without limb-sensing-and-saving technology.

Frustrated and exhausted from the constant vigilance, I figured a trip to a historical site would be harmless enough, so we ventured down to Chichen Itza on the Yucatán Peninsula to see

El Castillo, the famous Mesoamerican step pyramid that was part of a Mayan ruin.

Oh, how wrong I was.

The steps on that thing were maybe six inches deep, and crumbling, and went up seventy-nine feet at a forty-seven-degree slope. But did the Mexican government add guardrails? Anti-skid tape? Perhaps provide helmets and a carabiner line onto which one might clip? Did they even post a climb-at-your-own risk sign? No. Everyone else just blithely danced up the thing like they were Rocky Balboa at the Philadelphia Museum of Art. The kids were furious with me for forcing them to go up and down backward on their butts, but I was resolute. I was not about to have them tumble Jack and Jill style down the side of that thing. I kept saying to Chris, "People want to know what happened to the Mayans; I'll tell you what happened. They Darwined themselves out of existence with this place!"

A few years later the Mexican government closed El Castillo for climbing after a woman from San Diego fell to her death. Having been correct about the glaring safety issues was a hollow victory indeed. They really should have had signs, helmets, carabiner lines, guardrails, and anti-skid tape, is what I'm saying. So I'm deeply dismayed to hear that Chris was hurt, but not at all surprised.

I ask, "What are his injuries?"

Jessica slips onto a stool on the other side of the island. "He broke his fibula and tore his ACL because he tried to land on his feet. He's okay and Stassi's with him, of course. He had surgery and he came through fine and he's in good spirits. He says with the scar, this is going to ruin his career as a swimsuit model. Really, he's pretty banged up, but he's lucky. They're going to keep him a few days, and he'll be able to fly home on Saturday morning."

I finish putting plates in the dishwasher and I wash my hands. "Oh, poor Chris. He can handle pain, but he's the worst patient. He can't stand being sick or at all infirm. Remember when you were little and he tried to refinish the floors when he had that hundred and three temperature?"

She says, "I don't remember that, but I do remember him painting the trim in my room with his left hand after he'd sprained his right wrist."

"Stassi is not going to be dealing with a cooperative patient," I say. In no way is he my problem anymore, yet there's still a part of me that feels obligated to help, like somehow I'm better equipped. She can't possibly know how to manage him when he's down. He is *difficult* for the uninitiated. She doesn't yet have the experience. Does she realize that when he requests Gatorade, he means G2 (specifically Glacier Freeze) and not the regular version, because now that he's over fifty, he's starting to watch his sugar intake? Is she cognizant that he will turn up his nose if she brings him any variety of chicken soup other than Campbell's Chicken & Stars, including fancy homemade offerings from that wonderful Jewish deli in Skokie? And he needs oyster crackers, never saltines, damn it. And he likes applesauce, but not from a glass jar, only the single-serve plastic containers.

"Does she want me to call her? Do you have her number?"

Jessica selects an orange from the fruit bowl on the island but makes no attempt to peel it. Instead, she rolls it back and forth between her hands. "No, not now. She just wanted you to know because she wasn't sure the best way to reach Kelsey."

"Let's see," I say, trying to remember the itinerary my travel agent arranged for her, which is pretty much identical to the trip Chris and I were going to take for our twenty-fifth anniversary, except I'd just been promoted to managing director and we'd landed a massive project and I couldn't get away. I kept postponing until . . . smooth jazz. "They left Portofino today to return to Rome. The high-speed train will take them about five hours to get to Termini Station. They fly out of Rome tomorrow, which means they'll be home on Friday. Do you see any reason to get ahold of her? There's nothing she can do, you said he's okay, and I don't want to put a damper on the last day of her honeymoon."

"Agree. She'd go bitchcakes. She was already upset enough about the flights." Jessica bats the orange back and forth across the counter, like a cat toying with a ball of yarn. I can't tell whether or not Jessica is baiting me, so, naturally, I bite.

"What about her flights?" I ask. "Was there a problem? I haven't heard anything." I literally haven't heard a peep from her since she left here the night of her wedding to stay at the Peninsula downtown, also on my dime. (I forget why, but I was forced to right some grievous wrong by booking her a suite there—that much I know.)

"She was furious about being in business class and couldn't fathom why you didn't just book her in first class since you had the miles to spare. She said that the lie-flat seats were really narrow and the plane was old so they didn't have a built-in entertainment center. The flight attendants had to hand out tablets so people could watch movies, and she'd already seen most of what they had to offer."

Of course Jessica was baiting me.

Of course she was.

"That's what you call a first-world problem," I reply, keeping my tone light, while inside I'm raging. This goddamned wedding has been one opportunity for extortion after another, and now I'm hearing that even with everything I've done, I didn't get it right? An all-expense-paid business-class trip to Italy wasn't sufficient? Not satisfactory for Princess Kelsey? What is it the girls are always saying?

I can't even.

I give the counters a quick spritz with antibacterial spray and wipe them down with a paper towel, more vigorously than needed. "Okay, I'm off to bed. I'm glad you're here. I'm sure Stassi will appreciate your help once she gets home with your dad. Good night."

I don't even try to hug or kiss her. I simply head up the back stairs. The door to the guest room is closed. As it's too early for my folks to be in bed, they must be out. How nice that in their late seventies, their social life is more active than mine.

It's not until I've brushed my teeth and washed my face that I wonder how Jessica was able to make it to Chicago so quickly after hearing the news about Chris.

Curious.

• • • •

"Now, for the capital optimization project: Vanessa, you take the lead on the proposal. I'm sorry, Adrienne, do you need something?" I'm in the middle of my Friday managers' meeting in the glass-enclosed conference room with the lake view when Adrienne appears at the door. She never disturbs me when I'm with the team, so I'm immediately concerned that something terrible has happened.

"May I see you for a moment?" she asks.

"Excuse me," I say. "Please continue."

Everyone goes back to work, save for Vanessa, who seems more concerned with what Adrienne is about to tell me. I close the conference room door behind me and step out into the hallway, removing myself from Vanessa's line of sight.

"What's up?"

Adrienne grasps the cuffs of her cardigan. "I'm so sorry. I hate to bother you, but this seemed important."

"No need to apologize. I'm sure you have a good reason."

"Your Realtor called."

I immediately relax. I thought she was going to tell me something about Chris, who's had two restful nights and has been cracking jokes with the nurses in Spanish. "Kathy? Yes, she had a showing at the house today. Did she need something? Wasn't she able to work the lockbox? The code is 0320."

"She didn't have any trouble getting into the house, no. But there must have been some kind of miscommunication, because your parents and Jessica were all still home, so it was kind of awkward."

"Aw, you're kidding. I told them about the showing last night and this morning, and I had it marked on the big calendar in the kitchen. I don't know how they all forgot. I'll have to reschedule with her. Thank you for letting me know."

Adrienne makes no sign of leaving. "Um . . . they probably won't be back."

My stomach lurches. "What happened?"

She pulls at a loose thread on the cuff of her cardigan before she begins. "Well, the wife of the family who came to see the house is foreign—I think Kathy said she's from Argentina? Anyway, they loved your house, especially the room on the third floor. The wife wanted to run back up for one more look to see if there was space under the eaves for her son's drum set. As she was coming back down, your father ran into her in the hallway." She stops and clears her throat, visibly uncomfortable. "Your dad—um, Max—he pulled her into the bathroom off the guest room. He said he wanted her to see some spots on the grout that needed attention. He didn't think she'd been scrubbing hard enough and next time she should use bleach."

"Oh, Jesus, God, no," I say, feeling faint. "Please tell me Kathy explained that the old bigot does not convey."

Adrienne winces. "Kathy tried to lighten the situation by saying something like, 'You must be teasing! How could you confuse Mrs. Westerfield for a housekeeper when she's wearing such a gorgeous Armani suit?' and that's when Jessica walks by and says, 'Gorgeous . . . for a knockoff.'"

I double over with my arms clenched around my stomach. I feel like I've been kicked. I wonder if we're not seeing some early-stage dementia manifesting in his behavior now, and if so, what might be done about it. I believe the time's come to consult a gerontologist.

Jessica, on the other hand, is just a bitch.

"This violates all my rules, but I have to ask anyway. Can you ping Kathy and tell her I'll call her when I'm done?"

"Will do."

"Thanks."

I return to the conference room. "Sorry about that."

"Everything okay at home?" Vanessa asks, her voice saccharine sweet. She bats her eyes, which are circled in far too much black kohl liner. "Anything I can do?"

I give Vanessa my most competent, confident smile. "You can take the lead on the capital optimization project proposal. Other than that, no."

Terrific. She senses an opening. Now I have to play defense around Vanessa again, too.

I take my place at the head of the table and paste on a smile, trying to take comfort in the thought, Well, at least nothing else can go wrong.

• • • •

"No, really, I've got it. Don't worry about me," I call as I stagger through the back door under an armload of sacks from various grocery stores. With three extra people in the house, I've been running back and forth to the market all week. I had to shop twice on Saturday, and it's only Monday and we're already out of half a dozen staples again.

Since no one around here cooks, I buy a lot of premade items. My father is partial to the ready-made assortment of chops and roasts at Heinen's over in Glenview, while Marjorie prefers the salads from Sunset in Northbrook. Jessica only wants sushi from the Deerfield Whole Foods, but still complains about how much better the quality is in New York. As the only person who holds a day job, I have no idea why the hunting and gathering falls to me, yet here we are.

I'm out of space on the countertop due to all the dirty dishes, so I set the bag with the meat loaf, pot roast, St. Louis–style ribs, and barbecue pork chops (with Styrofoam containers of spinach au gratin, honey-glazed carrots, and jalapeño-studded corn bread) on the floor before returning to the Camry to retrieve the case of bottled water. Marjorie won't drink the filtered water from the cooler because apparently she *wants* to blow through the one point five million barrels of oil it takes to satisfy the United States' yearly demand for bottled water.

Argh.

I run down to the mailbox while I'm outside, and I spend a few minutes chatting with my neighbor before I return with the bottled water. When I step inside the kitchen this time, carrying the twenty-four pack of Aquafina, I catch myself as my foot slips in something. I glance down at the hardwood recently refinished in a pale, weathered gray, not expecting a crime scene. A swath of sticky, reddish brown fluid is spread six feet in every direction across the wide planks. Stray bits of bone are scattered from one end of the kitchen to the other, interspersed with clumps of green and orange and yellow and mangled bits of white.

What did—? How could—?

While I'm bent over, trying to make sense of this mess, I see in my peripheral vision an enormous black blob thundering into the kitchen. The creature plows into me, taking me out at the knees and knocking me onto my butt before pinning me entirely to the ground.

"Caroline! Come here, Caroline!" Kelsey comes charging into the room holding on to an empty leash. She surveys the damage to the kitchen and points toward the giant black Newfoundland now standing on my chest, cutting off most of my oxygen supply. "Uh-oh. Did she do all of that?"

"That would be my guess, yes," I gasp.

"Caroline, no. Bad girl."

Kelsey gives the dog a tentative shove. The beast lumbers off of me and I'm able to breathe again. I sit up and shake corn bread out of my hair. Caroline assists this process by eating all the stray bits that fall off. Then she nuzzles and snuffles me for a solid minute, searching for more, leaving me covered in strands of drool that are half an inch in circumference. She slurps me right across the face for good measure.

Somewhere in the ether, Barnaby is mortified.

"Explanation, please."

Kelsey pats the giant quadruped on its anvil-shaped head. Caroline begins to pant, revealing an alarmingly long pink tongue that produces heroic amounts of saliva. "This is my new dog, Caroline. I missed Barnaby, so as soon as we got home, I went out and adopted her."

"How does Milo feel about your naming your new dog after his ex-girlfriend?" I rise from the floor and try to brush off as much side dish and dog spit as I can, but I suspect this pantsuit is a loss. I head to the pantry and grab a dustpan and broom, but I may be better off with a wet-dry vac. Or an exorcist.

"*I* didn't name her; she was already called Caroline by the shelter."

"You can always rename her," I say, scooping up a wad of spinach and dumping it in the garbage disposal. Caroline begins to lick the barbecue sauce off one of the kitchen cabinets. "I'm sure Milo would prefer that. You guys can come up with a name together."

Kelsey's face darkens. "I don't give a crap what name he likes."

Oh, dear. Wait for it. . . . Wait for it. . . .

"Why do you say that?" I ask, as though I don't have a sinking feeling as to what's coming next.

"Because Milo is a jackass and we should never have gotten married. Like, who gets married that young? Did people really expect us to work? Well, that was their bad. Caroline and I are going to be staying here for a while until we figure out what to do next."

Caroline wags her massive plumed tail as she cleans the cabinet. Once she's removed all the sauce, she starts to chew on the wood.

So I was mistaken.

Something else can *always* go wrong.

CHAPTER ELEVEN

June 2006

"I can't do this right now," I say into the phone. "We're boarding momentarily."

The other passengers are already beginning to crowd the gate. They stand in an irascible clump, a sea of logo polo shirts and no-iron khakis. Many of them are holding bags from Auntie Anne's Pretzels, and the aroma of grease and dough mingled with cinnamon is almost intoxicating. The entire D gate at LaGuardia smells like Auntie Anne's, which is the best subliminal marketing plan ever. I'm not a huge fan of visible salt grains (due to salt's impact on blood pressure and its relationship to risk factors for heart disease, which is the leading cause of death in the United States) and I hate anything containing nitrates, yet I'm fighting the urge to mug one of them for their pretzel-coated hot dogs.

"I need a date, Penny," Chris insists, on the other end of the line, snapping me out of my would-be pretzel thuggery. "All of her friends have done their college visits. We're coming down to the wire here. Kids start applying to schools over the summer these days, and she can't apply if she hasn't seen any of the places she wants to go. You promised you'd take her. She only has a small window of time before she starts her camps."

With an eye on the gate, I select save on my spreadsheet and start shutting down my laptop while I keep my cell phone pinched between my shoulder and my ear. "Wouldn't she rather go with you?"

Chris sounds aggravated. "She asked to go with *you*."

"Why?" I press.

"Could be as simple as she doesn't want to share a hotel room with her dear old dad for a week. Or maybe she never sees you anymore and would like to spend a minute together before she graduates and goes away to college. You remember Jessica, right? She's the tall one, kind of a smart mouth?"

Okay, that was unfair. He should not be leveling this kind of guilt at me. The only reason we can even afford to send Jessica to the college of her choice is because of my sacrifices. We were almost wiped out in 1998 when Chris's house flip on Elm went awry—the one I privately refer to as the Nightmare on Elm Street. Between the cracked foundation, the zoning issues, the liens, the asbestos, and the black mold, we thought we'd have to sell our place and leave Glencoe entirely.

Thank God I'd finally become fully accredited by then and had enough experience to be hired at a consulting firm downtown at a healthy salary. Yes, I knew I'd have to put in more hours than when I went back to work part-time a few years after Topher was born. And while I loved Allstate's progressive job-sharing policies and the quick commute to their suburban campus, I wasn't making enough to save us from the financial Chernobyl that was the Nightmare on Elm Street. We'd get to keep our house, but the trade-off was that I'd be around less. Chris stepped up the daddy duties and all was well, except now he's trying to make me feel bad about choices I was forced to make because he didn't do his due diligence on that cursed house.

"For passengers on American Airlines flight 345 New York LaGuardia to Chicago O'Hare, we will be opening the doors for boarding momentarily."

In one fluid motion, I stow my laptop in a computer bag, scoop up my own roll-aboard, grab my Fiji water, and rise to get in line. This is the third project I've run with our huge New York client, so I've done this particular airport dance so many times on and off in the past two years that I could make it down the jet bridge and into my usual seat, 3B, with my eyes shut.

"I have to go; we're boarding. We can figure it out when I get home." Then I hang up before he can argue more.

"We'd now like to invite our first-class section to board."

I glance at the other Executive Platinum travelers in the priority lane, smiling and nodding at those I recognize, which is usually about half the plane. So many Chicago consultants take the same Monday-morning/Thursday-afternoon flights every week that we mostly know one another. We've bonded at one point or another, maybe in the Admirals Club over the last of the carrot sticks and ranch dip when LaGuardia's socked in with snow, or perhaps when lightning's struck the tail of our plane as we've flown over Pennsylvania during a wicked summer storm and we've all discovered religion at exactly the same time. I imagine we're like those expats hanging out in a tiki bar in some far-flung banana republic, singing along to "Hotel California," not because the Eagles are so great, but because they're familiar and they smack of home.

I hand my boarding pass to the gate agent and she says, "Welcome, Mrs. Sinclair. Have a nice flight home."

"Thanks, Leslie. See you next week."

I make my way down the gangway and up to the entrance of the plane. While I'm not superstitious, I always touch the right side of the door opening when I board. There's nothing about this empty, meaningless ritual that keeps the plane aloft, but I do it anyway. (Patrick says I'm an Episcopalian for the same reason. Sometimes Patrick is too cynical for his own good.)

I make my way to 3B, my most preferred seat. Because I'm right-handed, I want the aisle on that side for the elbow room. For most domestic flights, the seat numbers start at 3, not 1, so 3B is always bulkhead, which means more legroom. I'm just claustrophobic enough to need to spread out as much as possible. I arrive at my seat and stow everything in the overhead compartment, save for a padfolio and a pen. I'll take down my laptop once we reach cruising altitude. (By the way, I won't pay to sit in first class—instead, I use miles to upgrade. I have so many banked, I could take the whole family to Europe, a few times over. That is, if I could afford the time to get away.)

I'm reading e-mail on my BlackBerry when I hear a softly accented voice say, "Excuse me, is this seat taken?"

I look up, noting the neatly combed black hair and brilliant white smile in contrast to cocoa-colored skin. "Raj Bhalla! You're not Team Thursday Afternoon!"

I've flown to New York dozens of Monday mornings with Raj, as he's a Deloitte network security consultant currently working for a Wall Street client. He opts for 3A whenever it's available, so we're often seated next to each other on the ride out. Granted, we'd both be forty percent more likely to survive a crash were we seated near the tail of the plane, but as the risk of perishing in a crash is one out of eleven million, I'm willing to live on the edge to stretch my calves.

"I am today," he replies, placing his computer bag next to mine in the overhead bin. "My Simi—she's the youngest—has a violin recital tomorrow afternoon and I will not miss her performance. I could have left tomorrow morning, but with air travel today, you cannot be too careful."

I nod, cringing inside at everything I've missed through no fault of my own. The friendly skies have let me down so many times, and often for no good reason. Any road warrior can tell you horror stories about boarding a plane on time and pushing away from the gate only to then sit on the tarmac for four hours before the flight's eventually canceled. I've taken flights that have been diverted to other airports, that have turned around midair and returned to the airport of origin, that have been delayed for hours on end and then, just when you think you're finally going to leave, the crew's declared illegal because their time's run out and you end up waiting again while the airline rustles up fresh pilots.

My new assistant, Adrienne, tells me that Vanessa is attempting to frame my maternal duties as a reason I'm not qualified to run this project, and that's so upsetting. Who pulls something like that? I can't imagine this happening to a male coworker.

"Raj, has anyone given you grief about leaving a day early to attend a family event?"

"Who would give me grief?" he asks. "What I'm doing or why I am doing it is none of their concern. I perform well; that is all that matters." He knits his brow and peers at me. "Does someone give *you* grief, Penny?"

"Sort of, yes. There's a woman who wanted to be on the New

York job and she didn't get it. She's always asking after my kids, especially my daughter Jessica, who's about to go on her college visits—or will, as soon as I can figure out a time to take her. Turns out, she doesn't care about my family. She's just trying to use my responsibilities at home as leverage to advance herself. Right now my strategy is to clam up and tell her nothing."

Raj tents his hands and nods. "Here is what I believe, Penny. I believe someone will always gun for what you have. That is human nature. It is probably a wise choice not to share information with her. But be careful that she does not begin to occupy real estate within your head. Do not let her prevent you from fulfilling your family obligations out of fear she might use them against you. Your children will not make music for long, so go enjoy their concerts."

I want to comply, but I'm not sure how easy his advice will be to put into practice. I say, "Is Simi a talented violinist?"

He laughs. "Oh, no. No, no. She makes the sound of a cat caught in a food processor. Truly terrible. The screeching! Sharp to the point of pain!" He rubs his ears as he speaks. "But I would not miss this performance for my life. I do not go for the music. I go for the joy on her beautiful, beautiful, tone-deaf face as she massacres her Mozart. Really, she kills him until he is quite dead again."

The flight attendant comes down the aisle to make sure we're buckled in. "Why do you encourage her to keep playing if it's a lost cause?"

Raj slides closed the window shade and adjusts his air vent. "Ah, but nothing is a lost cause. I encourage her to keep trying, so she practices all the time and she finds ways to improve, like by seeking help from her music teacher and by looking at videos on the Internet. Right now she is terrible. But she is *less* terrible than she was six months ago. In another six months? Maybe I will not need to wear earplugs in the house. At present she does not have much talent, but she has *passion*. Talent can always be developed through practice, but passion is the fire that burns from the inside."

Kelsey and Jessica are just the opposite. They're both talented at so many things, but I don't know that they have any interior fires. Kelsey can master almost any kind of dance step after watching the choreography only once. Jessica can assume any character onstage, is an ace on the tennis court, and sees everything through the eyes of an artist. At the moment, Jessica says she wants to study fashion design, which is part of my hesitation on the college visits. I'm reluctant to spend a week on the road visiting universities she'll be bored with after a semester. She's only interested in schools like Parsons, FIT, and RISD right now. I'm trying to talk her into a traditional college with design options like Columbus College, University of Cincinnati, or Kent State, so if (and when) she changes her mind, at least her initial course work will count toward a different major. She can't exactly become a psychologist or marine biologist with credits in Intermediate Fabric Draping.

Why are both girls so mercurial? I don't remember being this changeable in my teens. I'm not so different now than I was back then. But those two? It's like they're constantly trying to reinvent themselves, along with all their likes and dislikes. For example, they say they love platform boots, they can't live without platform boots, so I'll surprise them with a couple of pairs from New York and then they'll tell me, "No, we hate platform boots; we want ballet flats." Or, I'll hear them go on and on about how much they adore Sydney Bristow, so I'll watch *Alias* on Netflix DVDs while I'm on the road only to find out they don't like *Alias* when I arrive home, that now they're into *Lost*. I'm perpetually two paces behind them.

"How do I figure out what my daughters' passions are?" I ask.

"You are asking the wrong question, Penny."

"Am I?"

"Oh, yes. The question is, 'How do my daughters discover their passions?'"

I lean forward in my seat, my mind already racing, anxious to book whatever guru could assist them, to send them to whichever camp would most benefit them, to sign them up for any program they need to figure out who they are and what it is that drives them so that they can have the best shot at becoming successful adults. "And the answer is?"

"They need you to be patient while they take their time."

I slump back into my seat.

Time and patience, those are my two most limited resources.

• • • •

"Why can't she just come with you and stay in your corporate apartment? You're *in* New York. Parsons is *in* New York. FIT is *in* New York. Fly out there together; you can work Monday and Tuesday if you have to, do NYC schools on Wednesday, rent a car and drive to Rhode Island on Thursday, fly to Savannah on Friday, and come home Saturday. You miss, what, three days? This seems pretty simple to me," Chris says. He's standing at the kitchen island, hands splayed on the marble countertop, in what seems to me like a very aggressive posture. I don't care for his tone. At all.

"It's not that simple," I argue. "I work twelve to fourteen-hour

days when I'm out there. I can't leave Jessica alone in some corporate apartment while I'm gone for that long. What will she do?"

"She'll figure something out. She's not a child, and she's not
incompetent."

"I am not comfortable with her being alone in the city. Anything could happen."

He throws his hands in the air. "Okay, then take the week off.
You're certainly owed the time. You can't just abdicate your family
because you're busy with your job. I mean, which is more important to you?"

"That's insulting. How can you even ask me that?"

"Because I legitimately want to know. In terms of priority, in
terms of attention, in terms of who you put first, I'm telling you
right now, from where I stand? It's not the Sinclairs."

I exhale heavily. "And whose fault is that?"

He clenches his jaw. "You're going to keep pinning this on *me?*
Yes, I made a bad investment. I know. You've mentioned this many,
many times. I realize I'm the reason you had to take this job until
we were back on solid ground. However, the decision to continue
to climb the corporate ladder was not something we made together.
That was all you. We were getting by on your initial salary."

"It wasn't enough."

"It *was.* You kept saying you wanted to advance because it
would mean more for the kids, but stop lying to yourself; you
wanted more responsibility because you liked it. Because you were
good at it. Because dealing with your facts and figures was easier
for you than figuring out your own flesh and blood. Your job gave
you an excuse to hide from what was hard."

I try to protest, but Chris doesn't let me interject.

"No, I don't want to hear it. I'm telling you this right now as your husband, as your partner, as your best friend: These kids don't want *stuff* from you; they want *time*."

Chris steps out from behind the counter and comes to sit by me at the table in the breakfast nook. "Don't you get it, Penny? These college visits are your opportunity to bond with Jessica. Take a road trip and listen to her shitty music—and I assure you, her music *is* shitty; in twenty years, no one is going to form a Nickelback tribute band. Have the experience. Buy terrible snacks at gas stations. Eat nachos made with liquid plastic cheese and petrified hot dogs from those roller things. Stop along the way and see the world's largest ball of twine. Have an adventure. Make some memories."

He puts my hand in his, rubbing my knuckles with his thumb. "Just take that week and figure out what makes her tick. She acts like she has her guard up, but I know she's still open to letting you see who she is. That won't always be the case. The door between you will eventually close. Get in while you can. I'm worried that if you don't do something to change your trajectory with her, you're going to wind up with the exact same kind of distant, formal, awkward relationship you have with Marjorie."

I snort. "Yes, but that's entirely *her* fault."

Chris looks at me for a long moment. "Is it?"

I bristle and snatch back my hand. "What's that supposed to mean?"

He gets up from the table. "That means figure out a way to get your daughter out on her college visits before it's too late."

• • • •

"So . . . what's happening with Jessica's college applications? I haven't heard anything!" Vanessa says with false bonhomie as she sidles up to me after our staff meeting. I tried to escape the conference room quickly, but apparently I wasn't quick enough.

"Are you going to be road-tripping soon?" she asks. "She's got to be excited! I understand most kids apply in the summer now. You'd better get on that, right? It's almost August! Will you need me to cover for you in New York? It's no problem. My schedule is wide-open, and I've been dying to become better acquainted with the clients."

"Handled," I reply. While I'd prefer to say nothing, I can't, because no response would be blatantly rude.

Vanessa stops in her tracks, her smug smile faltering ever so slightly. Her eyes seem especially hard behind all that heavy liner. What led her to believe that the key to success in corporate consulting is to steal Pat Benatar's look from the "Love Is a Battlefield" video? I wonder. "Handled?" she asks.

"Yes, handled. But thank you so much for your offer. If I do need to take time off, which is unlikely to happen before the New York project ends, seeing how we're almost done, you'll be the first one I call." I begin to walk down the hall in the opposite direction.

Vanessa scrambles after me. "Is she not going to college now?"

"What gave you that idea?"

"But her visits . . . You haven't been anywhere. . . ."

I reward Vanessa with my brightest smile. "They went *so* well, thanks for asking. She loved FIT *and* Parsons, so she may have a bit of a Sophie's Choice on her hands. We'll see what happens. Listen, Vanessa, I have to hop on a conference call. Bye!"

As Vanessa has been ratcheting up her level of aggression over the summer, I knew I couldn't let her take over the New York project, even for a week, so I came up with a compromise. I brought

Jessica and Marjorie out to NYC to visit schools. I put them up at the Plaza for the week, and the two of them hit a slew of New York colleges with fashion programs. Instead of road-tripping to Rhode Island and Georgia following New York, I promised she and I would do that together when my project is put to bed.

Except that's not going to happen because Jessica has found her passion and apparently that passion is New York City. After less than a week, she's more familiar with the place I've practically been living in for the past couple of years. She said she wanted to see the city like a real New Yorker, so she pocketed the cab money I left her and she and Marjorie figured out the subway system on their own. They visited all the schools on the list, but also made time to shop and sightsee and hit Bleecker Street for pizza (which is far superior to Chicago-style, according to them) and discover places I'd never even heard of, like the hidden waterfall at Greenacre Park.

Chris was right—spending a solid week with her is really all it took to figure out what makes her tick . . . at least according to Marjorie. Those two always had an amiable grandmother-granddaughter relationship, but now they're the best of friends, with inside jokes and the ability to communicate entire thoughts with nothing more than a wink or a raised eyebrow. When I'd meet them for dinner to download about the schools and how their day had gone, they behaved like sorority sisters and I was some unwanted rushee they were stuck entertaining for the hour. So the trip *was* a wonderful bonding experience.

Just not for Jessica and me.

CHAPTER TWELVE

To: christophersinclairjr@calmail.berkeley.edu
From: thefarmerfromthedells@hotmail.com
Date: June 22nd
Subject: Yes

I'm still thinking about you, too.

XO,

A

To: jessica@sinclairsartorial.com

From: interncassie@sinclairsartorial.com

Date: June 22nd

Subject: ???

Um ... do you, like, not live here anymore? There's someone else in your apartment, with, like, not your stuff. Am I fired? Is this because I ate your caviar?

If I don't hear back from you, I'm going to take the rest of the day off, cool?

XO, Cassie

BY THE NUMBERS

To: PenelopeBancroftSinclair@Facebook.com

From: AnastassiaLynnRickenbacher@Facebook.com

Date: June 22nd

Subject: You are amazing

You are beyond compare. You are the best. You rock my world.

. . . .

"**Y**ou are never going to guess who I heard from on Match!" I exclaim.

"Hold up, do I hear a car radio? Are you *driving*? You're actually talking to me on your mobile while you're *behind the wheel*, Miss Nine Americans Die Every Day Due to Distracted Driving? Miss One in Four Motor Vehicle Crashes Involve a Cellular Device? Miss Talking on the Phone While Operating a Car Makes You Four Times More Likely to Have an Accident?" Patrick fires back at me.

"I waited to dial until I pulled into the driveway, you jerk."

He immediately turns chatty. "Oh, okay, then who'd you hear from?"

"Remember Wyatt? Anagram Wyatt?"

"The world's most boring attorney, or the Natter Yo?"

"That's him. Interesting news. He lives in Lake Forest and he's recently divorced. We're going to meet up for a drink on Friday."

"Huh. On the one hand, congratulations; I'm proud of you. You're very brave to step outside of your comfort zone like this. And, on the other, I'm really underwhelmed and you can do better."

"Can you put Michael on the phone? Because I hate you and I'd like to speak with someone I don't despise."

"What?" he says, indignant. "You wanted me to lie? My job is to tell you the truth, so, yes, those pleated pants make your ass look wide, yes, you have spinach in your teeth, and yes, you've told me the story about how you once met Kelly Clarkson on a plane and, yes, it gets more boring with each and every retelling."

I grab my purse and computer bag and exit the Camry. I don't bother parking in the garage during the summer because I'm not trying to keep snow off the car. I head toward the back door and turn to double-check that I've pressed the remote locking key. The car's lights flash reassuringly and the horn rewards me with a jaunty honk. (I love this vehicle about a million times more than that horrid string of minivans.) I'm about to climb the stairs to the back porch when I realize they've been replaced with a very long wheelchair ramp.

"Mooooooootherfucker."

"Listen, Penny, if you want someone to sugarcoat things for you, call Karin. I'm sure Kelly Clarkson *was* sweet; no one's arguing that. But she—"

"No, no, that's not it. Oh God, no. This cannot be happening."

"What?" Patrick asks, suddenly on high alert. "What cannot be happening?"

I hiss, "My daughters are assholes."

"Tell me something I *don't* know."

"Damn it." I sit down on the ramp. "Their dad got back from Costa Rica Saturday night and they went down to the city to see him. I guess he and Stassi live in a walk-up loft with no elevator, which is almost impossible to manage on crutches, let alone in a wheelchair. I was sympathetic, because that's rough and I'm not a monster."

"Eh, debatable."

"Anyway, remember when Chris and I planned to move his mom in here about five years ago? We redid the bathroom in the den to be handicap accessible so Num-Num could have a first-floor bedroom?"

"But she went into assisted living instead."

"Right, and then she deteriorated pretty quickly, which was so sad. She was such a great lady."

"She was one hell of a broad." Being one hell of a broad is

Patrick's highest compliment. Even though Chris's mom was no relation to Patrick, she made sure he was willed her extensive Staffordshire dog collection because she knew he'd treasure it. She was famous for making thoughtful gestures like that.

"Anyway, I must have said something to the girls about it being too bad he didn't live here with the made-over den and all, not realizing that I should have said, 'It's too bad he had an affair and now we're divorced, or he could have used the den.'"

"Pen, when are you going to realize your kids are only going to hear the parts they want to hear?"

"Apparently never. Now the e-mail I received from Stassi today makes perfect sense. She sent a note that was all, 'You're the best; you're a rock star!'"

Patrick lets out a low whistle. "He was infirm and in her direct care for less than twenty-four hours and he already made her crazy. That's a new record, wouldn't you say? What do you think, she bought him saltines instead of oyster crackers and he lost it? So she found a way to foist him back off on your family? Hoo-boy, Michael is going to die when I tell him. I'm not kidding."

"Can I come live with you guys? I don't want to be in this house anymore."

I'm joking. Mostly.

He's quick to answer. "No. You're a shit magnet lately. I don't want your bad luck following you down here, messing up our lives."

He's joking. Mostly.

"Then I guess I'd better go inside and see my ex-husband, and my parents, and my two daughters, and the very large, very destructive dog who all live with me, each one of them an uninvited guest."

"On the bright side," Patrick says, "probably can't get any worse."

"Don't say that," I reply. "I'm learning it can always get worse."

$$\bullet \quad \bullet \quad \bullet \quad \bullet$$

"That'll be eleven dollars and eighty-one cents, please," the cashier tells me.

"I'm sorry? I just want the one pack, nothing else," I reply.

Yes. I'm breaking my own rule about smoking. I'm buying a pack of cigarettes. I know I normally have only one a year, but I normally don't have my two daughters who can barely conceal their contempt for me, my temporarily handicapped ex-husband, and my parents who may or may not be in the throes of dementia living under my roof for an undetermined amount of time. Oh, and I keep forgetting Sweet Caroline, who chewed her way through a solid oak door last night. Not a little hole, either. I'm talking the full-on "Here's-Johnny-in-*The-Shining*, minus Jack Nicholson and the ax" kind of hole. I'm beginning to understand how she ended up in a shelter in the first place.

The cashier bobs his head, which causes his septum piercing to swing like a door knocker. That piece of hardware's got to be a bitch when he has a cold. How would he blow his nose? Maybe he receives an employee discount on preventative meds like vitamin C and Zicam and never gets sick?

He tells me, "Right. That's how much one pack of Marlboro Reds costs."

"Really? The last time I bought cigarettes, they were a buck fifty," I say.

"Cool. I guess that was a while ago?"

"I guess it was."

"Would you like to enter your Walgreens rewards card number to earn points on your purchase?"

"I would not."

"Cool." I hand him a twenty and he makes change before placing my cigarettes in a plastic bag and passing the whole lot over to me. "Thank you and be well."

I pause before I walk away. "Does it strike you as odd, or at all hypocritical, to tell me to 'be well' when the only item I'm purchasing causes almost five hundred thousand mortalities *per annum*, which is more deaths than HIV, illegal drug use, alcohol use, car accidents, and incidents related to firearms *in toto*?"

He blinks at me a couple of times. "Did you need matches?"

Sheepishly, I reply, "Yes, please."

He reaches into a box under the counter and hands me a book. "Here ya go. Thanks. Be well."

I return to the car, drive home, hide behind the shed to smoke not one, but the better part of *two*, of my new, secret stash before finally stepping inside for the first time. I felt that the cigarettes would help me steel myself to have a stern discussion because everything about this setup is ridiculous.

I can't have Chris here.

I can't live like this.

While I'm sorry his living situation isn't ideal, that stopped being my problem when we signed the divorce papers. Correction: That stopped being my problem when he selected that fateful Kenny G album. How am I supposed to move on with my life with him *here?*

I stomp up the ramp and through the back door, where Caroline greets me with the mangled carcass of my favorite sandal in her mouth. No! Not these! Not my super-fancy summer favorites! I bought these little gold wedges with the T-straps, strung with little-bitty coins in mixed metals that jingle with each step because they're the perfect shoe for every hot-weather outfit, appropriate with anything from a swimsuit to a cocktail dress. I paid a ton for them, too, because they do the job of at least three pairs of shoes.

"No, Caroline, no! Bad girl! Give it here! No three-in-one super-fancies for you!"

I attempt to take the sandal from her, and this is apparently the most fun she's ever had. She lowers her front end, leaving her ample rump high in the air, and she begins to tug.

"Caroline, mine! MINE! Let go! Kelsey? Where are you? Come get your awful dog!"

Caroline's puffy tail swishes back and forth and she grunts with glee while keeping her teeth firmly clamped down on my shoe. She's got such a grip that she's starting to pull me across the room inch by inch.

"Caroline, drop it!" I command. She simply jerks harder. I try to imagine Barnaby behaving like this and I can't. I'd have a much easier time picturing him finding a qualified cobbler on Yelp and then making an appointment to have the shoes resoled in high-quality leather at a reasonable price, all without ever having been asked.

"I said *now!*" I give the shoe a solid yank just as Chris rolls into the room in his wheelchair, which frightens Caroline. She releases the super-fancy and bravely runs away while I'm mid-tug, which sends me reeling back into the kitchen island with a tremendous *thump*.

"You okay?"

I glance up at Chris from my spot on the floor. He looks both better and worse than I expected. On the plus side, his tan is deep and his hair bleached out from the hot Costa Rican sun. On the minus side, he's in a cast past his knee on the left side, he's wearing a neck brace, and he's covered in multiple cuts and bruises, with dark circles under his eyes. I didn't realize until this moment how lucky he is not to have been injured worse.

"You should have seen the other guy?" I reply, rubbing the back of my head where it hit the cabinet. "So . . . um, hi."

"That dog is no Barnaby," he says.

"Tell me about it."

He wheels closer to me and offers me a hand to help me up. I wave him off. He says, "Are we planning to talk about my being here, or is it just going to be this awkward thing? Since you're smoking again, I'm guessing you want to talk and I shouldn't get too comfortable in the den?"

I'm dumbfounded. "You can tell I smoked? How?"

"Please. This is not exactly *CSI*-level detective work. I've known what you smelled like since 1980."

"You have not."

"Of course I have."

"Prove it."

"You wore Love's Baby Soft until college—"

"So did everyone."

"Ralph Lauren until you graduated—"

I roll my eyes. "Again, so did everyone."

"You were big on that super-sweet stuff, um . . . Poison until we got married, nothing when you were pregnant because everything made you queasy, and in the past few years you've been on a quest to find the perfect neroli-oil-based scent. Thus far, Tom Ford's Neroli Portofino is the best. What? I *told* you so. You were prematurely smug. Stop looking at me with your mouth open. My not listening to you was never our problem. Also, you installed motion-sensor lights, and I can see behind the shed from the den."

I have no idea how to respond, so I just laugh. He could always do this—he could always defuse any tense situation, if he chose to. "Did you know cigarettes are twelve bucks a pack now?"

"You're kidding! They used to be a buck fifty! When did we get old?"

"Who's old? You're the one in a wheelchair, Grandpa, not me."

"Ouch. I mean that literally and figuratively—I'm due for another pain pill. They are not as much fun as you'd hope. Do me a favor and don't fall from a jungle canopy; one star, do not recommend." He wheels a couple of inches back and forth, in a motion that's sort of like pacing. His face takes on a more serious expression. "So, you want to have a discussion? You cannot be thrilled to see me here."

"Honestly, I'm not, especially because I didn't agree to this. You have to sense that. The girls didn't clear you being here with me, and all of a sudden I come home and, hey! Guess what! We're ADA compliant. You know how I am with surprises."

Chris nods slowly and only as much as the brace will allow, as though he's agreeing with me, although his lips are pressed together tightly. "Yeah, I wondered about that. They both said it was fine and I said I wanted to talk to you, but somehow it didn't happen. Don't worry about it. I will figure out somewhere to go, but it might take me until tomorrow, if that's okay. I appreciate your being a decent sport, though. I don't think I could have handled fireworks today."

He begins to wheel out of the kitchen, and I watch him maneuver past the doorframe, careful not to ding the paint. "You'll just go back to Stassi's, right?"

"Yeah, probably not."

"Because of the stairs?"

He turns back to face me. "No, because of the breakup."

"What? What happened?"

He runs his good hand through his hair. "Stassi said she couldn't handle my injuries. She said she wasn't going to be able to take care of me. She said she truly didn't realize how old I was until I was helpless."

"Are you freaking kidding me?" I point to his lap. "Correct me if I'm wrong, but it's just a broken leg and torn ACL right? The bruises aren't that cute, but those will be gone in a week. Otherwise, you're good, and the girls said you can do the whole, you know, bathroom thing by yourself. Wait, you didn't sprain anything . . . *else*, right?"

The tips of his ears turn red. "All of my parts are functioning normally, thank you. And here I thought we were going to avoid awkwardness."

"I'm sorry, but she's a bitch!" I fume. "That is *bullshit*. That is *ageist*. That is *not right*. I thought you were serious with her. I thought marriage was a possibility. In sickness and in health, for better or worse? Well, this is worse and a little bit of sickness and her first instinct is to cut and run? Not cool. One thousand percent not cool."

Chris takes a deep breath and he suddenly looks very fragile in his chair. "Ultimately, it's my fault for not choosing well. Actions have consequences, and I have become painfully aware of them. Okay, I'm going to make some calls and figure some things out. I can probably go to my sister Sophie's. She's the closest, and she's already going to take me to physical therapy anyway until I can drive." He does a three-point turn and goes to leave, but I catch his wheelchair by the handles before he can roll off.

Before I can even think through my idea, I find that I'm already talking. "Listen, I could actually use your input. There's a lot going on with our daughters, and neither one of them will tell me anything. Kelsey's left Milo and I have no idea why. And I suspect Jess has gotten herself into some trouble in New York. I saw a couple of weird comments on her blog about her owing people money and now the whole site is down. She says it's a technical glitch, but I have a bad feeling there's more to the story. Between them and whatever is up with my folks—I can't even begin to pick apart that mystery—having you tool around the first floor really would be the least of my problems. I know you're going to have to find your own place at some point because you guys broke up. I'm just saying it doesn't have to be today. Take a minute. Slow your roll."

I can't read Chris's expression as he searches my face. "I'm not sure what you're trying to say, Penny. Do you want my input, or do you want my *help*? I realize it's hard for you to admit you require assistance, but I'm here; I just need confirmation."

I have to swallow hard to get the words out. They feel foreign on my lips. "I want your help."

He lets out a soft chuckle. "Then I guess you've got yourself a temporary new roommate."

"One thing, though?" I ask.

"What's that?"

"If anyone asks, I don't smoke."

· · · ·

"Penny Bancroft, my goodness, it's like you're still twenty-three years old," Wyatt says, greeting me with a brief formal hug.

Time has been kind to Wyatt, rounding out the places where he was once too angular. The fire of his ginger hair has softened and the volume thinned, but not drastically. He's definitely matured, but he also appears a lot less anxious than he used to. He no longer seems on the cusp of being shaken down for his lunch money.

"You flatter me, but it's Penny Sinclair," I remind him. "Married. Divorced, but first married."

"Penny Sinclair, Replicas Ninny."

"You can say that again." I motion toward the bar. We'd decided to meet on his turf, at an elegant old English-style pub on the first floor of a timbered Tudor boutique hotel in downtown Lake Forest. The walls are covered in dark panels of oiled wood, and beneath them, the banquettes are comprised of tufted leather. All of the gilded framed paintings are of hunting dogs. What is the North Shore's obsession with making everything look exactly like the local country clubs? Doesn't anyone else get tired of all the plaid and brass? Would all of Lake County implode if someone decorated modern or minimalist for once?

"Shall we sit?"

He pulls out my chair and we're seated. "I'm sorry. I didn't know what to order for you; it's been a very long time. I mean, Zima and ice beers have come and gone since I saw you last, although no one would know that to look at you. I hope you don't mind that I got started," he says, holding up his rocks glass.

"Oh, please, how could you remember what I drink? It's been more than twenty-five years! What are you having?" I ask.

"Right now, club soda with a twist of lime."

"Whoa, slow down there, cowboy. Hope you're not driving tonight."

He smiles at me over the rim of his glass. "It's wonderful to see you, Penny. What are you in the mood for? I hear they make a nice Moscow Mule here, which is vodka, lime, and ginger beer served in a copper cup."

"Mmm, that sounds nice."

"But wait—before you decide, their signature cocktail is the French 75, which is gin, lemon juice, simple syrup, and prosecco. The story is that it's supposed to pack such a kick that drinking one felt like being shelled by a French 75-millimeter field gun. If I may be so bold, might I suggest we get one of each, we taste them both, and decide from there who drinks what?"

"You have a beautiful mind," I reply.

Hold up, is that flirting? I can't tell if I'm flirting. Holy cow, I'm rusty at this. Is this a date? I'm not sure, since we're not actually consuming a meal. Let's say it's a date, though. If this is a date, then it would stand to reason that I would act the coquette. Maybe my body is involuntarily reacting to this situation by making me say flirty things, sort of like how my pulse would quicken and dump cortisol and adrenaline in my system and my muscles would automatically contract to protect me from pain if I were in a situation where I felt fear. Also like if I were on a date.

(Is it too late to go back to my idea of getting fifteen cats?)

Wyatt *is* someone I used to quite like. He and I have been exchanging e-mails all week, and his witty banter is reminding me of what I enjoyed about our relationship. Did he ever rock my world, in so many words? No. Yet there's something to be said for quiet, clever companionship. And let's be frank here—I'm a fifty-something actuary who's basically married to her job. Hot monkey sex is not at the top of my to-do list. Karin says it should be, but Karin spends way too much time talking to Ryan and Sasha about their hookups. (Which is disturbing, if you ask me, and exactly why we never let our kids watch HBO.)

He places our order and I'm reminded of what a gentleman he always was. While I'm loath to do the Wyatt-did-this and Chris-did-that comparison, I do recall Wyatt having impeccable etiquette. Chris was always my hero—until he wasn't—but Wyatt was certainly diligent in his own way. I forgot how well mannered he was. I don't think I touched a car door or picked up a check once the entire time we dated, no matter how hard I protested. At the time I found his chivalry painfully old-fashioned, but now I grasp the appeal.

"Sounds like you have a bit of a three-ring circus going on at your house," he says. I've been giving him the broad strokes so I didn't just spring my bizarre new living situation on him in person.

"Yes, a total circus, complete with wild animals. My daughter brought home this wrecking crew in a black shag coat. Caroline—that's the dog—ate my phone in the middle of the night. She literally snuck into my room and chewed it to bits. This is problematic for a number of reasons, but mainly because I use my phone as my alarm clock. Normally I'd have just woken up on my own—I'm an early riser—"

"Still?"

"Still," I confirm, blushing a bit, having forgotten that I've woken up with this man before. However, it seems too soon to delve into that portion of our past, so I acknowledge this comment no further. "Thing is, I was exhausted because she kept waking me up all night with her incessant barking. I guess she heard an owl hooting outside? Anyway, I missed a huge breakfast meeting this morning because of this. Slept right through it. And no one could call me because my phone was in thousands of pieces."

Wyatt chuckles politely. He never did let out giant guffaws like Chris, which isn't a bad thing. "You missed your meeting because your dog ate your phone? That's one shade past your dog eating your homework. Did people believe you?"

"Would *you* believe me? I've never in my life been late for a meeting, let alone missed one, and this was with a big new client we've been trying to land. Luckily one of my colleagues was there and she covered for me, so it was fine for the firm, but not so great for me." Vanessa was practically running victory laps around the nineteenth floor by the time I arrived at the office at noon.

"I'm sure no one will judge you too harshly for one indiscretion." He gives me a reassuring pat on the shoulder.

"I hope not."

Except I haven't had just the one indiscretion. Chaos has ensued over the past five days since Chris has been in the house, and truly none of it has been his fault. For example, I had to rearrange this initial client meeting more than once to make some accommodations, such as when the girls were using my car to bring Chris to his doctor's appointment, which would have been fine had they told me first. Stassi did bring up Chris's truck, but apparently neither of them can drive stick shift. Nor can I, which would have been good to know before I tried to take it to the train.

And then there are my parents. I was able to get my dad in to see the gerontologist, but only because of a midday cancelation, which meant I had to take a day off at the last minute, hence more rescheduling. Max surprised me by coming to the appointment without complaint and then was sharp as a damn tack the entire time the doctor ran his evaluation. While we were there, Dr. Vora drew blood and took a urine sample and we're waiting for those results. Once we know what's happening there, we can proceed with next-level testing to check on his memory skills and problem-solving abilities, and if those prove inconclusive, we move on to a CT scan and possibly an MRI.

In a private conversation, Dr. Vora wanted to know if there was a possibility that my dad might have trended a bit bigoted because of the times in which he grew up. He says this isn't terribly unusual in his patients and thus far that seems to be his only issue. I'll have to talk to Foster and Judith about this, because . . . maybe? I'm not sure what to root for here, dementia or small-mindedness. The doctor also wanted to know if my father had been under any undue stress lately, but what kind of strain could he be facing, unless Bunky Cushman suddenly, drastically improved his short game?

Regardless, my personal life is wreaking havoc on my work life right now, which has never been an issue with me. I am not Personal Problem Gal. I am not Crying in the Bathroom Lady. I am not Woebegone Sigh as You Walk Past My Desk So You'll Ask Me What's Wrong Woman. No one even knew I was divorcing until someone noticed I no longer wore my wedding ring. (Thanks to Vanessa, I learned long ago to stop mentioning anything vaguely home-related in the office.) And yet despite my best efforts, home is now having an impact on my performance. I mean, this afternoon, Mr. Waterstone stopped me in the hallway to ask if everything is okay with me and if I needed to take any of my vacation time. I'm desperately unhappy about having registered on his radar, particularly so close to our upcoming meeting about my promotion, and that needs to stop right quick.

Our drinks arrive and Wyatt sets them both in front of me.

"Please, ladies first. You have the honor of choosing."

"I'll try the Moscow Mule, but you have to taste the French 75 at the same time so we can toast," I say.

"If you insist." He lifts the cocktail, which is served in one of those wide old French champagne glasses, and says, "May we kiss those we please and please those we kiss."

Aha! Looks like I'm not the only one trying to flirt here. I give him a coy smile, and we clink glasses. We each take a sip of our respective drinks. Mine tastes strongly of ginger, which I appreciate. I always forget I enjoy the flavor of ginger, having relied on it so heavily to settle my stomach when I was pregnant. Chris was forever on the lookout for ginger-based food and drink back in the day. The day he found ginger root in the grocery store? You'd have thought he'd located the Dead Sea Scrolls.

Wait, why am I thinking about Chris right now? Stop it.

"Mmm, very citrusy," he says of the 75.

"Shall we switch?" I ask. We swap and I take a sip of his, which I immediately want to spit out because it's like a mouthful of liquid Lemonhead candies. His face is equally puckered after his taste of the Moscow Mule. Without a word, we each take back our original drinks.

Wyatt wipes his mouth with a napkin and clears his palate with some wasabi peas. "I have a small-world story for you."

"Oh, yeah?"

"Mmm-hmm. Apparently my neighbors bought your parents' old place in West Palm."

"I beg your pardon?" He has to be mistaken. My parents haven't sold their place in West Palm. They would have mentioned it. You don't just conduct a major real estate transaction and move out of the state without telling your kids.

Unless there's a problem the gerontologist has yet to diagnose. Damn it.

"Yes. The Hanovers are very excited. Apparently it's almost impossible to find something available in Vista Pines, especially a home right on the fourteenth green. They told me to say hello to Marjorie and Max."

"I'll do that," I say.

I have a great deal of difficulty concentrating on anything Wyatt says for the rest of our time together. We touch upon his divorce, (amicable, no kids) and his job (amicable, no kids) and everything else he's been up to for the past twenty-five years (amicable, no kids). We part with a kiss on the cheek and the promise to get together soon for a proper dinner. I hustle off to the Camry, digging out my new phone before I even reach for my keys.

I stay parked while I call Foster.

"Hey, little sister, what's going on?" he says by way of greeting.

"Did you know Max and Marjorie sold their place in Vista Pines?"

"I'm sorry, *what?* Hello? Penny?"

"Yes, hi, it's me. So you didn't know."

"Hell, no. We just bought our tickets to go down there for Christmas! Shoot. You think they're refundable? We booked on JetBlue. They have free in-flight entertainment and brand-name snacks."

"Fos, I need you to focus. Do you find it odd that they sold their place without mentioning it to us? Don't you think that's worthy of a conversation?"

Foster doesn't seem too upset. "Eh, maybe a little? But we don't have the kind of parents who want to share their *feeeelings* with us. They're old-school, so it's not too surprising. I wouldn't read that much into it."

I'm not satisfied with his lack of urgency here. "Have you spent much time with Max lately?"

"I've seen him at the club. Why?"

"Are you noticing any changes in him?"

"Hmm. His backswing's been for shit. Too short. The pro calls it 'old man swing.' I think his rotator cuff's been acting up. I keep saying he should look into physical therapy, or at least get a massage to open things up, but no one listens to me."

I try to remain calm. "*Mental* changes. I'm talking about his faculties. I'm worried he may have an onset of dementia."

"Dementia? Definitely not. He just read me the riot act about the new payroll system I installed. Said I was nuts to change what had worked for so many years. He walked me through every part of why his old system was superior. Gotta tell ya, he was right. Turns out the new software is super-glitchy, so I went back to the old way."

Huh. "Does he seem on edge at all? Agitated? Quick to escalate?"

"Yes. I've definitely witnessed that."

"How long would you say he's been that way?"

"Every day for my entire life."

"Foster, you're not helping."

"What? I'm trying here. What do you want? Max seems completely normal, again, save for his backswing. I wonder if chondroitin would help? Or a cortisone shot?"

I begin to drum the steering wheel in agitation. "Give me something, anything. There's weirdness afoot he won't tell me about, and I can't figure it out. Until I get to the root of the problem, I can't help him. And until I can help him, I'm not sure I can get him out of my house."

"Yeah, I could see how that'd be a problem. Judith lasted, what, a week with them?" Foster says. He's laughing, but I know Judith didn't think any of this was funny. "Marjorie called her a 'harridan.' What is that, like, a belly dancer? Let's see . . . something.

Something about Max. Well, okay, here you go—my financial department ran across a weird recurring Accounts Payable to an M. Ramos, and I asked Max about it. He said he'd talk to his old accountant about it. He must have taken care of it, because it's off the books now. But that's it."

"That doesn't seem like a big deal."

"Exactly."

I exhale so hard I fog a bit of my windshield. "This has been a useless phone call, Foster."

"Hurtful language! You can make it up to me by having me and Judith over for dinner. Chris is up for visitors, right? Did he get the fruit basket I sent?"

"He did, but what do you expect him to do with *two dozen* cactus pears? He's one person."

"I wanted to give him the most expensive stuff I could find to let him know how much I care."

"Why didn't you send something with more of a shelf life, like wine or scotch?"

"Where were you Monday, when I was placing orders on the Internet?"

"Okay, Fos, I've gotta go. Tell Judith I'll call her this weekend."

"Cool. Bye, sis. TELL CHRIS I MISS HIM."

I put away my phone and pull out of the parking space to head for home. Regardless of what Foster thinks, something major is up with my father, and I'm making it my job to find out what it is.

CHAPTER THIRTEEN

May 1974

"Penelope, darling, can you please answer the door?"

"Yeah, Mom!" I run down the stairs as fast as I can in my shiny church shoes.

"Say 'yes,' not 'yeah,' Penelope, and walk down the stairs like a lady, not a charging bull, please," my mom instructs me from the depths of her bedroom, where she's setting her hair with hot rollers.

How does she know I was running when she can't even see me? Still, I slow to a walk.

She's been extra-bossy since we moved to this house. Lately I feel like she's trying to create this image that we are some kind of perfect family from a magazine. She used to be more easygoing. Now she's always all, "I don't want the neighbors to get the wrong impression!" when I do stuff like yell out a window to tell Foster to come inside for supper.

Since when is that not okay?

She used to do that on our old street, like, all the time!

Oh, and we're not supposed to call supper "supper" anymore—it's "dinner" now.

She hates when I throw my bike on the lawn instead of parking it in the garage now, too. Sometimes I forget, and I swear that whenever I do, she automatically knows and sends me back outside to put it away right.

The weirdest thing is she doesn't call me "Penny" anymore. I'm always "Penelope" now, and she only used to use my full name when I was in trouble. My first thought is always that I've somehow screwed up when I hear her say my name.

Still, I'm real happy we moved, even with the changes. Our new house has a double set of front doors, which is pretty neat. They open extra-wide. Our old house just had the one door, which was way less exciting. We didn't move very far from our old neighborhood, and I didn't even have to change schools, but my parents tell me this is a giant leap for mankind, like the astronaut Neil Armstrong says. I'll say—we have one hundred percent more front door now! Our last door was made mostly from aluminum, so it was real light, but these big wooden dealies weigh about a million pounds each. I really have to yank to get 'em open.

When I finally pry the big ol' wooden guys apart, Karin is here. Karin goes to my school and is in my fifth-grade class. We always got along, but now that I live down the street from her, she's become my best friend. Her mom and dad are divorced, which makes me sad for her. I feel like that would be lonely, but she says she is great friends with her mom and it's fine. I can't imagine being friends with my mom because she's too busy telling me what to do.

"Hey! Wanna come outside? A bunch of kids are playing TV

tag, and I figured you wouldn't want to miss it." Karin's wearing dungarees and a T-shirt, so she's ready to play.

I *love* TV tag. Even though I'm not the fastest runner, I have a really good memory, so I can always come up with the name of a television show that hasn't been used. I'm smart because most of the other kids only call out Saturday-morning cartoons. Once they run through *Scooby-Doo*, *The Yogi Bear Show*, and the *Harlem Globetrotters*, they're fresh out of ideas. But I make sure to read the *TV Guide* so I can throw out crazy stuff like *60 Minutes* or *Mannix*.

"I wish," I say. I point to my ugly ruffled dress with the weird, stiff petticoat underneath. I feel like one of those creepy Victorian dolls with the glass eyes. Nobody wears outfits like this. My mom wanted me to look fancy to impress my gam-gam.

Here's a news flash: An expensive party dress is going to have the opposite effect. Gam-Gam gets real mad and kind of resentful when things are too nice. I just don't see her appreciating a dress with this much lace for no good reason, especially since I'm not getting confirmed in it. Might be what she calls a venal sin, if I remember my CCD classes right? (No one has told Gam-Gam we go to the Episcopal church now instead of the Catholic one. I suspect it's a very bad idea to bring up the subject.)

I tell Karin, "I have to go to a Mother's Day brunch at our new country club with my grandmother and my aunt and uncle and stuff. Maybe I can play when I'm done."

Karin slumps against the doorframe. Even her pigtails droop with disappointment. "Aw, man. I won't have any fun without you."

"I'm not going to have any fun, either. My gam-gam is a big crab. I thought grandmothers were supposed to be nice old ladies who make cookies and stuff, but she mostly just smokes and says things that hurt people's feelings. I don't know why we have to go eat waffles with her. Mom and my auntie Marilyn will be all excited for Gam-Gam to be here, and then she will say awful stuff to both of them the whole time until she leaves. Then my mom will be in a bad mood for a couple of days. It's like everyone loses."

Karin's eyes grow huge. "Really? My grandma knits me fuzzy sweaters and sneaks me candy when my dad says I can't have any more and sends me fifty dollars for my birthday."

"See? That's what they're supposed to do," I say, monkeying with the itchy lace hem of my dress, yanking on it so hard I think something might have ripped underneath.

"Penelope, leave your dress alone!" I hear my mother call.

"Okay!" I say.

How does she know?

To Karin, I say, "Gam-Gam always tells me I'm lucky to not be working in a button factory. What does that even mean?"

Karin kicks at the welcome mat with the toe of her Buster Brown oxford. "I dunno. Well, call me when you get home."

"I will. Hey, for your game, use *Doctor Who*, *Nova*, and *Monty Python's Flying Circus*. You will win. See you later!"

"Ooh, those are *good*." She runs down our cobblestone walk to a waiting group of kids farther down the block. The ones who see me wave and I wave back.

I really like this neighborhood. I liked our old one, but this one is so much nicer; plus I still see my old friends at school, so I'm not missing anything. The houses are a lot farther apart and they are much bigger, with more trees and flowers. When we pulled up here for the first time, I thought maybe my parents were joking that this was ours, because it is huge.

Auntie Marilyn is the only other one of Gam-Gam's kids who even lives in the suburbs—everyone else is still in the city. The way all the brothers and sisters talk about Glencoe, you'd think we had cows or something out here! That's crazy. We're less than a mile from the grocery store, and we can walk to the train station and to buy ice-cream cones—that's hardly the boonies. We're still in Cook County!

Anyway, that day, my mom and dad took out their key and opened the door and let us in and then the movers showed up with all our stuff. If our being in this house is a joke, it's a really elaborate one that's gone on for two whole months.

While I'm standing outside watching everyone start the game, Auntie Marilyn, Uncle Leo (he works for my dad—that's how he and Auntie Marilyn met), Cousin Patrick, and Gam-Gam pull into the driveway in their Country Squire station wagon. From the expression on Patrick's face, he is not having a fun time with our grandmother. He practically bolts out of the car.

"Kool-Aid. Now. Please. I need some sugar to wash the drive from picking up Gam-Gam out of my brain," he demands. He looks very handsome in his plaid pants and double-breasted, belted vest. I like the long lapels on his silky shirt, too. "Why is she convinced we should be working in a button factory? It's 1974, and (a) we're in grade school and (b) there are child labor laws."

I hold up my hands. "Maybe because our fingers are small?"

He takes a look at my dress and says, "I hate everything about what you're wearing, up to and including the ankle socks. Especially the ankle socks."

I nod in agreement. "Me, too. Come on in. I think we have red Kool-Aid," I say.

"Perfect."

"Should we wait for everyone else?" I glance back to see Gam-Gam dawdling at the front of the house.

"No. Gam-Gam will want to spend some time criticizing the landscaping before moving inside. She's going to have a field day with the shag carpet and all the wood paneling. I'd say we have a few minutes."

Oh, no. Is Gam-Gam really going to be nasty about the new house, too? My parents are so proud of how nice it is, with the automatic dishwasher that's the same mustardy gold as the fridge and the stove and the trash compactor. Dad can't stop talking about how great his custom cabinets look in there, too. He may even use pictures of our kitchen in a magazine ad! Plus, we have the built-in kind of air-conditioning here instead of the window units like in the old house. We haven't had a real hot day yet, but when we do, I bet we won't have one room that is stifling.

You should hear my dad when he shows everybody the den with his hi-fi system and reel-to-reel audio player. When he played "Bad, Bad Leroy Brown," it sounded like Jim Croce himself was in the room singing to us! My dad bought a horseshoe-shaped bar and stocked it with a bunch of bottles of scotch. (Which does not taste like butterscotch *at all*. Ask me how I know.) (Well, ask Foster, technically.) He said he heard our fancy neighbors the Cushmans really like scotch, so if they ever want to come over, he will be ready to entertain them.

So I guess what I'm saying is I will be mad if Gam-Gam craps on this for my parents, especially because they try to be so generous with her, except she won't ever take anything from them. Why is that? I once overheard my auntie Marilyn say that if Gam-Gam allowed them to do nice things for her, she'd be giving up control and it wouldn't be worth it. That Gam-Gam would rather be miserable. I didn't understand what any of that meant—who would ever choose misery?

Sometimes I don't understand people.

Patrick and I walk inside, and I yell up the stairs, "They're here! I'm getting Patrick a cold drink!"

Mom replies, "No Kool-Aid for you, Penelope! I don't want you to stain your dress before brunch!"

How does she always know?

• • • •

The eight of us are seated in the main dining room at Centennial Hills, having just taken a walk around the grounds. Everything is so pretty and green here, and you can see the lake! I hadn't been anywhere but the dining room before today. This place is so big, with a pool and a golf course and lots of racquet courts and a stable, and there's even a shooting range!

My mom says now that the weather is getting warm and school will be out, there are lots of activities she expects me to participate in. She says it's important for our futures for her to meet "the right kind of moms," and she'll do that if Foster and I get involved in all the kids' sports here. A lot of the stuff sounds fun, so I am up to try. I do pretty good in PE when we have sit-up and pull-up challenges, but less so when there is a ball involved, so I guess we'll see. I start tennis lessons next weekend. I already got new sneakers and a white skirt outfit with little shorts sewn in underneath and some cute, short socks with fuzzy pom-poms on the back of them. Karin says tennis is hard and I should do gymnastics with her in Wilmette, but they don't offer gymnastics at the club, so my mom says no. I wonder if that's because Karin's mom is divorced. The way my mother talks, divorce is worse than cancer.

A very nice man named Miguel is waiting on us. My dad gave him a real big smile and a handshake when he seated us at the table, so I guess my dad likes him, too. When Miguel was taking drink orders, he offered to bring Shirley Temples for me, Patrick, and Foster. A Shirley Temple is ginger ale and grenadine, garnished with maraschino cherries, and it's the best thing I've ever tasted. Foster has put away three so far.

"What do you think about the country club, Bernadette?" my dad asks. I can tell he's trying to sound real casual, but he's sitting there with his chest all puffed up and I know how proud he is of finally becoming a member. He's talked about belonging here for a long, long time. I don't know what changed to make the snooty people finally let him in, but they did, and then it was like ten thousand Christmas mornings for him. When he found out our family was accepted, he and my mom danced around the kitchen holding hands for about five minutes. I think he even cried a little.

Patrick and I give each other the side-eye. We know what's coming. We can tell you what Gam-Gam is going to say. In school, I've been learning about how math helps predict patterns, which lets you know what's going to happen next. But I don't need arithmetic to predict that my dad's about to have his feelings hurt, because it happens every time.

Gam-Gam's steel-gray eyes dart around the room, taking in all the other families enjoying their Mother's Day brunch. There's nothing about her that's relaxed or friendly. For example, her hair is all scraped back into a bun that's so tight it must make her whole scalp ache. Maybe that's why she's cranky. (I know I don't like it when my mom pulls my braids too tight, but I tell her and she loosens them, so it's okay.) Her mouth is all small and pinched into a bitty little dot in the center of her face. She's got that flappy arm skin that you think would make her feel soft and doughy when you're forced to hug her, but no. The flaps are more like something she'd use to suffocate her prey. She kind of reminds me of a lizard, except a lizard might be more warm-blooded.

"Ridiculous," she spits. "This club is ridiculous."

My dad looks like he's had the wind sucked clean out of him. My mom's teeth are still smiling, but none of the rest of her face is.

"Mama, membership here is everything Max has been working toward!" Mom calls him Max now. She used to call my dad "Sully" because his middle name is "Sullivan." Everyone in his old neighborhood where he grew up still calls him Sully, but he doesn't go there much anymore. "The connections he's made already are invaluable! The new business tipped the scales and helped us buy the house!"

My mom's eyes look really sad, but she's still wearing that big toothpaste-commercial grin. Actually, people ask her all the time if she's on television, because she's very glamorous. People used to say she was a dead ringer for Angie Dickinson, and then they'd add words like, "Va-va-voom!" which always made me feel funny. But over the past few years, her style has changed. Now when she goes to the beauty salon, she brings pictures of Princess Grace of Monaco and says she wants to be like that. People still admire her looks, but more quietly now.

I probably will not be pretty like her when I grow up. I take after my dad, who is more plain, but he's very smart even though he did not have a chance to go far in school. My mom says Gam-Gam was so beautiful when she was young, but I don't see it. Maybe it's because her personality makes her ugly.

Why can't Gam-Gam try to be nice? Why can't she just tell my mom and aunt they did a good job? When we go to other relatives' houses, there are a lot of dirty kids in bad-fitting diapers without enough grown-ups paying attention to them. Why isn't Gam-Gam saying to my family, "Wow! Look how far you have come!"

Gam-Gam tosses her napkin on the table, and her tiny dot of a mouth gets even more puckered. "The house is ostentatious." I know what "ostentatious means," and this makes me mad. We don't have plastic on a single piece of furniture, unlike at her house, and there's no crocheted doilies covering up our toilet paper, either, because we have plenty of cabinet space. *Custom* cabinet space. "Cobblestones? Turrets? All that landscaping and four bathrooms? You're four people. You two forget where you come from all of a sudden? You move twenty miles north and all of a sudden you have to put on airs? Makes me sick."

When is my mom going to learn that Gam-Gam only seems to feel better when she's making other people feel bad? She is a MEAN MISTREATER. She is the Grinch and it's not even Christmas.

"Mama, you're being very hard on Marjorie. That's simply not fair," Auntie Marilyn says.

"'That's simply not fair,'" Gam-Gam repeats in a voice that is meant to mock Auntie Marilyn. She says this with her pinkie finger raised in the air. "You're as big a faker as Margie; you're just not as good at it yet, *Mary*. Oh, and I didn't name you Marilyn, so I'm not calling you that either."

My brother isn't paying any attention to what's happening at the table because he's snuck a *Sports Illustrated* into the dining room. The magazine is sitting on his lap, and he's glancing at it between bites of his salad. But Patrick and I are taking in the whole scene, and it's so uncomfortable. He reaches for my hand under the table and gives it a squeeze. His palms are really cold and dry. I can feel his pulse racing. Mine is, too.

Why is Gam-Gam so awful?

There's so much tension at the table I'm not even sure how anyone's going to be able to chew or swallow their food, when Miguel practically runs up to us with a tray full of drinks. "Oh, no!" he says, his voice real bright and cheery. "You asked for coffee and orange juice, but I accidentally bring a big, huge tray full of Bloody Marys. It's my mistake, so I am happy to leave the drinks for no charge. Otherwise I will have to throw them away. Can you help me out, please, and take them?"

The cocktails disappear off his tray, and I swear my parents look really grateful. After that, the meal is a little bit better, because the liquor takes some of the bite out of Gam-Gam. She stops telling Mom and Auntie Marilyn what's wrong with them and starts complaining about her other kids. Gam-Gam doesn't seem to like any of her children. She says they are all bums, worthless bums. I wonder if some of my aunts and uncles would have their acts together more if my Gam-Gam weren't so hard on them. They probably all stopped trying after a while.

I suspect my mom is never going to stop trying to get Gam-Gam's approval; nor is Auntie Marilyn, and that is too bad. They are both real good ladies, and they deserve to have come from someone better than Gam-Gam. They tell me all the time about the neat stuff Gam-Gam did when she was younger and about all of her business smarts. They say if she were raised in different times, Gam-Gam would be running a big company like Pepsi or Coke and that she used to be decent to them and rather sweet, but I sort of doubt it. I think she kind of ignored them.

Maybe Gam-Gam is why my mom is always after me to walk down the stairs instead of run, make a good first impression, use my napkin, chew with my mouth closed, pick up my bike, et cetera. Maybe she thinks if I turn out good enough, Gam-Gam will finally be happy.

Now that I'm thinking about it, sometimes my mom's constant instructions feel as suffocating as being hugged with Gam-Gam's arm flaps.

At least it's better than having a mother who ignores you. I know she wouldn't boss me around so much if she didn't love me.

CHAPTER FOURTEEN

To: christophersinclairjr@calmail.berkeley.edu

From: thefarmerfromthedells@hotmail.com

Date: June 26th

Subject: I bought a ticket

Hey—I'll make this brief because I know you're busy, but I bought my ticket to come out to San Francisco over the 4th of July. Let me just say this—expect to see fireworks.

XO

To: the_bride@kelseylovesmilo.com

From: the_groom@kelseylovesmilo.com

Date: June 26th

Subject: I'm so confused

Kelsey,

You're not answering texts, so I'm e-mailing you because I don't know what else to do.

Should I get you a ticket or not to see Owl City at the House of Blues in October?

I think I will err on the side of yes.

Hope to see you then!

Love,

Milo

BY THE NUMBERS

To: jessica@sinclairsartorial.com

From: interncassie@sinclairsartorial.com

Date: June 26th

Subject: awkward, but . . .

Hi, Jess,

I know this is, like, an unpaid internship and all, but I'm kinda broke, so I'm wondering if you can start giving me some money for all the work I'm doing? Because that would be supes great! Maybe just PayPal me five hundo to start, kewl? Kewl.

XO,

Cassie

. . . .

Jessica is sitting at the island in the kitchen when I come home. She's eating a bowl of miso soup and snorting derisively as she looks at fashion blogs on her iPad. When she finally notices me, she asks, "Where have you been?"

"Have you seen your grandparents?" I say by way of reply. Hey, check me out. I can be brusque, too.

"I have. They're old, they're fabulous, and the lady always smells like juniper berries and Shalimar."

"True, but not helpful. Specifically, where are they?"

"Specifically, they said they were playing bridge with the Cushmans, so they're probably at their house. Ew, how twisted would it be if they were actually all old swingers? Gross. Regardless, I bet *someone's* driving home twelve miles an hour with the blinker on the whole time tonight. Now, *specifically*, where were you?"

I actually feel a bit of pride in telling her where I've been. See? I'm young. I'm vibrant. I can do things. "I had a date."

"Pfft. Not in that outfit you didn't."

Well, that feeling of pride was short-lived.

"I think your mother looks nice," Chris says. He clatters into the kitchen on his Mobilegs crutches. (His neck brace is also gone.) He says he felt like FDR in the wheelchair, so he's been giving the crutches a whirl instead. I'm amazed at the advances in crutch technology since I used to bang myself up in pursuit of country club sportsmanship back in the seventies. I had these wooden Tiny Tim–style deals, with odd-smelling rubber grips and pads. I had to stuff washcloths under my arms to keep my skin from rubbing off, and I was perpetually sore. But Chris's Mobilegs are these ergonomic lunar-landing-looking things that are ventilated and spring-loaded and in no way appear to have come from a Charles Dickens novel. Sure they're still durable medical equipment, which is inherently not sexy, but they're the Lamborghini of durable medical equipment, so that has to count for something.

He says, "I'm just spitballing here, Jess, but if I showed up at someone's house uninvited and without a lot of explanation as to why I was there, I might try to be, you know, not horrible, as opposed to horrible."

"I'm here to help *you*, Dad," she replies, snapping shut her iPad, moral indignation set to eleven.

"I'm managing nicely and Sophie's taking me to PT, so you can probably go back to New York now," he says. "The worst of it's over. You should apologize or pack."

Jessica replies, "Listen, I'm not used to dealing with people from the Midwest anymore. I forgot that I have to sugarcoat every little thing here instead of just offering the truth as it is. My mistake."

"We should write down that apology and send it to all the greeting card companies because, *damn*," Chris says.

Chris claims he didn't hit his head when he fell and also that he was wearing a helmet, but I am not so sure. Where is the guy who constantly babies his daughters? Who perpetually gives them the benefit of the doubt? He's not letting her get away with any of her usual lip right now and *it is amazing!*

From the expression on Jessica's face, she's surprised, too, but she quickly composes herself. "What I meant, as a *professional stylist*, is that you went out to a social activity in a daytime, business look. It's late June and it's evening, so you could wear anything— you could do a sundress, a halter, a tunic, a romper—even, God help us all, capri pants—yet you opted for a summer-weight gray pantsuit with a white shell. No colorful scarves, no chunky jewelry, no strappy sandals. Nothing festive. An absence of joy or whimsy. Let me ask you something: Did you even take off your jacket so your date could get a peep of your reasonably toned arms?"

"I don't recall," I mumble.

"You arrived home five minutes ago. You don't recall what happened prior to five minutes ago?" she presses.

"The bar was chilly, so, no, I must have left my jacket on," I admit.

"This is what bothers me about your generation," Jessica says. "It's like you guys have given up. You don't even try. What, you think it's all over because you're fifty? Well, news flash, look at Mimsy. She's how old?"

"She tells people she's sixty."

"And they believe her because she's *fantastic!* She's got it going on. Follow her lead—she always has her hair set, her lipstick on, her nails just so, and the outfit always matches the occasion. No matter what, she's impeccable. I bet if Mimsy were a fashion blogger, she'd make a zillion dollars, because that shit is genuine."

"What's your point, Jessica?" Chris asks.

"I'm just saying that your generation is the first to claim, 'We can do it all!' but that is not necessarily true. Stuff has fallen through the cracks. Stuff like knowing how to present yourself for a date during your second act in life. You, PBS, have one speed, and that speed is set to business. You approach everything like it's a professional opportunity. Anything that falls outside the realm of business? Not your forte."

"Again, your not-horrible, guest-in-this-home point is?" Chris queries.

She shrugs. "I can better prepare you for your next date, if there is a next date, if the full Angela Merkel you're currently working didn't send him away screaming for mercy."

"*Bzzt.* Close, but still wrong. Try, 'Mom'—not PBS—'Mom, let me help you get ready before your next date. I have some ideas,'" Chris says.

Whoa. This is new.

Chris was not often one to straight-up take my side when it came to the kids. He'd do that infuriating devil's advocate business the times he wasn't openly supporting the opposing side when it came to anything having to do with them.

Jessica rolls her eyes. "Yes, Mom, I mean *that.*"

To Jessica, I say, "Thanks. I would welcome your input. Maybe we could go shopping? I'm sure I could use a little spice in my wardrobe. Patrick says my taste is way too vanilla."

Jessica rises, leaving her soup bowl exactly where it lies and her bar stool ajar. "What he calls vanilla, I call tragic. But with my help, you could probably avoid future train wrecks. Maybe not be basic as fuck, right? After all, you aren't getting any younger." With that, she trots up the back stairs.

Chris turns to me and says, "She's our perfect little angel sent straight from heaven."

We're silent for a beat and then both crack up for about thirty seconds. I can't remember the last time he and I stood in this kitchen and laughed together, and I didn't realize how much I missed it until right now.

Okay, why is this happening?

What am I *doing* here? I finally go on my first sort-of date and I spend the whole time comparing him to the guy I just divorced? I mean, yes, I really appreciate Chris stepping in and defending me to Jessica, because that's brand-new, but it doesn't exactly make up for everything that went awry. Come on, I need to be reasonable. A couple of laughs are nostalgic at best, but they can't change the past.

I need to focus. I have other priorities. I need to figure out what's going on with my folks, but since they aren't home right now, I have to get to the bottom of what's happening with the girls. I have a feeling that until I do, they aren't going anywhere. As in, my Realtor's having a lot of trouble showing the house with everyone hanging around here, so my primary mission needs to be Operation Empty Nest.

I compose myself and clear my throat. "Any guesses as to what's going on with Jessica?"

Chris replies, "Money trouble, but I don't know the extent. I've gotten a couple of odd calls from people looking for her, so what else could it be? I'd guess she can't afford to go back to New York right now, or else she would; hence the nonstop bitching about what's wrong with Glencoe. She's not here to take care of me. She came to one doctor's appointment and then asked me to make her a grilled cheese afterward. I think she swiped a few of my pain pills before I hid them, too. I didn't say anything because I didn't have it in me to fight."

I ease into Jessica's abandoned bar stool and push aside her bowl. "Why am I not surprised to hear this? The rules have never quite applied to her, have they?"

Chris takes the seat next to me. "I'm not playing the blame game here. All I'm saying is we spared the rod on that one."

"We should have spanked her?" I ask. "We both agreed corporal punishment was barbaric."

"I'm saying she's spoiled."

I nod vigorously. "Oh, yeah, that I see now. Hundred percent. Mostly my fault, too."

Chris gawps at me. "You've never said that out loud before."

I wave him off. "Of course I have."

"No, you haven't." He traces patterns in the marble with his fingertips as we speak. "Trust me here; this was an issue with us."

I say, "But it's so obvious. Her level of disrespect, her sense of entitlement, the idea that she's the center of the universe, the fact that she's never satisfied no matter what she's been given? All signs point to spoiled."

"I can't believe you admit she's spoiled."

I throw up my hands and let them drop in defeat. "Fine, I admit it. She's spoiled and I'm to blame. But where does that knowledge leave us? I can see with her being spoiled, she might feel like she deserves things she can't afford, and I imagine it's easy to get into trouble in such an expensive city. Chicago isn't cheap by any stretch of the imagination, yet if you do a cost-of-living comparison between the two cities, New York is twice as much. Then look at the goods and services index, the housing index, the transportation index—it's all so far above the national average. And let's be honest, she has *your* math skills, so . . ."

"So she can't do long division, but I still didn't spoil her." He taps the counter to punctuate his point.

"Oh, stop looking so damn smug. I've admitted I've been wrong before." Chris tries to wipe the smile off his self-righteous maw but is wholly unsuccessful. "The question is not about who was right here—"

He points to his chest. "Because the answer would be me."

"Not so fast, pal—let's figure out what the definition of 'spoiled' is. If you just mean giving her things she didn't deserve or earn, yes, that's all me, but if you're talking about making life a bit too easy in general, we probably share the blame. You were always there, clearing the path for her, toppling any obstacle in her way. The great love of accumulating stuff? That was all me. The sense of entitlement? Maybe more of a gray area."

"I suddenly feel slightly less smug."

"The question is, what do we do for her? Do we ask her? Do we have her tell us what's going on? Do we offer to help? I have an emergency fund set aside for her, although maybe that's the wrong move. However, I was skeptical when President Bush signed the TARP legislation, but ultimately the 2008 bailout was beneficial and the banks have paid back those loans with interest, so maybe that's the right way to go. There *is* precedent."

"Penny, Jessica's an adult. We let her figure it out. We can't parent her forever. We can't keep throwing goods and services at her."

I suck air in through my teeth. "And toppling the obstacles for her."

"Touché."

"So I should leave it alone for now?"

"I would, at least short-term."

"What about the other one?" I ask, referring to Kelsey. "Has she told you anything? Have you spoken with Milo?"

"You know what? He's been texting me and I haven't gotten back to him yet. I'll give him a buzz right now. Let me put him on speakerphone and you can listen in."

"Is she home?" I ask.

"No. Zara came and got her and Caroline earlier."

"Ah," I say. "I thought things seem less destroyed around here."

"You're probably not going to say that when you see the dining room." He dials, and Milo picks up on the second ring. "Hi, Milo. It's Chris. I've got you on speakerphone here with me and Penny."

"Hey, good to talk to you. Thanks for calling me. It's funny. I kinda forgot what my ringtone was on this thing. No one ever calls me. Wow, ringtones, man, right? So, how you gettin' along? You feeling okay?"

"I've been better, but thanks for asking," Chris says. "Listen, Milo, Kelsey hasn't told us anything, and we really don't want to be in the middle of this. But if there's anything we can do to facilitate or mediate between the two of you . . ." He trails off, unsure of how to continue. Neither one of us has a clue as to what grievous trespass Milo has committed, but it must be significant for Kelsey to abandon her whole new marriage/life.

Milo says, "You guys know about Caroline."

"Sort of," Chris says. He shrugs at me, and I do the same. Neither of us have heard anything about his ex coming back into the picture, so this is a surprise. No wonder Kelsey was furious. "But why don't you give us your perspective?"

"We just need to find this peaceable coexistence thing, right?" Milo says.

"Sure," I say. I mouth, *I thought she moved away,* and Chris bobs his head in agreement.

"But Kelsey won't, like, let it go, man. She keeps bringing it up," he says.

"She keeps bringing up what specifically?" Chris asks.

"Sleeping with Caroline."

We both grimace. This is not an appropriate in-law discussion, yet here we are. We had an HR seminar at the firm recently about millennials in the workplace, and one of the facts we learned is that they crave a personal connection with their boss. This must somehow extend to families, and it seems that Milo would like that same kind of buddy-buddy relationship with us.

Aces.

Milo tells us, "I don't want to sleep with Caroline."

We also learned that millennials thrive on lots of positive feedback. "Well, that's outstanding!" I say, and Chris tilts his head at me, confused at my reaction.

"I mean, have you gotten a whiff of her?"

"A whiff of Caroline?" Chris clarifies.

"Yeah, she smells like old sourdough rolls or a wet welcome mat."

Millennials also appreciate the feeling of having been heard. I say, "Oh, does she use that crystal deodorant because she's afraid of the aluminum in traditional antiperspirant? You know, the National Cancer Institute found no conclusive evidence linking antiperspirants to the development of tumors in breast tissue. Of course, she should still conduct her regular monthly self-exam, but do tell her she could put Secret back on her shopping list."

"What?" Milo says.

I notice Chris silently shaking, with tears streaming down his cheeks. He holds up his hands like he's begging for a treat, sticks out his tongue, and begins to pant.

Oh.

Different Caroline. Dog Caroline, not person Caroline.

Chris has to blot his eyes while Milo speaks. "Anyway, we only have a queen-sized mattress, and she's, like, a really big, huge dog. I'm, like, 'We can put a dog bed in our room—that would be totally chill—but she's too massive to snooze in our bed,' but Kelsey kept insisting."

"And that's why she left?" I confirm.

"Mostly, yeah, but some of it was about the money."

"What money is that?" Chris asks.

"My trust," he replies. "Kelsey wants to use money out of it to hire someone to cook and clean around here, but that's cray-cray. I said, 'You don't even have anything else going on until the baby comes. At least you could take care of the household stuff.'"

"Um, Milo? Can you repeat that?" Chris says, suddenly quite sober.

"Which part? The part about hiring a cleaning lady or the part where I said, 'You don't even have anything else going on until the baby comes. At least you could take care of the household stuff.'"

I find myself inadvertently squeezing the stuffing out of Chris's arm. He gently loosens my grip around his biceps, and he clears his throat. "So would you say your fight was more about the child the two of you are expecting together and less about a dog? Is that what you're telling me? Am I getting a clear picture here?"

Milo considers this. "I guess that's accurate, yeah."

I catch my breath and say, "Milo, are you familiar with the concept of burying the lede?"

"Is that, like, a college thing?" he asks.

"It's a journalism thing," I reply. "The lede is where you start with the most important part of the story." I sigh. "Now, what's this about a trust? Is that important? I don't want to pry as it's none of my business, but are these funds enough to cover paying someone to work in your home?"

Milo says, "Aw, yeah. My family owns the largest dairy farm

in Ohio and a bunch of Wendy's restaurants. Maybe we're up to twenty by now? Didn't Kelsey ever tell you that?"

"Apparently Kelsey doesn't tell me a lot of things," I say.

"But it's real important to me to make it on my own. That's why I don't want to touch any of the money," he says. "Anyway, the whole dog thing was a test run for us being parents. We're young, you know. Most people in our generation wait until their thirties to start having kids, if they're gonna have them at all. We're—what do you call it on a bell curve—outfielders? Outhousers?"

"Outliers," I supply.

"Yeah, we're those. Anyway, I figure she'll calm down soon enough and we'll figure it all out. I just wanted to touch base with you guys and see where she was at, since she's not talking to me."

"She and the dog are out with Zara, so I can't speak to what she's thinking right this minute," Chris says. "Soon as I know more, I'll get back to you. That sound okay?"

"Most definitely."

"We'll talk soon then, Milo. Good-bye," Chris says.

"Bye," I add.

"Later, GeMaw and PePaw!" He hangs up.

I point a finger at Chris. "Oh, *hell*, no. We are not using those as our names. We are going to be Grandmother and Grandfather or something of the like. This family has an unlimited propensity for generating stupid grandparent names, and that stops right here. No more Gam-Gam. No more Num-Num. No more Mimsy or Gumpy or Bonpa. None of it. Not happening."

"Jesus tap-dancing Christ, we're going to be grandparents," Chris says, holding his face between his palms, with his arms propped up on the counter.

"Yeah, happens sometimes, despite precautions," I say. "Happened early for us. Now we know why her dress didn't fit."

Chris is taking this a lot harder than I am. "I'm going to be someone's grandfather. How does that work? Do I buy a cardigan and a bunch of hard candies? Am I going to start carrying around bags of bread so I can feed ducks? I'm not ready to be a grandfather. I never even bought my motorcycle."

"You wanted a motorcycle? Since when?"

He seems awfully upset. "No, but I wanted the *option* to buy a motorcycle."

"I'm sure someone will still sell you a motorcycle. There's no grandparent portion of the credit check."

"What, they're going to try to put me on one of those massive three-wheeled kinds? Or one of the four-wheeled jobs with so much trim it may as well be a riding lawn mower?"

I cover his hand with mine and run my thumb over his knuckles. "You're missing the bigger point here."

He takes a couple of breaths and tries to collect himself. "That our childlike daughter is going to be a parent herself in the next nine months?"

"No, that if Stassi hadn't dumped you already, you'd definitely be over now." Then I bust out laughing while he turns fifty shades of red.

I get up and grab a bottle of wine from the fridge and two glasses from the cabinet next to it.

He glowers at me. "We are NOT cool."

I place one glass in front of him and one in front of me, pouring a healthy measure of chardonnay in each. He's stiff when I come in behind him for a hug and kiss him on the cheek.

"You're absolutely wrong, Christopher Sinclair. We are finally cool."

· · · ·

I read the guide's description for *Love, Again* on the Hallmark Channel. "A couple on the brink of divorce decides to keep their marital woes a secret as they help their daughter plan her wedding. As the two work together on the happy occasion, they discover their own marriage might just be worth saving."

"Hey, that sounds just like us," Chris says.

"Go home; you're drunk," I tell him. "(A) We were already divorced at Kelsey's wedding, (b) there was no secret about it, and (c) my glass is empty. Do you need a refill?"

"Just bring the bottle. So we're not watching this movie, right?"

"Oh, no, we're absolutely watching the movie; we're just not identifying with it."

"Okay."

I pour more wine for both of us and settle back into the family room couch. After hearing the news about Kelsey, Chris seemed to be on the verge of a midlife freak-out, so I decided he could use a friend. And a drink. He hasn't had any pain pills in a few days, so he figures he's okay as long as he doesn't go crazy and pound shots, even though he's tempted.

The movie begins, but he grabs the remote and presses pause. "You spoiled Jessica. Mostly."

"We established that earlier. What's your point?"

"I think Kelsey might be my fault. Mostly."

I sit up straight. "How do you figure?"

Chris grips his wineglass. "I didn't allow her to fail. I let her quit when things got hard, or I fixed them for her, but I never permitted her just to go belly-up. She never felt the consequences of her actions. I meant to protect her. I didn't want her to know what it felt like to screw up so spectacularly that she almost lost everything, like I did with Elm Street."

"But you had the best of intentions there. And it's not like I jumped in and said, 'No, no, let her ship sink.' I probably wasn't even there enough to see that she wasn't being allowed to go down like the wreck of the *Edmund Fitzgerald*. Let's be honest—if I had noticed, then I wouldn't have let her fail, either. This isn't all you; it's on both of us."

"Her problem is she now goes through life like Mr. Bean, setting calamities in motion behind her and never once looking back to see the havoc she's created. I've done her a terrible disservice and I don't know how to fix her."

I place my arm around Chris and put my head on his shoulder. "We weren't great at this parenting thing, were we? For all our education and our plans and our hopes and our lofty dreams, we kind of sucked out loud."

"Why is that?" he asks. "How did we go wrong?"

"I don't know. What's sad is that our parents with their three-martini lunches, smoking while we were in utero, not making us wear seat belts or bike helmets, and telling us to go play outside and not come home until dark did a better job than we did."

"They sort of did. That's bullshit."

"Right? You and I? We turned out to be two fairly well-adjusted grown-ups. For all our big talk about happiness and success, we have two miserable daughters trapped in a state of arrested development."

"We tried so hard. We tried so goddamned hard," he says,

laying his head on mine. "How do you work so hard and mess it up so much?"

"I have no idea. Statistically, it seems impossible, yet here we are. Will we be better at grandchildren? Maybe if it's a boy, he'll be—whoa. Wait. Wait a hot damn minute." I grab Chris's arm. "Topher is okay."

"What?"

"Topher. He's happy. He's well-adjusted. He graduated and got a phenomenal job. He takes care of himself. He doesn't live here. We have a thirty-three percent success rate! We're not total failures!"

Chris's entire face lights up with joy at realizing we're not complete washouts. "You're right! He's a great kid with his act fully together. He's pretty mad at me, but I kind of deserve it."

I poke him hard in the gut, and he grunts. "Hell, yes, you deserve it! You wrecked smooth jazz for everyone, but otherwise, TOPHER IS OKAY! We didn't ruin him!"

We both high-five and cheer and hug each other, and suddenly I'm enveloped in his familiar citrus and cinnamon cologne and I don't care about my stupid rules or what's most logical. I can only say that this feels right in this moment. He holds me tightly, too, and when we do finally release, we stay locked in each other's gaze.

I can't predict what might have happened next, given the intoxicating combination of the news of the night, the profound level of honesty, and the aphrodisiac better known as the Hallmark Movie Channel, but the spell is broken when we hear my parents come clattering in the back door and up the stairs in the kitchen.

We pull apart, saying our good nights immediately, and heading to bed separately.

Which is probably for the best.

I think.

CHAPTER FIFTEEN

To: penelopesinclair@colbyaustinwaterstone.com

From: doctorstephenvora@
northwesternmedicalphysiciansgroup.com

Date: June 26th

Subject: All clear

Dear Mrs. Sinclair,

Per my voice mail, I'm attaching the results from Maxwell
Sinclair's CT scan and MRI. As stated, there is no evidence
of stroke, brain tumor, blood vessel damage, or shrinking of
the frontal or temporal lobe. In short, this is good news that
we can discuss further at your father's next appointment.

Please call the office if you have additional questions before
then.

Sincerely,

Dr. S. Vora

. . . .

n my dream, I'm coming home from my internship at the insurance company during the summer of 1984, clad in Reeboks and one of Marjorie's old suits with the giant David Byrne–type shoulder pads. I can't say if the jacket was really this wide in the shoulders or if everything is slightly exaggerated in this illusory state, but most other parts of the memory remain true to life, rather than surreal, like how the other commuters are reading the *Sun-Times* or listening to their Walkmans or sipping Old Style tallboys.

Chris is picking me up from the train station, fresh off the day's roofing job. We make an odd pair, me in my grown-up business attire and him in grimy jeans, work boots, and a sweat-stained Elvis Costello T-shirt. When Marjorie witnessed this dichotomy for herself the first time, she had a fit. She began to meddle relentlessly, and I allowed her to get into my head. I let her convince me that being with Chris was a risk I couldn't afford to take, not if I wanted a proper future.

It's Tuesday, the third of July, the day I tell Chris that our relationship isn't going anywhere and we need to break up. I feel a sense of dread and loss because of this. I know how this dream goes because it reoccurs whenever I'm under stress or going through a transitional period.

The tiny part of me that is conscious tries to fully wake myself. I know that if I can just rouse myself, everything will be okay. Barring that, I can reach out and Chris will be next to me.

I'm too tired to open my eyes, so I roll over and there he is. I can feel the warmth from his body and I press up against him. I smile to myself. It was only a bad dream. I can relax again. I inhale, expecting the faint scent of cloves and cinnamon and citrus.

Instead, I smell . . . a wet welcome mat?

I open my eyes in the gray light of predawn to find myself snuggled up next to Caroline, who's resting her massive head on the pillow next to me. She's spread out along the length of the bed. She's literally the size of another person. No wonder Milo didn't want her in bed with them. She notices me looking at her and gazes back at me with her soulful cocoa-colored eyes. She thumps her tail and gently touches my shoulder with one of her massive paws. I believe she's trying to hug me, like the large, cuddly, foul-smelling teddy bear that she is.

You know what? I'm not made of stone.

I allow this.

I bet with a trip to the groomer and a few (dozen) sessions with a trainer, Caroline has the potential to be a fine family dog. She shifts and rests her massive head on my hip, exhaling with pure contentment.

Yeah, this is sweet.

As I lie here with my new best friend, I try to interpret my reaction to the dream. Is it odd that my subconscious is still root-ing for me/expecting me to be with Chris? I mean, we definitely have a history together, and I can't discount that. If the past few weeks are any indication, we'll absolutely be friends going for-ward. And, there's still chemistry. There never wasn't chemistry. Hell, at times all we had was chemistry.

The hurdle I can't leap over, the part that gives me pause, what I'm afraid I can't get past, what made me march up the stairs last night instead of dive into the pullout bed in the den was the numbers.

I say to Caroline, "How can I trust him again when there's so little empirical evidence that getting back together is a good idea?

According to one survey, up to sixty percent of men who have cheated would cheat again. I can't go through this again. I can't put my friends through this again. I can't buy more spite-pillows. I can't add more weight to my kettlebell workouts; *I'll* start looking like the Rock."

Caroline keeps her gaze focused on me. I know she can't understand anything I'm saying, but it feels as though she's listening to me.

I tell her, "Another study shows that men who cheat are three point five times more likely to do it again. These aren't even men who claim to be unhappy in their marriages! I recently read about a poll in which seventy-four percent of male respondents admitted they'd have an affair if they knew they wouldn't get caught. What? Women aren't much better, with sixty-eight percent ready to hop into bed with someone else, provided it's risk-free."

She nudges my hand to indicate her desire to be petted. Her fur, aromatic though it may be, is surprisingly silky.

"Why, Caroline? What is so wrong with everyone's lives that this sounds like a fine alternative? Doesn't anyone just want to watch television sometimes? *Empire* is a really good show. Maybe you'll see it with me sometime and we can have cheese. I bet you'd like that. But my point is, isn't anybody guided by a moral compass anymore? Doesn't anyone want to be with their one and only not because they're afraid they'll be busted but because they can't imagine life with someone else? Don't they long to grow old with their original lobster? (It's a *Friends* reference, Caroline. That was a good show, too.) Why are so many willing to do the unspeakable as long as no one's looking? Isn't the definition of a decent human being someone who does the right thing even when no one can see it? Would people also be as likely to commit crimes like robbery or murder if there were no chance of getting caught? Oh, Caroline. I don't get people. I really don't."

She burrows in close to me as if to say, *You raise many valid questions, and yet it's still so very early. Perhaps we'll find some answers if we quiet ourselves for a moment.* She lays her paw on my chest, as if to calm me.

The dog may be onto something.

Perhaps I will sleep on this a bit more.

· · · ·

When I wake up, Caroline is gone, having left a trail of destruction in her wake. For a minute I think it's snowed in my bedroom and I'm reminded of the early days in the house when that was a real possibility. I quickly realize Caroline has discovered the cache of pillows on the window seat, and now there's a solid foot of free-floating down along the side of my bed. I'm not angry with Caroline, though; I can't be mad at her for never having been taught the rules.

I can certainly be mad at Kelsey for her level of irresponsibility, however. I wonder if Kelsey can even have a dog in her apartment. It would be just like her to not bother checking first. This frustrates me because almost thirty percent of all animals relinquished to shelters are there because their residences don't allow pets.

I take my iPhone out of the nightstand drawer and snap a couple of shots. I'm not on Facebook much (when I'm not stalking), but this should make for a funny visual.

By the time I have everything cleaned up, the house is empty. Even Chris is gone. His sister Sophie lives a couple of towns to the west, and she's been chauffeuring him to his physical therapy appointments. I find myself disappointed not to be able to share the feather carnage photos with him in person. I thought he'd get a real "I told you extra bed pillows were trouble" kind of kick out of them.

I run my normal Saturday errands, and when I arrive home, I notice Blanca, my cleaning lady, sitting on my front porch. I park out front and jog up the front steps.

"Hey, Blanca, what are you doing here on a Saturday? Did I forget to leave you a check?"

When she stands, I realize the woman I'm speaking to isn't Blanca, but a beautifully dressed doppelgänger. They have the same caramel-colored hair, tawny skin, and green eyes and are quite similar in height and weight.

I say, "I'm so sorry—I thought you were someone else. Can I help you with something?"

"Yes, hello. You're Mrs. Sinclair? Hi. I'm Lise Westerfield. Kathy showed me your house a few weeks ago."

I redden, remembering the incident. "Oh, yes, I'm so sorry about that. You met my daughter and my father. Lucky you."

"Your father also called me Blanca. I must resemble her quite closely. Anyway, Kathy tells me you have temporarily pulled your listing. Is this true? My husband and I have looked at so many homes since then, and none of them hold a candle to this place." She gives an embarrassed laugh and shifts her weight. "I'm not even sure why I'm here. I was driving by and I just wanted to see it again so badly."

"Well, I'm not taking the house off the market, per se," I explain. "I'm just having a few family issues—as you witnessed— so I'm holding off on showing the place for a few weeks."

"You have not accepted another bid, then?"

"No, I haven't done that," I say.

She begins to bounce on her heels and then catches herself. "My husband says I should never play poker because I would be so terrible. But I am very happy to know that. You will hear from us soon. Thank you!"

Mrs. Westerfield practically dances down the walkway into her car. No, she should definitely not play poker. While I'm excited about a potential offer on the house, what's really caught my attention is my father mistaking her for Blanca, whom he's met only a few times. What I assumed was garden-variety racism on his part was actually fairly astute recall on a small detail. And terrible manners, but not straight-up xenophobia.

Between this and his clean test results, I'm more confused than ever as to what's going on with him. But I'm going to get some clarity, and soon.

I open the front door, and the house is still quiet. I'm surprised Chris isn't back yet. He's never at PT this long—I hope everything's okay. I head down to the den to drop off the bag of miniature Milky Way bars I bought for him (no nuts; God help everyone if there are nuts in his chocolate), and I'm taken aback when I find his room empty. All of his things are gone, and there's a note with my name on it tented on the coffee table in front of the couch.

Hey, Pen,

I feel like my being here is muddying the waters for you, so I'm going to bunk at Soph's while I find a new place. Thank you so much for having me here. I'll have my crew swing by at the beginning of the week to disassemble the ramp. If you need more

help with the girls, give me a shout. But, remember, you can't
go wrong if you simply acknowledge and proceed.

Your partner in thirty-three percent success,
Chris

I read his note a couple of times.

Yes.

This is logical. Him leaving makes the most sense. What were we doing, trying to play house all over again, like the past had never happened? We had proceeded but we never quite acknowledged, and ultimately that was never going to work.

This is for the best.

So why do I feel like I want to cry?

• • • •

"Are you sitting down?"

"I'm at my desk, so, yes, I'm seated," I reply. I've been in a daze ever since this weekend. I feel like there's been a thick fog in my head and I'm having trouble concentrating on anything. I completely slept through my workout this morning and had to be prompted twice in my first meeting of the day. What's wrong with me? I'm supposed to meet with Mr. Waterstone and the rest of the EVPs later today to make my promotion official, and I have to snap out of it by then, lest they believe they've made a huge mistake.

"Well," Kathy says, "we received an offer on the house from the Westerfields and it's a good one. They're an all-cash buyer, no contingencies, they're asking for a quick close and—here's where I want you to be sitting—they're coming in *above* your asking price."

"Wow."

Is Mercury in retrograde or something? I don't actually believe in astrology, but surely there's some explanation for why everything feels so off, why my rhythms are so out of sync.

I can't concentrate on any of my work because every single thing at home is an unfinished piece of business. Is Kelsey going to be a single mother? Is Kelsey going to be a single mother in my house? Is Kelsey going to decide she's bored with being a single mother and just run off and leave her baby with me like so many unwanted chapati pans? When am I even allowed to approach her about her whole situation?

What about Jessica? Who keeps calling for her? Exactly how much does she owe? At what point can I intervene? Is there anything I can do to guide her in the direction of maybe, possibly being slightly less miserable even for a minute?

And how about Marjorie and Max? What is going on there? Are they actually dodging me, or are they truly that popular? Who has a social calendar like that? What are the both of them hiding? Why won't anyone tell me anything?

"*Wow?*" she repeats. "You don't even want to know how *much* wow? There's a lot of wow to be had."

"Oh, yeah, I guess so."

We discuss numbers, and for the first time in my life, they're utterly and completely meaningless. I don't even bother writing them down. All they represent is a doorway to everything unknown. This whole time I've been saying that I need a change, but . . . what if I don't? What if a change is the one thing that will make me less happy? What if boxing up twenty-seven years' worth of memories, for lack of a better term, blows goats? What if change is the worst possible choice?

What if the familiarity of my present surroundings is the one thing that's keeping me from flying off the rails right now? I'm on the cusp of being promoted to executive vice president; it's all done save for the handshakes later today. Do I really need to add a change of scenery on top of the already great transformations to come professionally?

Hold on. . . . Am I even interested in the great transformations to come professionally?

Do I *want* to be an executive vice president with all the additional duties and responsibilities the position entails? Do I actually *want* to completely and entirely give up on the math and focus on the management?

The great irony here is that I spend all day, every day, enmeshed in analysis, and at no point have I truly examined the data points of the new position. Chances are, this will be a job I'll hate for a dozen reasons, but mostly because instead of playing to my strengths, I'll have to forgo numbers for people. This dynamic didn't work out with Smith Barney when the stakes were minimal, and I can't imagine what might happen now that they're so high.

In this moment of self-reflection, I feel like those ladies on the dating show Patrick makes me watch. A few seasons ago, all these beautiful women were fighting like mad to win the heart of an Iowa hog farmer. They were ruthless in trying to capture his interest, employing every single one of their feminine wiles. Toward the end of the show, it began to dawn on some of the gals that the victory, sweet though it might be, ultimately would result in the grand prize of *life on an Iowa hog farm.*

That's because it's one thing to say, "I love you so much, Bachelor Chris, that I would be happy to imagine my life on a hog farm in Iowa," and it's another thing entirely to actually go there and smell the place for yourself.

I believe today's the first day I've actually stood downwind (metaphorically) of the EVP position and I'm honestly wondering if I wouldn't be a lot happier just buying my (metaphorical) bacon in the little plastic packages at the grocery store.

Plus, I'm going to be someone's mother's mother in less than nine months. (I haven't figured out the specific term I want to be called yet.) Regardless of name, the position is not insignificant. Do I look forward to spending the next ten years on a plane or in a meeting while this kid turns into a preteen without ever having gotten to know me? I feel like I'm right on the edge of vast and limitless space, and if I don't put on the brakes, I'm going to careen endlessly, tumbling head over foot for all eternity like Sandra Bullock's character in *Gravity*, except I don't have a George Clooney to catch me by the ankle before it's too late.

A bead of sweat travels from my temple down my cheek. I feel like I'm fighting to pull air into my lungs and my heart is pounding so loudly that I'm surprised Adrienne can't hear it from her desk on the other side of the wall. Am I having a panic attack? Or is this the actual, physical manifestation of a midlife crisis?

Am I leaving here to buy a convertible and procure a spray tan? Or am I Chris and his mythological motorcycle right now?

My head hurts.

I hear Kathy clear her throat on the other end of the line.

I try to regain my senses. "Kathy, this sounds great, but clearly this is a big decision and I will need to look at the deal from all angles," I tell her.

"Of course. I don't expect a reply now. This offer's on the table for the next forty-eight hours; please give it your full consideration, but know it's a great deal."

"Okay, thanks for all your hard work, Kathy. Bye-bye." I try to regulate my breath. Calming yogic breath in through the nose, exhale through the mouth. Again. I do this a couple of times, and it seems to help.

I hang up and dial Patrick. His assistant answers the phone. "Hello. You've reached Walsh, Kahn, and Partners Integrated Marketing Solutions. This is Alysin, Patrick Walsh's assistant. How may I help you?"

"Hi, Alysin; it's Penny. Is he in?" I ask.

"He's not in the office, but I'll put you through to his cell phone," she says. "This will just take a second."

For all of my complaints about the millennial generation, they are at ease doing the kinds of things with technology I never dreamed possible, like transferring a phone call from a landline to a mobile device.

After a couple of long beeps, I hear Patrick pick up.

"Penny! What's up?"

Without any preamble, I ask him, "Am I crazy?"

Without hesitation, he answers, "Yes."

"Really?"

"No. But how else do you expect me to answer when you ask like that? What's going on?"

"I'm on the verge of getting everything I've been working for, and now I'm not sure I want any of it."

"Intriguing. Continue."

"I want to know if that's crazy."

"Do you mean, is it crazy to change your mind? No. You're

allowed to change your mind. What is it you're not sure you want now?"

"For starters, I'm not sure I want to sell my house."

"Fair enough. You've been there half your life."

"And I'm not sure I want to be an EVP."

"Hmmm. In the immortal words of the Notorious B.I.G, 'Mo money, mo problems.' You saw how that worked out for him, so that might not be the worst decision."

"Actually, I'm not familiar with him. Was he a drag queen, too?"

Patrick barks with laughter. "Definitely not. But Biggie is not germane to the discussion. Your takeaway is that only you know what's right for you."

"The last thing is I'm not sure I'm ready to date Wyatt."

"Again, intriguing. I thought after the whole Moscow Mule thing—Close Mum Ow, and damn it, he's got me doing it now— you kind of liked his vibe. How much of this is because of your almost mash-session on the couch with the former Mr. Penelope Bancroft Sinclair afterward?"

I can keep no secrets from Patrick, whether I like it or not. Within five minutes of casual chatter on Saturday, he had me spilling each and every bean.

"At least thirty-three percent," I admit.

"Penny, you always say you don't know people; you know numbers. Well, guess what. *I* know people. As a marketer, I'm paid to read people for a living. What you have to realize is that people can change. You're so afraid of history repeating itself that *you fail to recognize that history can also learn from itself.* I said that part in italics because it's that important. Now, I'm going to do you a tremendous favor. We're ending this conversation and you're just going to sit with what I've said. Mull it over. Let it sink in."

In the background I hear a voice say, "That'll be seven dollars and twenty-nine cents, please. Do you need any ketchup for your fries, sir?"

"Hold on, Patrick, are you at a *drive-through*?"

"What? Are you kidding? Ew, I would never! No!"

"Thank you for stopping at McDonald's and have a nice day!" the voice says.

I laugh. "You're *so* busted."

He sputters, "I didn't—you can't—"

"The good news, Patrick, is you just illustrated your own point. People *can* change. Thank you. Please enjoy your Quarter Pounder with cheese."

"Listen, it's not a Quarter Pounder. It's a Filet-O—whatever." He sighs with resignation. "Just don't tell Michael, okay?"

"Pinkie swear."

By the time we hang up, my path is clear.

• • • •

I don't know whether or not I made the right decision, but what's important is that I made a decision. I could have hemmed and hawed for the next day, the next week, the next month, debating my options, weighing the odds, running the numbers. Instead, I looked deep into myself and went with how I felt.

Granted, a lot of people make a lot of stupid decisions following this very protocol. But if that's the case, then I live with the results. Again, at least it's a decision.

So, while I'm not overjoyed or jubilant when I walk in the

back door, I do feel a sense of calm. Surprisingly enough, Max is there at the counter, reading the paper.

"I feel like I haven't seen you in ages," I say. "We need to talk."

"So talk," he says, patting the seat next to him. "What's stopping you?"

"Mainly your never being here. My God, it's like I need to give you a curfew or something. The two of you are out gallivanting at all hours! You know that the Center for Disease Control says that STDs are spreading like wildfire through the senior population? Syphilis is up fifty-two percent."

He cocks an eyebrow at me. "This is what you think your mother and I are doing? Giving the Cushmans the clap? Get your mind out of the toilet, Penelope. We're usually playing bridge. If we're feeling wild? Canasta."

"No, that's not what I'm saying. I mean, it sounds like yours is the only generation out there having any fun."

"That's a problem? Didn't we earn the right?"

Before I can answer him, Caroline comes shuffling into the kitchen, which is about fifteen miles an hour slower than she usually travels. "Hey, does she seem okay to you?" I ask.

"I don't know. I just got home. She doesn't have her normal level of enthusiasm, though. I'll say that," he replies. "She didn't even try to knock me over when I came in. I said to her, 'Dog, you're slipping.'"

"Is Kelsey here?"

He gestures with his thumb. "Upstairs."

Caroline begins to hack and lets forth a small pool of clear vomit. I grab some paper towels to mop up after her. She vomits again, and this time I notice something odd in the pool.

A Milky Way wrapper.

Oh, no.

I could have sworn I put the chocolates on a high shelf in the pantry, far away from anywhere Caroline could reach, even if she stood on her back paws. I run up the stairs to Kelsey's room, where I find her watching a show on her laptop, the package of Milky Ways open and scattered across the bed. There are only a few of them left.

"Kelsey, did the dog get into the chocolate?"

She presses pause on her computer. "Well, hello to you, too."

"Kelsey, please, this is important. Did the dog get into the chocolate?"

"What chocolate?"

"This chocolate, here? All around you? That is toxic to her. Did she eat any while you were sitting here?"

"Um, I don't know?" She shrugs and presses play.

"You don't know? Were you paying attention? You understand what 'toxic' means, right?"

"Don't talk to me like I'm a dummy," she says. "I know what 'toxic' means."

Instead of getting louder, my voice becomes very quiet. "Then do you understand that this dog—your dog—may have consumed an amount of a substance that could not only hurt her but could cause her to die?"

"Uh-huh?"

"This life—that you are responsible for—is possibly in jeopardy. What are you going to do about it?"

She stretches and puts a hand on her stomach. "Can you not yell at me for once? I don't know what to do. I don't feel well."

"Yes. Caroline doesn't feel well either. She's vomiting all over the kitchen."

"Gross."

I am incredulous. "Gross? Is that all you have to offer here?"

"What am I supposed to do?" Kelsey whines. "Dogs don't come with a manual or anything. Do I Google 'Milky Way'? This is hard. How am I supposed to figure this out? Maybe you could just do it?"

"Do you not feel your maternal instinct kicking in? Don't you want to scoop this dog up and protect her and do everything you can to make it right for her?"

She pats her abdomen. "I can't lift the dog or anything; I feel like it would be bad for the baby."

"I'm taking Caroline to the emergency vet now."

"Cool. Later."

"La-ter?" I repeat, enunciating both syllables.

"As in 'see you'?"

That's it. I'm done here. "You will be gone when I get back."

"Did you not hear me? I said I don't feel good. I don't know what else you want me to do."

"Kelsey, I'm going to do you a tremendous favor that you won't understand or appreciate right now, but someday you and your baby will thank me. GET OUT OF MY HOUSE. GET OUT NOW. TAKE YOUR SHIT AND GO. YOU ARE NO LONGER WELCOME HERE. I DON'T CARE WHERE YOU GO. I DON'T CARE WHAT YOU DO. I SUGGEST YOU GO BACK TO MILO AND GROW THE HELL UP BEFORE YOU BRING ANOTHER LIFE INTO THIS WORLD, BUT IF YOU DON'T, THAT IS NO LONGER MY PROBLEM."

Kelsey's chin is pretty much resting on her chest when I'm finished and her eyes are saucers.

"By the way, Kelsey? *That* was yelling. And Caroline belongs to me now."

CHAPTER SIXTEEN

To: penelopebancroftsinclair@yahoo.com

From: wyattchapin@hotmail.com

Date: July 1st

Subject: Fireworks!

Hello, Penny!

I tried calling you, but I'm not sure if your cell phone is still at the bottom of a Newfoundland, so I'm e-mailing just in case. I'd like to cordially invite you to our first official dinner date of the new millennium. If you're free, please join me on Friday night at Michael in Winnetka at 8:00 p.m.

Looking forward to hearing from you!

Wyatt

. . . .

"So . . . how's tricks?"

"Chris, I'm kind of in the middle of something," I reply.

"I know," he says, taking on a more somber tone. "I wanted to see how Caroline's faring."

I'm sitting in the waiting area of the twenty-four-hour emergency vet twelve miles to the west. I don't even want to consider the traffic laws I broke to get here, but I arrived in less than seven minutes. "The vet believes she's going to be okay because I got her here in time. Right now they're forcing vomiting and they'll pump her stomach with fluids. Poor thing. She was starting to convulse. They're doing something with charcoal to keep the toxins from getting into her bloodstream, too. I'm just thankful you don't like dark chocolate or almonds, or we'd have really been in trouble."

"Why is that?"

"She ate the medicinal bag of Milky Ways I bought for you."

"Oh." He's quiet for a beat. "Anyway . . . Kelsey called."

It's my turn to pause before replying. "Yes, I imagine she did. What did you say to her?"

"I apologized."

"Terrific. Listen, I've got to—"

"No, you're misunderstanding, Penny. I apologized to her for having made things too easy her whole life. I said I was sorry that I never let her fail, that I never let her experience consequences. I told her that my belated wedding present was to allow her to handle this situation with you on her own. Then I wished her well and asked her to let me know where she was planning to settle. Told her I loved her and then I hung up."

"Whoa. How badly do you want to go and help her right now anyway?"

"I made Sophie confiscate my crutches and my chair; I can't be trusted. Every fiber in my being is like, 'Daddy's coming!'"

I can't help but laugh. "When do you anticipate she starts speaking to us again?"

"Hard to say. But Milo texted me. He's on his way to pick her up. She's going home. To her home."

"You're telling me we did the right thing? Both of us? Does this bring us up to a sixty-six percent success rate?"

"Maybe so."

"Ha! We're on a winning streak. Hot damn. I should buy a Lotto ticket, because I even managed to run into Max today. You know, all of his tests came back fine? Even the MRI and CT scan. And he seems totally present. He helped me load the dog in the car. As I was leaving, he said if I wanted to talk to him, I should meet him at the Green Bay Café tomorrow in Winnetka. Says he has lunch there every week with Miguel."

"Miguel? How do I know Miguel? The nice old waiter from the club?"

"Yeah."

"That can't be right."

"I know. But I'll at least try him there tomorrow and see who he actually meant."

"You're not working?"

"Interesting development. I—" Before I can explain what trans-pired, the vet tech calls me into the room where Caroline's being treated. "Oh, shoot. They're ready for me. I have to sign off. But, Chris? Thank you for having my back. You're kind of my hero right now."

"Penny, that has always been my goal."

I feel my cheeks flush as I turn off my phone.

I follow the tech through the sprawling waiting area, populated with other nervous pet owners. This clinic serves many special pet needs during the day, from hydrotherapy to animal behavior to oncology to nephrology. But if anyone is here after hours, they're experiencing an emergency, and I pray their outcomes will be positive, too.

I enter the room where Caroline is being treated. Three techs had to hoist her up onto the table where she's currently in restraints because of the IV, but if she weren't, she'd have bounded up to greet me. No one's pinned down her tail, and it slaps merrily against the stainless steel. The pink color has returned to her tongue, which had been pale, and her breath is no longer labored.

I can tell she feels considerably better.

Well, guess what, Caroline—so do I.

• • • •

I park on the street in front of the Green Bay Café, noting that Max's car is indeed here. As I gather up my purse, I see someone who looks a lot like Miguel leaving the restaurant and getting into a Maserati. He waves, so I return the gesture.

Curiouser and curiouser.

The café is a tiny neighborhood joint one town to the south of Glencoe. The atmosphere is homey and charming, with mismatched novelty coffee mugs and an eclectic collection of plates. A menu is handwritten in chalk above an antique cash register. I like the place immediately, but I can't for the life of me imagine what my dad would be doing here, knowing his propensity for white-glove service.

However, as the café boasts only a few tables and booths, I spot him immediately.

"Was that Miguel I just saw?" I ask.

"Yes. I told you I have lunch with him every week," Max replies.

"Miguel, the waiter from the club?"

"Do you know a lot of other Miguels?"

"Just the one."

"Then that's him. Do you want some coffee? Excuse me, Wendy, can we get a cup o' joe over here?" my dad says, pointing at the waitress and then pointing at me. "Thanks."

"I swear I just saw him getting into a Maserati."

"Is he driving the GranTurismo or the Quattroporte today?"

"Miguel, the waiter from the club, has more than one Maserati?"

My father stirs some sugar into his coffee. "He's a bit of a gearhead."

I repeat, "Miguel, the waiter from the club, is a bit of a *gearhead*."

"Penelope, you sound like the Mad Hatter. Are you investigating things that begin with the letter 'M'?"

"Am *I* having a stroke? Do *I* have dementia?"

He puts down his spoon. "What, just because he's a waiter, he can't have nice things? That's kind of a racist attitude; I thought I raised you better than that."

I feel like I'm through the looking glass right now. I begin to crane my head around.

"Penelope, dear, what are you doing?"

"I'm searching for the cameras. Clearly this is some sort of elaborate setup. I thought *Betty White's Off Their Rockers* was canceled, but I guess not?"

"You're talking gibberish."

"Join the club." My coffee arrives in a mug that has "Drama Queen" written on it in curling script. I take a big sip, and in so doing, I scald most of the interior of my mouth. I can already feel fleshy stalagtites forming from the burn. So at least it's not prop coffee; that much is real. "Humor me. Let's backtrack. You know Miguel."

"And you know Miguel."

No, it's *me* who's talking to the Mad Hatter here, not vice versa. *I'm* the Alice, not him. "Let me try this again—you are friends with Miguel."

"Obviously. We have lunch every week."

"On the days he's not serving you lunch."

"He has Thursdays off."

"Of course he does." I drink some more boiling coffee, assuming I will need the caffeine to help every piston in my brain fire. I had no problem in college wrapping my mind around how Stokes' theorem relates a surface integral with curls of vector fields and line integrals, but this? This is above my pay grade.

I ask, "How do you know Miguel?"

"I've known Miguel forever."

"This is impossible."

He swirls the coffee in his Bannockburn Fire Chief mug. "Only if you believe it is."

Did Alice ever punch the Mad Hatter right in his enormous hat? I feel like I'd remember if she did; ergo, I will continue to question him calmly, but if he asks me why a raven is like a writing desk, it's all over.

"Max, if you had to stick a pin in the specific date when 'forever' may have started, that would be . . . when?"

"Hmm. I'd say more than fifty-five years ago. Miguel was my first employee. He was a young, young kid back then who cleaned up the shop at night."

"You're just mentioning this *now*? You've known him my whole life and you're only telling me now?"

He shrugs. "You never asked."

Fair enough.

"Then what's the connection to Centennial Hills?"

"I couldn't pay him much back then. When he had the opportunity to work at the club with his cousin, I wished him well and gave him a couple of shares in the company because he was a good kid. We kept in touch—we were friends. Years later, when we moved to Glencoe, he kept his ear to the ground around the club. Told me who I needed to know and what I needed to know about them. That's the thing about service professionals—people in power believe they're invisible. They let their guard down around them. I was able to get in because of Miguel."

"Seriously?" I exclaim. "Your whole country club membership is predicated on *extortion*? You *blackmailed* people into making you a member? You built our lives on a lie?"

He raises his eyebrows at me. "Really, Penelope, that's what you think of your old man? That's crazy! What I did was develop similar interests. Miguel told me who was important, told me who made the decisions. They all lived here in town, so I paid attention to their habits. I followed their patterns. If they bought a Town Car, I bought a Town Car. If they used Joe the barber, then I used Joe the barber. I wasn't insidious. I was ubiquitous. I blended. I became part of the scenery. I was someone who was always there. I did this until my membership seemed a mere formality, because they assumed I was already one of them."

I have never been more surprised by anything my father has told me. "You used math to become successful."

He nods and sips his coffee. "I guess I did. Club membership was important to me because it was important to your mother. She knew it was the key to opening a new world for us, and she was right. She wanted to be able to give you everything you'd ever need to be successful, and I'd say that's mission accomplished."

I sit with this information for a moment. I guess I never looked at her social climbing from this perspective before. I'd always assumed her purposes were more self-serving, and that distinctly changes my narrative about her.

Wendy comes up behind us and refills both our cups. Max says, "Careful, this stuff is usually pretty hot," bringing me back into the moment.

"Can you explain how Miguel has so many Maseratis?"

"Oh, he's *rich.*"

"What? How many shares did you give him?"

"Not enough to get rich. Just enough to wet his beak. He took the money and began investing. Here's the rub again—invisibility. He's like that little wizard boy with the cloak from the movie. With the scar."

"Harry Potter?"

"That's him. All anyone wants to talk about at the club is their money. Bit of a bore sometimes, actually. Enough already! Everyone was always, 'I bought Apple at twelve dollars. I bought Pfizer at fifteen dollars.' Finally, Miguel goes, 'I'm going to buy Apple at twelve dollars and Pfizer at fifteen dollars, too.' Then he did. The rest is history."

"When people think he's standing there being solicitous, he's actually eavesdropping and perpetrating the ultimate in insider trading and the whole thing is a scam?"

"No."

"No?"

"He's a great waiter and he loves what he does. He's a people person. He could have retired years ago. He's there by choice."

"No wonder he's always so happy."

Max shrugs and taps his watch. "Works for him. Listen, I've got a tee time soon. Anything else?"

"Wait, yes! Everything else. You sold the place in Florida and didn't tell me."

"Didn't concern you."

I scoot over so I'm blocking his exit from the booth. "What's going on? Do you even own the condo up here anymore? No one will give me a straight answer, and you guys are perpetually out running around. The doctor says you're fine, but nothing is adding up."

My father gives me an imploring look. "Think about it. You're the smart one. You'll figure it out."

"I've done nothing but think about it!" I reply. "Wait, does that mean you think Foster isn't smart?"

He shrugs. "Foster has a fine long drive. That's important, too."

"Really not here to talk about Foster's golf prowess."

"All those fancy certificates and accreditations and you still don't see it." He slumps against the back of the booth. He seems defeated in his posture, and I don't understand why, as clearly he's still winning this battle of wills. He gestures to Wendy for more coffee. She trots over and fills his cup with an eager grin.

"Sure you don't want a scone or anything?" he asks. "Their cinnamon chip with maple icing? The best on the North Shore.

Or they have lemon poppy seed. Maybe you'd like savory? I think they might have a few bacon cheddar chive left."

"No! I don't want a damn scone," I bark. This man is in a master class when it comes to stalling techniques. "I want you to stop speaking in riddles and baked goods. It would be so nice if something would make sense for a change."

He sighs. "The problem ain't me, kiddo."

"What?"

He begins to rub his knuckles. He hasn't built anything himself in many years, but all of his early days wielding a hammer have taken their toll and some days his arthritis really acts up.

"Your mother. Your mother is beginning to have a few problems—just a few memory lapses here and there and some trouble with judgment. She . . . Well, she made a bad investment without discussing it with me first. We're fine and have enough to live out our lives, but I had to sell the place in Florida to cover the loss. We still have the condo up here, and we legitimately did have water damage. However, we had water damage because your mother left the faucet running. She keeps forgetting that part."

"Oh, no. She will hate every part of this," I say. Poor Marjorie. She'd rather die—literally—than have any part of her be perceived as less than flawless.

"I'm aware. But she's going through a good phase right now. She's bright and alert and not lapsing into the British that much."

"Wait, that's not a drinking or a *Downton Abbey* thing?"

"No. Right now we're seeing as much of our friends as we can before a lot of them go away for the fall and winter. I can't predict where her mind will be next year, so I want everyone to spend time with her now while she's still fully herself. The place should be done next week, so we'll be out of your hair soon enough."

I realize something. "That's why you were so compliant about seeing the gerontologist. You wanted her to see it was no big deal?"

"Perceptive. Like I said, you're the smart one. At some point we'll sell our current unit and move into a senior living place with progressive levels of care, which hopefully she'll agree to, because it'll be about both of us."

"You're so much craftier than I ever gave you credit for."

"And what else did you learn from this conversation?" He wipes his hands on his napkin before placing it on the table. "I'm thinking about things that begin with the letter 'M.'"

"She doesn't know you're friends with Miguel, does she? She'd hate everything about that relationship."

"Every marriage needs a little bit of mystery," he says. "And, of course, you will keep this conversation between us. You know how your mother needs to maintain the facade of everything being perfect."

"I may have noticed that once or twice."

An anxious look crosses his face. "Are you going to tell Foster what we discussed?"

"Yes, of course. I have to."

He breathes a sigh of relief as he slides out of the booth. "Oh, thank God. I'm too old to have to do this twice, and you know I'd have to talk slowly for him. Pick up the check, won't you? I have to go right now. You don't keep Bunky Cushman waiting, after all."

• • • •

Caroline has quickly rallied and is greatly enjoying what I call our "discipline walks" around the neighborhood. I'm teaching her basic commands, and she's responding beautifully. This is a dog that wants to learn. However, our path today does not include the lake-front. As we found out yesterday, you cannot walk one hundred and thirty pounds of a web-footed creature genetically programmed to rescue drowning fishermen past a lake without incident. The boaters had a great sense of humor about the whole thing, but still, it was mortifying.

I imagine once we start with her new trainer, I'll learn how to handle her around larger bodies of water, but until then, she has to content herself with the baby pool in the backyard.

As soon as we come in the back door, she collapses on her bed. My strategy has been to walk the naughty out of her, and in the past two days, she's barely touched any of my delicious shoes, while her attempts to eat the ottoman were weak at best.

I feel Barnaby would be proud.

When I go upstairs, I notice Jessica's door is partially open, but I knock anyway.

"Enter," she says.

"Hey," I say. "I'm going shopping. Do you feel like joining me? I have a date, and I thought you could work your magic."

Jessica's attitude has warmed toward me since Kelsey went home. Although we haven't spoken about it directly, Jessica did say in passing, "I can't believe you told her no." Baby steps are still steps.

I wait for whatever snappy rejoinder she plans to hurl at me, but instead she says, "You're in luck. I'm free. Let me save what I'm working on and then we can go." She hurriedly taps at her iPad and then scans the screen, a smile playing at the corners of her mouth. "This is genius." Jessica glances up at me. "You should see this."

I'm taken aback that she wants me to participate in anything, but I reply, "Sure."

I look down at a gorgeous fashion pictorial, featuring the Chicago lakefront in all its summer glory. I scroll past shots of her standing on the stone wall where Sloane Peterson comforted Cameron in *Ferris Bueller's Day Off,* past pictures of her poised on the swings in the sand, one shapely leg raised to catch the sun. There's even a snap of her from behind, looking impossibly chic in a vintage Chanel suit, white gloves, and wide straw hat while yanking the leash of a large black dog who's terribly interested in a pack of seagulls. "Maybe it's not New York, but it's not too shabby," I say.

"No, it's not," Jessica agrees.

I look closer at the pictures and I realize that Jessica isn't modeling the styles herself. The effortless blonde with the bloodred lips and the signature shades and the pricey bag is . . . Marjorie. Then I notice the site's new URL—SeniorSartorial.

"Is it just me, or is this amazing?"

Jessica is full-on grinning now. "It's not just you. The *Huffington Post* agrees. The phone's been ringing nonstop with new advertisers."

"Are you too important to shop with me?" I ask.

"Not today," she replies. She looks me up and down. "But you will change out of yoga pants before we go, of course."

"Of course."

. . . .

"How are we doing in here?" Brenda, the Nordstrom sales associate, asks.

"Everything is fine, Brenda," I reply.

"Everything is *horrible*, Brenda," Jessica says. "I'm going to need you to find something not horrible. Hint: That means no midriff bows. She's not a toddler. And what is she going to do with military-style buttons? She's going on a date, not presenting a white paper. I need tits or ass, okay? I need to think 'sex' when I see her and not 'systems analysis.' If you can't imagine whatever dress you bring her in a ball on the bedroom floor, then don't bring it. Got it?"

Chastened, Brenda runs away.

"We're never going to see Brenda again. You realize that, right?" I say.

Jessica flips her hair. "Mission accomplished." She paws through the stack of dresses in the room. "Try this."

"But it's so skimpy," I reply.

"Have you listened to a single thing I've said?"

I take the dress from her and pull it on over my head. I get caught in the complicated web of straps, and Jessica has to help me angle the dress into place. Nothing about this garment is my style, and yet it's not so bad once I have all the cutouts lined up in a way that's not pornographic.

"Not bad, but we can do better," Jessica says. She snaps her fingers. "Off."

She has to assist me in getting out of the garment, too.

Brenda gives a tentative knock on the door.

"You're not here with pantsuits, right? God help you if you brought us a pantsuit," Jessica says.

Brenda vanishes without a sound.

"I'm considering sticking around," Jessica says, apropos of nothing.

"I would like that," I say. "I'm sure your father and your grand-parents would like that, too. Can't really speak for Kelsey."

I pull a linen Eileen Fisher piece off the rack, and before I can even remove it from the hanger, Jessica yanks it away from me, replacing it with a Tadashi Shoji embellished lace sheath dress.

"I had some trouble in New York," she volunteers. "God, it's so expensive there. Not easy to keep up. Remember how I used to complain about how hard it was to compete in Glencoe? Yeah, New York was a wake-up call. I had it easy in Chicago. Thing is, I . . . ended up cutting some corners professionally and that eventually came back to bite me in the ass, so I'm kind of starting over right now. I racked up some debt. Nothing I can't get out from behind eventually, but I will have to live on the cheap for a while."

I'm not sure what I should do here in terms of offering help, volunteering to write checks, or make calls, so I just listen.

Maybe all she ever wanted me to do was listen.

"I think if I rebuild now, I can do it on a more solid foundation. I don't really want to design—too cutthroat—and I'm sort of over the whole New York thing. I want to help regular people look their best. Doesn't have to be celebrities. Actually, it's easy to make famous people look fab. You can put them in anything and they're amazing. Fixing someone like you is a lot harder."

I zip into the sheath dress while I try to figure out the best way to say what I need to say. "Those sound like achievable goals, and I'm proud of you for coming to those conclusions. My only suggestion is that you maybe tone down the blunt honesty. Offer up a little sugar to counteract the salt."

"Do people not like that? I hate when people try to bullshit me."

"People appreciate the truth as long as it's not delivered in a way that hurts their feelings," I say.

"Huh." This seems like brand-new information to her.

"You know what, Jessica? I blame myself for you not knowing some basic stuff like this," I say, having a seat on the padded banquette of the dressing room. Jessica watches me via the threefold mirror. "Your only role model has been Marjorie, which is basically

like learning from a lesser Disney villain. I wasn't around enough
during your critical, formative years. I thought I was doing right by
you, but in retrospect, that was a mistake. I provided you things
instead of time and attention. The worst of it is, I convinced myself
that everything I did, I did for you, but that's not true. I liked the
person I was at work. I liked being in charge. I liked being competent. Ultimately, I did us both a disservice, and I'm sorry."

Jessica is still holding my gaze in the mirror. "You've never
said that before."

"I'm saying it now."

She nods. "I waited a long time to hear that. Thank you." She
narrows her eyes at me. "We're not going to hug now, are we?"

"Not if that makes you uncomfortable."

"Okay." She helps me out of the lace sheath and sets it to the
side. "This is the one. Did you see how it clung to all of your curves
and showed off your arms and back but covered your knees?"

"Is there a problem with my knees?" I ask.

"Oh, look, a baby wolf," she says.

"Is that you trying to not hurt my feelings?"

"Yes."

"Thanks."

"Can I ask you something?" she says, as we gather up our purses
before we leave the fitting room. "Did you ever apologize to Daddy?"

"Did I apologize to him? Why would I apologize?"

"Because affairs don't start in a vacuum."

Before I can respond, before I can even parse out her meaning, Jessica is halfway across the department, urging a middle-
aged woman to put the capri pants down.

By the time we leave Nordstrom, I have the dress, a shopping
bag full of new cosmetics courtesy of MAC, shoes with an actual

heel, and underwear that does not cause me great shame. And Jessica has a part-time job as a personal shopper. (Apparently Brenda's boss liked Jessica's hustle.)

By the time we leave Old Orchard Mall, my grays are gone via a trip to the In Style salon and I have subtle amber and russet highlights, à la Kate Middleton. Karin and Patrick are going to be thrilled. Jessica and I both got mani-pedis, too. Her nails are a matte aqua, while mine are (surprise) taupe.

Who knew that having a daughter could be kind of fun?

· · · ·

I'm sitting at my dressing table, putting the finishing touches on my makeup, when Marjorie wanders into my bedroom and perches on the edge of my bed.

"Hi. Are we out of gin?" I ask.

She winks at me. "I always knew you were the clever one, darling. Boodles, please."

"I'll bring some home after my date."

"Are you going out with someone lovely?"

I dab some Tom Ford behind my ears and wrists. "Yes."

"You planning to marry him?"

I laugh. "Not tonight, no. It's our first official dinner date."

"I knew with your father on our first date. He was fourteen years old and didn't have a dime to his name, so we went for a walk. I'll never forget how he said, 'Stick with me, kid, and I'll give you the world.' He used to find interesting rocks and tell me to hold on to them; one day I could redeem them for diamonds. He kept his word, and I had a lot of rocks."

"That is so incredibly sweet," I say.

"Mmm," she says, nodding and sipping her drink. "Hard to believe it all began almost forty years ago."

I rise from my dressing table. "I have to go, Marjorie. I'll be sure to pick up your gin."

I grab my evening bag and begin my tentative trip down the back stairs on these precarious heels. I can hear Marjorie muttering to herself.

"Bloody hell, it's always, 'Marjorie this' and 'Marjorie that.' Such disrespect. Oh, for the days when these children called me 'Mother.'"

. . . .

I arrive at the restaurant after him, and he's already at the table when I approach. "No, I insist. Don't get up."

He gets up anyway. "You look beautiful, by the way."

"Thanks. My daughter styled me."

He sits back down. "So, we're really doing this." He hands me a glass of chardonnay from the bottle that's already open on the table.

"We are. I'm ready. I had to figure out if I was ready, and turns out I am."

"Do we start with small talk?" he asks. "I'm so rusty at this. I don't remember how to date you. It's been too long."

"Like I'm not? I don't remember how to date you either."

"Why don't we start with small talk?" he suggests. "How's work?"

"Interesting," I say. "I was supposed to be promoted to executive vice president this week, except I decided I didn't want to be an executive vice president. I declined the position, and now I'm on vacation for the next few weeks."

He seems surprised. "You turned down the job! Why?"

"Well, when I was married, I spent a lot of time jockeying for position within my company. Too much time. I kept angling for promotions that in retrospect did nothing to advance my family. They only advanced me. My forward motion only fed *my* ego, only fulfilled *my* needs."

"That sounds like a problem."

"Yeah, turns out it was. What ended up happening is my job drove a wedge between my husband and me, only I wouldn't admit it because I didn't see it. Instead, I used my work as some kind of moral high ground, my get-out-of-jail-free pass."

He studies me in the candlelight. "That had to be hard for your husband."

"I imagine it was. Eventually, I was gone so much and so completely checked out of our lives that he ended up turning to someone else in a moment of weakness, and I was furious. I was unforgiving. I wouldn't talk to him afterward. I wouldn't go to marriage counseling. I wouldn't consider trying to work through how we got there in the first place. I just put all the blame on his shoulders. I was so mad."

He runs his finger up and down the stem of his glass. "I can see your point. You had every right to be angry. You didn't break your vows."

"True, but I never owned up to my responsibility for the whole situation. I was so busy being the injured party that it never occurred to me that I was just as much to blame. Today my daughter told me, 'An affair doesn't happen in a vacuum.' She's right."

"She sounds like a smart kid."

"She is. I'm going to get to know her better because she's sticking around for a while. She can't afford to rent her own place, so she's planning to fix up the little apartment over the garage and move in there. That'll give her some privacy—because who wants to live with her mother, especially when her mom is starting to date?"

"Aren't you selling your house? I thought you were moving to the city."

"I had an offer—crazy high; you wouldn't believe the number. But I'm learning the numbers aren't everything. There's no math in the world that makes me ready to sell. I've got a big new dog and a grandkid on the way and an adult kid who needs the garage space. Looks like I'm tethered to the place for a while."

"I'm really glad to hear that," he says. He takes my hand and begins to trace this thumb back and forth across my knuckles.

"Are you even hungry?" I ask.

"Not really," he says.

"Thing is, I promised my mother a bottle of Boodles, and she gets antsy because she's old. She says she's not old, but she's a liar. Would you mind terribly if we just settled up and picked up her gin and went back to my house? I mean, to *our* house?"

He smiles at me. "There's nothing I'd rather do."

I rise from my seat and hand him his crutches. "Then let's go home, Chris. Let's go home."